ONE
AN IMPRINT OF PUSHKIN PRESS

Queen Mab

'A young woman's travels to and through the lands of motherhood and mental illness are chronicled with brutal clarity in McBride's debut novel. . . A harrowing tale of mothering and myth'

Kirkus Reviews

'McBride establishes herself as someone ready to write (and be read) alongside authors of Helen Oyeyemi's skill with this powerful exploration of the poetics and politics of motherhood'

Library Journal

'Seamlessly weaves fantasy into the increasingly suspenseful narrative, which builds to a powerful crescendo'

Publishers Weekly

'McBride writes with both poetic force and clarity, her powerful prose weaving a fairy world of its own'

Lana Bastašić, author of *Catch the Rabbit*

'Plunges deep into the specific loneliness of new motherhood and the way it rewrites our world order. . . Its peculiar beauties and horrors are told through an unclouded lens, never not funny and always tender, and in prose that is alive, charged by its own velocity'

Claudia Dey, author of *Daughter*

© Silvia Poch

EMILY McBRIDE is a Canadian-born editor, writer and translator living in Barcelona. Her work has been published in *The Stinging Fly*, *The Nation*, and *The Rumpus*. *Queen Mab* is her debut novel.

Queen Mab

Emily McBride

ONE

AN IMPRINT OF PUSHKIN PRESS

ONE
An imprint of Pushkin Press
Somerset House, Strand
London WC2R 1LA

First published by Pushkin Press in 2026

ISBN 13: 978-1-80533-806-2

A CIP catalogue record for this title is available from the British Library

The authorised representative in the EEA is eucomply OÜ,
Pärnu mnt. 139b-14, 11317, Tallinn, Estonia,
hello@eucompliancepartner.com, +33757690241

Offset by Tetragon, London
Printed and bound in the United Kingdom by Clays Ltd, Elcograf S.p.A.

MIX
Paper | Supporting responsible forestry
FSC® C018072
FSC www.fsc.org

www.pushkinpress.com

1 3 5 7 9 8 6 4 2

For my parents

Queen Mab

At dawn on the street of princely foxes and senile cats, a pigeon cooed and the first traffic purred by. A woman in a fluffy green bathrobe sat at the bus stop. Minutes earlier, she had emerged from a nearby gate with the recycling box, but it was the wrong day, or the wrong box, and it had all seemed too complicated.

Now she watched the sky catch fire in a sublime, unholy dawn. Pink mist crept along the asphalt, and clouds clustered the horizon like heavy fruit. Across the street, her own flat on the second floor of a seventies low-rise building was still in shadow. And what shadow. The blank façade, the vacant windows, the malevolent black wink of the one she left open. Out here was all the world, with its promise of fulfilment and demise. In there, one great unknown.

People in daytime clothes arrived at the bus stop and shot her wary glances. The light grew feverish bright, enough to reveal a purple smear on the road: the remains of a squirrel with its skull crushed and its body mangled. One little paw remained whole, angled back towards her house.

PART I

The Lady of Shalott

One's sympathies, of course,
were all on the side of life.

—"The Death of the Moth," VIRGINIA WOOLF

The first flicker of life was a moth. It was dusty, threadlike legs and Rorschach wings. It was what I had wanted, but immediately I no longer wanted it. I was only twenty-three. What had I been thinking?

Flicker.

I was on the way to see my tutor, a woman of massive intellect who was a cult figure in my discipline. I was on the verge of being late, but at the first flicker I stopped. I went and leaned against one of the pillars and saw the sunlight on the Victorian towers, and watched the whole shape of my life change.

Flicker, again. The word "moth" came to me, and an image of a moth crouched in darkness.

It rustled its wings, almost like it was saying *ahem.*

Ahem, said the moth. *Here I am.*

I leaned against the pillar, counted the days backwards, and felt: comprehension, inner rebellion, tug of responsibility, panic.

"No," I said. "No. This is a mistake." I remembered the circumstances that had led me here. "It was the night after the funeral, a night with a full moon. I wasn't thinking clearly that night. There was this sense of lingering magic, a belief in the transmigration of souls. I don't believe in all that in the daytime, moth."

Even so, the moth said. *I'm here.*

I was teaching *An Introduction to Nineteenth Century Literature* that term. A parade of fallen women, ruined women, clustered around me.

"They will make me wear a scarlet A," I said. "For accident."

Tom would say it didn't matter what people thought, but I cringed to think of telling anyone, because I liked to project an aura of control, and in the second year of my PhD this could only indicate the opposite, total lack of control and lack of foresight. I could hardly even bear to tell Tom.

Don't worry about Tom, said the moth. *He likes the idea of me. Even you like the idea of me. A blood relative for you.*

"But not now," I said. I fretted, I rocked back on my heels, I felt sick. I rummaged in my mind through all the books I had ever read, which was always my first response in a crisis. But what help were books now? "Perhaps like that short story Marie told me of," I said. "A woman goes for an abortion but it goes a bit science fiction. The doctor gives her something to make the baby fold back into her body, an embryo postponed. When she does have a baby, years later, it's that same baby." The grooves of the pillar cut into my back.

You can't fold me back into your body, said the moth, tiny and trying to contort away from me. But it was an honest moth. *You could do away with me, of course.*

No, I couldn't do that. I had a bad history. It didn't take much to see that snuffing out the moth would be a betrayal, bad karma.

I'm raw potential, said the moth.

I was used to thinking of myself as raw potential. The sun had moved on from the tower. I was late. I could not go and see my tutor now.

Tom will make a wonderful daddy, the moth said anxiously,

still worried I might actually snuff it out to protect everything: my twenties, stretching ahead full of reading, travel, dancing, impromptu feasts with Tom at two in the morning. And my strong, empty, young body.

It will make your mother happy, said the moth.

But by then I was feeling something divorced from reason. I was feeling the delicate tickle of silken legs, the vibration of the dry, quavery voice. I was feeling the thump of new blood. It was a lure. It was a mystery. I was imagining Tom as a wonderful daddy. The baby would be Tom's and it would be mine. It would be something different; it would be complex and disruptive.

Tom would say we could make it work.

"Tom," I practiced saying, for later. Or maybe I was talking to the moth. "It seems that *life* is stronger than I am."

Afternoon falls fast in September. The air was as sharp as the vertical thrust of the tower, but I was warm with a new desire.

But for him it was his last afternoon as himself

—"In Memory of W. B. Yeats," W. H. AUDEN

"Tomorrow is my birthday," Marie said. "I've always hated being born in November. There's no excuse for it. Based on totally anecdotal evidence I think it must be tied with February as everyone's most despised month. When is your birthday?"

"June twenty-third." We faced each other across a lacquered wooden table, in a froufrou bar in an upscale neighbourhood, waiting. It was the kind of place where the ceiling was tiled pastel pink, the walls painted mint green, and there was a hodgepodge of framed aspirational pop-art prints, polished wood, mood lighting. I was here for a meeting. Marie was not supposed to be here at all as far as I knew, and I hadn't been pleased to see her.

"Summer child. Not to be mystical about things, but I feel that says everything. Why you're all sorted and loved up with the perfect man and already underway on your PhD, while I'm such a princess of darkness. I just flounder about."

I hadn't been paying much attention to what she was saying. For weeks, being in public had been a test of my attention span. I seemed to have two frequencies running at once, constantly. Finding Marie here ruptured my inner monologue, but it was still there, under the surface. Tonight was both a meeting to plan a trailblazing project between the university and the wider community, and also the night I must tell Angela. I had said to Tom, yes, I would, yes, why not, yes. But I dreaded it. It was one thing to be excited with Tom, at home, discussing names and debating first board books, speculating whose eyes, whose chin. Another to reveal my private life in public, invite everyone to observe my body and question my choices. But the time had come. We'd had the ultrasound this morning, paisley squiggle, moth portraits in black and white that made the whole thing real, and it was doubly real because we'd called my parents in Ontario when the time difference allowed and—well, I was still digesting that conversation. They had been polite rather than thrilled.

Marie had her lips pursed, was staring out into the early gloom, tapping her fingers lightly on the table. Next to her on the mini red leather chesterfield was all her usual chaos, a cracked phone, free newspapers, a collapsing tote bag, a stack of library books that wouldn't fit inside it. I pulled back to the conversation.

"Flounder about. I don't think anyone else would describe you that way," I said.

We looked like mirror images, two women drawn by a child who only knows one type, and so makes one fair and one dark. We were both tall and leggy with long and permanently tangled hair; Marie's was light brown, mine very dark. Her face was wide and mobile, mine was narrow like a bird of prey. But our faces lied: Marie was the bird of prey, and I was the ingenue. She had transferred into the department last year, fleeing her previous university after a sexual assault ("I can't even look at that place again," she'd said). She was a year younger, but my only real competition. I had been accepted to study under Angela, and that meant something, but my inner critic whispered that I wasn't brilliant. I just had an excellent memory. I remembered things I had read years ago, almost verbatim. But Marie might actually be brilliant. She read close to two hundred books a year. She had taught herself to read Spanish. Her research was feminist and unapologetically personal, grounded in her lived experiences. She wasn't intimidated by the lauded old professors, and didn't hesitate to attack a friend on intellectual grounds either, which is how we'd come to public argument about "The Lady of Shalott" in my nineteenth-century seminar.

The interpretation I taught was unassailable. The Lady Elaine abandons her tower, mirror, and loom to go after Lancelot in search of love and colour; and yes, she dies, but she has still chosen life over shadow half-life. Marie had demanded to know how choosing Lancelot could possibly be choosing life, and why, if Lancelot was so wonderful, did he have that awful final line about the Lady having a lovely face, as if that were all that mattered? The other twelve young women in the class nodded along with Marie. The Lady had it wrong, my students said. The loom was life, creative energy, manifestation of self through work. And she abandoned it for a man. The room was quiet then. "Fine," I said, aiming for Angela's crystalline diction but coming across distant, possibly snooty. "Support it in your essays." It wasn't so serious. It was just that I loathed standing in front of people and being appraised, loathed being the focal point of the room. In that moment I loathed Marie too. I wanted to be left alone with my Victorians.

So her "perfect man" comment rang false. Tom was indeed the perfect man. But was she mocking me, and fishing for compliments at the same time?

There was a vibration from my phone inside my bag. I dug it out, and Marie went up to the bar.

After four hours of silence, I could tell my mother wanted to please me because she was texting select feelings in quotation marks.

> **Mum:** I'm sorry if I was maybe a little "dry" earlier.
>
> **Mum:** Delighted for your news, thrilled.
>
> **Mum:** I only wish you had told me before the ultrasound. Just my little "hangup." You know I always miss the parentheses of life. First days and last days. You know. After Nan and Grandy, I would have loved to have known about this from the start.

After five minutes had passed:

> **Mum:** I just mean I would have liked to share the "early days of excitement" with you.

My mother had once said "tick, tock" to me about having babies. I was a teenager at the time. But she had not been able to have any herself, so she was sensitive about this.

The earliest of her messages had come through half an hour before, when I was walking up from the bus stop through a drab no-man's-land of laundrettes and betting shops. The city spread before me, its bright ribbon of river, ruddy brick, patches of ugly towers, tufts of tree-filled parks. I turned away from it and cut in among leafy streets and Georgian terraces. Angela had called this meeting not far from her own terraced house.

My mother was still online. She was at work at the licensing office of the municipality where I grew up. It was five hours earlier there; she was in her afternoon slump and distracting herself by looking up prenatal yoga classes in my new English city.

Mum: I know you're "not into yoga" but building core strength is important when expecting! I've been looking it up . . . it reduces stress and strengthens muscles and endurance needed for childbirth!!
Me: Ok we'll see
Mum: Oh, Maddie. "Humour me."
Me: Can you find a class for cynical graduate students without $200 leggings?

I deleted those words carefully, letter by letter, before I could send them. My mother with her minimalist spirituality, her forced cheeriness. I had run away from her. The least I could do was let her be involved.

Tom messaged that he was leaving work and would meet me soon.

Marie was back with a packet of crisps. "The prices in this place," she said. "I wanted the cheese plate but then I wouldn't make my rent. Now, important! Do you have room in your bag? I'd rather Angela's novelist doesn't know I've been reading his books. I'll be forced to find something nice to say about them."

"Did you read them all?" I asked, astonished. "I only read the newest one." Angela's novelist was another person she had roped in for the scheme we were here to discuss. Angela and I and a social worker and the novelist were to run a program that would create links between the university and the local community, bringing at-risk youth together to read literary texts and learn how to express themselves in writing. It would culminate in a publication and a series of performances that would prove the relevance of literature and the untapped potential of the youth. Angela strongly believed it was our role to engage with the world, but I was quite nervous; I liked the distancing effect of university, and even my seminars meant being a little too close to other people sometimes.

"There are only three. But I've no intention," she said, lowering her voice conspiratorially, jabbing out words in her flat Midlands diction, "of talking about them with him. Or talking with him much at all. I think he's basically a vampire. As you go through them, you see a man ever more in desperate need of a subject that isn't himself. I bet he takes notes on everyone he meets."

At moments like this I could lower my hackles and remember how much I'd wanted Marie as a friend when she'd first appeared on the scene—before I suspected her of sniffing around me for what she might get out of it. I had been as glamoured by her as everyone else. I'd started angling my chin just like her, and tossing my hair around. She'd come around mine for dinner; we'd gone together to protest the planned Tesco that threatened to undermine local commerce in my neighbourhood. We still went for coffee every week with other graduate students. I smiled and opened my bag for the novelist's books.

Then my attention drifted. There was no point trying to get closer. Our life paths were about to diverge. She had somehow invited herself along to what was meant to be my project; and I knew she would worm her way into it. Actually . . . and here my attention drifted again, counting weeks and days forwards. There was a strong possibility it would just be handed over to her. It was meant for March, and the moth was expected in April, but Angela never stayed on schedule.

And there was Angela, coming through the door, her waxlike face framed by platinum hair. Dressed as always in voluminous black clothing of many textures, and exclamatory jewellery, she filled the space, reducing the floor-to-ceiling windows to background, towering above the little lacquered tables. The clientele, mostly slim, groomed women also dressed in black, were wraiths next to her. She held the door open for someone she had glimpsed approaching, and the November wind rattled in.

Angela was the kind of serious, frightening older woman I worshipped, women who were effortlessly themselves and spoke their minds without needing to be constantly speaking. There had been a collection of women like her in my life: a drama teacher, a neighbour back home, the boss at my first summer camp job. Women like suns: I moved in orbit. Since I had come to study with her a year and a half ago, life was tremblings and epiphanies. Crushing insecurity, shyness, transcendence. I was terrified of slipping up and having her despise me. I had no idea how I should tell her my news. I desperately did not want to. Angela shared another trait with the other fearsome but inspiring women in my collection: she had no children.

In came the social worker, so similar to Angela in type and passion, so different in background and field. Angela was a renowned scholar of medieval poetry and literary Modernism; Dorrie a longtime activist and advocate for young people who had aged out of the care system. Angela was widely considered a genius. I often worried I didn't need a genius supervisor; I needed a musty one, one who would let me read and write but not insist on our galumphing back out into the world. I hardly knew how to speak to Dorrie; she seemed to represent a hard reality, which might easily have been mine, because I had been adopted out of the care system as a baby in Canada. I had not mentioned this to either of them.

Angela was still holding the door open. Throughout the warm bar people were raising their heads in protest, tsking and fretting, but Angela ignored them all and waited until a slight man of about forty with a goatee hurried in.

"Thank you for coming all the way out here to meet me practically on my own doorstep," Angela called as they advanced to meet us. "Oh, you two have been catching up. Maddie, Marie told me yesterday she was hoping to take on more responsibilities, so I invited her along tonight. Now, you've met Dorrie, I think. And this is the Lord of Misrule, who needs no introduction, Marie and Madeleine." (How naturally our names went together.) The novelist was recognizable from his book jacket photo. Flustered, I forgot that I had not liked the one book I had read.

"So, you're the writer," said Marie.

"I am. And one of you is Angela's French graduate student, who sends the emails?"

"Only I'm not French," I said.

"No you're not, are you? How so, with a name so *Gallic* as Madeleine Brodeur?"

"I have one French-Canadian grandparent," I said, which was a half-truth. A brief silence followed.

"What do you study?" A question he was obliged to ask and we to answer, with words we'd repeated so often that they had lost most of their meaning. Marie's topic was the monstrous feminine, literary body horror, but she was bad at explaining it, throwing in names like everyone knew them, lobbing in theory, tossing her hair around.

It was nice to be undeniably better than her, at this one thing. "The non-human in Modernism."

"Non-human as in machines?" asked the novelist. "Cyborgs and whatnot?"

"There is that," I said. "It includes machines and streets and the alienating features of the modern landscape. And also animals—quite a few of those—and a few fairies courtesy of Yeats." It was Tom who'd gotten me into bed with the Modernists, or rather I'd fallen into Tom's bed when we were both undergraduates, and the Modernists just happened to be there. I'd been a pure Victorian maiden before he got his hands on me. I was still a bit pastoral, for a Modernist.

"Oh, fairies," said the novelist with a comedy grimace that banished me to an intellectual corner. I smiled. My mother had been delighted with this angle of my thesis topic, picturing me studious among flowers and acorns. I'd heard every possible reaction. Fantasy fairies, not *real*, all made up. Sometimes I heard this from people who had no problem with zombies or ghosts. Other people I suspected of harbouring secret passions for fairies, asking had I read such-and-such, did I know about Arthur Conan Doyle and the photos at the bottom of the garden? Did I know about brownies, pinkies, pixies? Lots of people liked dallying in the aesthetics and magic.

Of course, I could explain my topic without going into all of that. Most of what I studied had nothing to do with fairies: I could frame it around Marianne Moore's animals or Hope Mirrlees's urban soundscapes or Delmore Schwartz's movie theatre. I loved them all equally. I had come to posthumanism via the animals; my master's thesis used horses to reframe wildness and labour in Victorian texts. I had been animal-mad as a child, but also allergic to all of them. My studies became one more way to extend childhood into maturity. I rather liked getting raised eyebrows about the fairies. Just my mother and I against the world, for once, a high-five across the distance.

"Not real," I could hear the novelist saying confidentially to Marie. She laughed and twirled a piece of hair.

"I've got an icebreaker in mind." Angela glided forwards, cleaving them cleanly apart. She pushed him over by Dorrie. "Let's all have wine, maybe some cheese. My treat."

"How is your wife?" Dorrie asked the novelist pointedly.

"We're separated." He smiled at Marie and me once more.

"That's a shame," Dorrie said. "I liked her so much."

Wine gurgled forth like blood. I was handed a glass, and should have spoken up then, but didn't. I was unable to say anything at all. There were too many personalities in the room. Conversation was a football match; the novelist and Marie were vying for possession of the ball with Angela and the outreach worker, conversing about art and text and sex and society and money, everything except babies. I hadn't a hope of keeping up, with my own thoughts running on another track entirely. I wanted it to be over, but I didn't want to do it. I would be cast out of this magic circle.

Angela finally called us to order. She spoke in the clipped tones that were her trademark in lecture halls, in office hours, on the phone. "Our job throughout this project is to help people who aren't used to expressing themselves." She gave me little shivers of excitement; she seemed to confirm that it all *mattered*, what we were doing, even if all we were doing was reading. "We have to remember that many of these young people are wearing masks, of one kind or another."

"Often several," added Dorrie.

Across from me, Marie smiled and nodded.

My phone vibrated and I excused myself. Tom was almost here, and I would go meet him at the bus stop. Outside in the cold, I read a message from my father, my old conspirator and best friend, my recent enemy. He wanted to get down to the nuts and bolts of things, the who-did-what-in-the-night-with-whom, the from-where, the why-didn't-we-know-about, the narrowing of horizons into a manageable line of descendancy, genealogy.

> **Papa:** I'll be happy to sponsor the baby's first DNA test, and we'll see how stern a stuff he or she is made of. ;-) Once arrived, of course.

I hissed like a kettle letting off steam.

But Tom was coming, so I forced all that down and put the phone away for good. There was a tranquillity that spread through me at the sight of him, at the delight of him. You could see everything about Tom at a glance. He was flushed and freckled, sandy-haired and grey-eyed, often laughing, and you knew immediately that he was warm-hearted and approachable, and funny and incisive.

"Hello, *baby*," he said, all good cheer and double entendre, laying a sly hand on my stomach. We giggled like teenage lovers. "How is your work meeting or drinks night or whatever this is?"

"Marie is plotting a coup. There's a vampire. Angela's got all her biggest jewellery on."

"Excellent." Tom rearranged a crimson scarf. He was always more dressed up than I was, and more effortlessly at home in the stylish corners of cities. This came at the cost, as he often told me, of being horribly, irrevocably out of place in the rough coastal town he'd left at eighteen, and with the family that never expected our marriage, any marriage, to work out. We *had* married young, but it was part romance, part pragmatism, at least

50 percent the fault of the passport office who considered me un-British despite my mother, who had been born and grown up in the north of England. A story I had told too many times. *I'm adopted. Yes, later they changed the law to include people like me, but it doesn't apply to the year I was born.*

"Have you told her yet?" he asked.

"No."

"Why not?" Tom would not have hesitated. He would have swept in, pink-cheeked, announcing the news in the first minute.

"It feels complicated. And I've realized I'll be rather unprofessionally having the baby right in the middle of this project."

"They can't blame you for that. Life is complicated. Embrace complexity."

Always Tom's attitude. If something was difficult, he was the first in line for it. Manual film photography. The Modernists at university. The Postmodernists. None of my Victorians and their moral certainties. He enjoyed complexity because he didn't, despite his disadvantageous background, actually find life all that complex. He enjoyed alienation, from his peers, from his place of origin, because he never in fact felt alienated. Everything was a new adventure. Even getting an adult job, which he'd accomplished last year by lobbing off almost a hundred CVs. His enthusiasm for doing new things was catching. He made me see the pleasure in being clever enough. But I did not like things to be complicated; I thought they were complicated enough. Angela and her expectations, Marie and her aspirations. My father and his dead relatives.

"How was work?" I managed, stealing more time alone, even though it depressed me to talk about Tom's work. I had managed to avoid grown-up life so far.

"Oh, fine. The usual. I can never decide if I'm selling my

soul or just paying my dues, and this job is a stop on the way to one that does some good in the world. What though?" A question complex enough even for Tom. He worked in communications for a brand agency, where he wrote copy, took photographs, and was learning to shoot promotional videos. He often moaned that in one fell swoop they had reduced most of his hobbies to filthy lucre. The company was lucky to get someone with all Tom's skills on an intern's contract. When they couldn't string him along further, they'd promoted him to the minimum entry wage. Youth unemployment was high, so he stayed. And I was lucky too; I could study for years on a barely sufficient stipend and introduce the moth into the equation because his salary might—would—go up. And yet.

"I wouldn't mind one of these houses," Tom was saying, looking around.

"These are just the little ones," I said. "I told you we should explore the city more. The houses get bigger further in."

"These would be perfect for a growing family."

"The neighbourhood is boring and the shops cost a fortune. Anyway we'll be able to afford one when we're dead." Angela came from the generation when becoming an academic allowed a person this minor luxury, a house, three little bedrooms, a small garden. Everything finished properly. An electricity plan that didn't involve running to the corner shop to top up.

"Angela has no heirs, does she, Queen Mab? Perhaps she'll let us live in her garden shed in exchange for caring for her when she's ancient. They look worth a gander anyway," he said, angling his head to peer through a kitchen window. I was taller and could easily see the bespoke-looking cabinets in robin's-egg blue, the expensive taps.

"And 'love likes a gander,'" I said. Tentative.

I thought he wouldn't reply but he murmured, almost absently, "'And . . . and adores a goose.'"

I smiled like an idiot. A few days ago he had failed to notice one of my quotes. We had always gone around dropping quotes for each other into conversation; all our shared loves, Eliot, Lawrence, Woolf. He had not recognized an obvious one the other day, and when I had jokingly pointed it out, he'd said, "God, I never thought that would happen. It's amazing how it all starts to seem unreal—uni, I mean, talking about books all day." It was a small thing. But I had taken such joy in finding Tom, in finding Lancelot, when we were barely twenty, and in being freed by it, not entrapped or cursed. My world was still a patchwork of other people's words. It had shape as long as I could find a quote for all the pivotal moments. But I didn't want to be alone in the narrative.

"Come on," Tom said as another gust of November wind barrelled through. "It's Baltic out here."

When we reentered the café, I saw that the mask metaphor had been brought to life. Angela had actually brought masks with her, old-fashioned painted cardboard half-faces with ribbons to tie behind the head. Dorrie was a vintage nurse, the novelist a mid-century housewife with a curly blond updo, Marie a little girl. Angela was, so far as I could tell, Mother Goose. If we weren't the oddest group in the bar before, we certainly were now.

"Hullo Angela," said Tom, sitting across from her. "I like your area. I'd not been out this end of town since we moved in. I bet you get lots of birds, with all the greenery. I love to take pictures of birds, but our neighbourhood is so full of borderline evil cats and foxes that we don't see so many."

Tom and I lived nearly forty minutes away by bus, in a

rundown but vibrant district officially called Saint Peter's Wood, though the wood, if there had ever been one, was long gone. Around town it was universally known as Splinters Wood, or just Splinters.

"I like to take pictures of them myself," said Angela. "But I've heard you're a proper photographer. I'm very much the armchair kind. I use my phone with the zoom, which a photographer friend has told me is a cardinal sin, pardon my pun. But I quite like the sound of evil neighbourhood cats."

"Ah, well mine is just a hobby too, really. But I like doing birds in particular. Everyone wants to see them as delicate and poetic, but when you get down to it and home in on their bright little eyes, you see something that's just bent on, you know, brute survival. Long-winded way to say, something wild. The same with squirrels, of course, but people don't tend to get so romantic about squirrels. Are these going free?" Tom was going through the masks, slipping on one of a bearded old codger. "One for you, Maddie?" The masks of faces were gone now but there were a few that looked like animals at the bottom of the box.

"Wolf?"

"Erm."

"The badger looks more like a cow. Evil Splinters fox or cat, then. Which do you prefer?"

"It doesn't matter," I said, and he tied one over my face while introducing himself to the others. I turned a vixen or feline gaze on the novelist, and wondered why I couldn't make such easy conversation as Tom.

"So I hear you're gestating a new project," Tom said slyly to Angela. Here was my cue; all I needed to do was jump in with our news. I said nothing. Angela and Dorrie described the history of the project and this year's iteration while I sat frozen.

"And the due date is in the spring?" Tom followed up politely. But still I said nothing. I was safe behind my mask.

Tom continued. Did Dorrie consider herself as mentor to the at-risk youth, or as surrogate parent? Had the last such project had a difficult delivery? What teething pains were they anticipating with this one? Well not to worry, you had to crawl before you could walk, wasn't that what they said?

"Does he always talk like an investment banker?" Marie whispered.

But then Angela, reaching forwards to pour more wine, said, "Madeleine, you don't seem to need a top-up. That's not like you." And suddenly it left me like a last breath leaving the body.

"I'm not drinking tonight, Angela. The fact is, well." There was nothing for it. "I'm having a baby. Tom and I are having a baby."

"Oh," said Angela.

There was a short silence.

"What? Impossible!" Marie pushed her mask up onto her head.

"That's wonderful news, congratulations," Angela said a moment later. She patted me on the shoulder. Silence fell. She patted my shoulder again.

It was Dorrie who rescued me, smiling like Christmas and jumping up to kiss us both on the cheek. Tom pushed up his mask. I was so startled, I kept my mask on and so my kiss landed on the chin, which made everyone laugh.

"Tom is blooming," said Angela. "Surely that is Madeleine's job."

"When?" Marie demanded, dumbfounded. "When for, I mean. When is the due date?" She shot a quick look at Tom.

"Spring," I said hesitantly. "Mid-April."

"April is the cruellest month," said the novelist.

"Haha," I said. "So, Angela we'll need to work some things out, though obviously I'll work right to the end . . ." The words came uncertainly, grovellingly. I had never let anyone down before.

"Of course," said Angela. She lapsed into silence a moment. "Your classes, of course . . . maybe Bronwen. Though . . . well never mind, we'll find someone. Maybe . . ." her eyes moved musingly across the table. I felt a flush of rage and was glad of my impassive animal face.

But it was over, and on a wave of relief, I truly entered into the drunkenness of things being various. Polite questions about how I was feeling from Dorrie. Marie, of course, asking *but why*, and insinuating that it was an accident. We both ended up embarrassed, and Marie finally said, drunkenly, that she supported my right to be a young mother even if she thought I was completely crazy, at which point the novelist, of all people, leapt in to save me, or so he thought, asking if I would choose a baby name from my heritage, which was what, then, since I wasn't French? This led to the old speech about not knowing my heritage, closed adoption, et cetera. Growing up, my friends liked to play guessing games, because I looked so different from my parents. They would say, "Maybe part-Italian, or part-Iranian?" Some people even guessed part-French, just to confuse everything. Everyone was agreed on the "part" part. Yes, I knew about DNA tests. No, I had not done one. Yes, I knew people sometimes found surprise skeletons in the family cupboard, discovered their fathers were not their fathers and so on. In my case this was a bit of a foregone conclusion.

"But *why* don't you want to know?" Marie demanded. Tom

had drawn Angela and Dorrie back into more conventional conversation, and I could see he was trying to think how to jump into mine too, and save me from all this. But I was used to *all this*; I had been telling this story forever.

"I decided years ago that I am a product of my adoptive parents," I said. "I know that isn't true genetically, and I know that generally you can't choose your family but, in my case, my family chose me and I've decided to return the favour. There are inconveniences, but also surprising moments of freedom. And the gate to the past is shut. I don't plan to pick the lock."

For years I had been able to hit the perfect tone delivering this speech, a note between inspirational and forbidding. In recent months it had been harder. My chosen family wasn't keeping the faith. And I'd had my own covert flickers of warmth for the past two months, an eagerness to look into the face of the coming someone who would be my first blood relative. I was glad I was wearing a mask, to keep my secret joy away from all these eyes.

"But still," said Marie, mutinous. I saw that she couldn't handle uncertainty, or ambivalence, and in that moment I didn't feel threatened by her; I was almost sorry for her in fact. This was something that Tom would understand. This was something my Modernists would understand. A world in flux. Life and death in a moth. Complexity and not knowing.

Angela and Dorrie laughed loudly enough to drown out our conversation. Tom had led them to discuss our news to just the right degree without derailing the purpose of the evening. The conversation was moving on. I was still in the magic circle, a circle that grew tipsier and pushed masks up onto foreheads. I kept mine down.

"Happy birthday a day early," Tom was saying to Marie.

A line had been beating about in my head all week as this day approached, a quote of course.

"'But for him, it was his last afternoon as himself,'" I said, making quote marks with my fingers. I smiled at Marie as though it was a silly joke about her changing year. But she would wake tomorrow the same person as always, and I, now that the cat was out of the bag, was forever changed. Or that had been my fear. I was wrong of course. My last afternoon as myself came six months later.

But there comes a time, after the first pains have passed, when you swim down a silver river running like a torrent, with the convulsive, corkscrew movements of a great fish, threshing from its neck to its tail.

—The Squire, **ENID BAGNOLD**

In the last days of my pregnancy, my body perched at an odd angle to everything else. It kept me at arm's length from tables, from the bedroom window and its spy hole into the back gardens of my neighbours. In bed, on my back or my side, I was warped, obscene, protruding. I looked absurd walking, or trying to put my shoes on, but there was a kind of holy-vesselness about me. People smiled on the street.

The neighbourhood foxes screamed their mating calls in January and gave birth silently in March. There were cubs in the garden shed of the family home out back. I stood by the window one morning watching the teenage daughter drinking her tea in the garden. She squinted towards the shed, jumped up, and called and ran to the house. They all came crowding out, the parents and two younger brothers, and smiled and cooed. I loomed behind the curtain like a pregnant Mrs. Danvers. After they'd gone, I pulled out Tom's birding binoculars and trained them on the yard. A wobbly fox cub appeared at the shed door and stood in the morning cold with a beleaguered look. "Look at their sweet little faces," I moaned joyfully to Tom, and promptly burst into tears of happiness. Pregnancy was ridiculous. I was looking forward to our own baby's face, and also to getting back something of my usual, unsentimental self. But I was frightened of the process.

I could not ask my mother, of course, nor Angela, nor any of my friends. I read accounts online of the three stages of labour until I was riven with anxiety and paranoia, and dreamed of them. Parturition. Dilation. Expulsion. Horrible words. Afterbirth, urgh. I tried to replace them with other three-step processes. Labour as the three-volume novel or three-act play; labour as the Fibonacci sequence. Labour as the father, son, and holy ghost. Labour as a joke that is funniest on the third repetition.

Finally I broke down and called my uncle Julian's wife, Angharad.

"It can be wildly different depending on the woman, love. They say a lot of it's genetic. You don't know how it was for your birth mother, I suppose?"

"I'll just have to hope for the best on that front, Auntie Harry. But what's it like *generally*? What was it like for you?"

She thought a bit and said that labour was boring, like waiting for a pot to boil, and horrifying, like being a lobster in that pot. On a physical level it was made up of contractions—I knew about those, yes? You were fine in between contractions, but they became longer and more intense until the times you felt fine were far between. Her recommendation was not to try to be heroic about the pain. Take whatever they offered. It was bad, but then it was over.

"Right," I said. And then, "Don't mention I asked. If you speak to my mother, I mean."

"Ah," my aunt said dubiously.

I could handle it, I thought. I was a quiet and self-contained person. I had been doing yoga for some months already, finally ceding to my mother's offer to pay for it. Everyone in the classes was at least a decade older than me and spoke in gentle sing-song tones. There wasn't too much chanting, thankfully, but a good deal of cradling the belly, communing with the unborn child. I didn't enjoy this at the studio, though at home I could lie for hours touching my stomach, murmuring to my soon-to-be companion, reading poetry aloud and trying to imagine the features; would they be mine, would they be Tom's? Would there be a little of me at least—I so wished to find out.

It was the end of March, Easter break, and I was coming home from yoga class at ten in the morning. The studio was quite far away, on the other side of the high street, where everything was gentrifying quickly. My back was in agony as I trailed slowly through the side streets of the neighbourhood, past the foxes' house. There was nothing to be seen from the front but an enormous hydrangea bush, which had been a beautiful powder blue the previous summer but was bare, waiting to bud. It was a nice little house. Tom and I lived on a busier street behind it, where everything looked dingier and greyer and more oppressed.

I caught sight of a bird crouched near the foot of the hydrangea, a bird so bizarre looking that I stopped and stared at it. It was large . . . larger anyway than the usual sparrows and robins. It was grey and hideously ugly, like an experiment gone wrong, like some evolutionary throwback. It huddled near the bush with an expression of misery.

I finally realized it was a young pigeon, whose beak was still misshapen and whose adult feathers had not come in. It had either fallen or jumped from the nest and, flightless, had hidden in the bush. The chick heaved to its feet when it saw me and moved gloomily away.

I didn't realize where it was going until it was too late. "No, no!" I called after it as it went around the back of the house. I waved my hands over my head. The chick looked alarmed and moved faster. I seized a few crumbs of broken brick from the building site next door and tried to lob them past, to frighten it back to safety, but they fell short. With a last terrified glance back, it disappeared around the side of the house to the family of foxes.

Oh, my back.

A large woman wearing a smock coat with the name of a hairdresser on the high street was coming down the road, saw me, and hesitated.

"Do you need help?"

I gazed through a film of pain into her brown eyes.

"Don't worry," I said. It came out on the edge of a gasp. "It's to be expected. Just two more weeks to go."

"Oh, I don't think so, love," she said, looking me over. "Not so long as that. Why don't you go home and put your feet up? You'll need your strength."

I was optimistic when the contractions started in earnest. I was young and strong. It would all be fine, and in any case, the contractions weren't so terrible; painful, yes, but I knew I could get through them.

"Contractions" was a word that had implied pushing or tightening, and before all this I wouldn't have thought it meant back pain.

Nor that it was a pain that was very bearable until, after many, many hours, it wasn't; it was like being eaten alive by a famished wolf that couldn't be bothered to kill me properly. Though that was later, at the hospital, some twelve hours after I saw the baby pigeon.

In between I was at home, where the raving of the downstairs neighbour on a bender kept time with the rise and fall of pain.

"Breathe, breathe, breathe," I muttered, rolling and tossing on the bed, turning and turning in discomfort, turning and turning in the widening gyre, or perhaps that wasn't the best quote for the occasion. I felt a strange excitement, a strange jubilation underneath it all of being at a pivotal moment of my life; an impatience to meet the baby coupled with a reticence, a need to feel every shiver, every gasp, every icicle stab in the spine, an endless curiosity about what the baby was, when he or she would make an entrance. I couldn't lie in the bed anymore, although I was the one to tell Tom we should try and get some rest, the night would be a long one. He was a collapsed form, breathing easily, but I paced around, making piles of books to create some order in my life, books that then loomed around me like deserted high-rises. It was almost 10:00 p.m.

"Thieves!" howled the neighbour below, one of his favourite tirades. "You come and fucking take it all away."

"We should go back to the hospital," Tom said. He flicked on the bedside lamp and looked at me: he was tired but bright-eyed with excitement. I had been stuffing a corner of the duvet into my mouth so as not to disturb him with the small moans I could no longer keep in. I nodded, and he was up at once, dressing clumsily, picking up the bag that had been gathering dust in a corner for weeks, saying he was just off to get a taxi and disappearing, leaving me deciding on glasses over contact lenses—it seemed safer—and struggling into my coat and wondering how

I would get down the stairs by myself before remembering this was all part of the nonsensical narrative of pregnancy from the movies, that you were incapable of doing anything. Really, it came in waves as Aunt Angharad had said, and I was fine, felt great in fact, and confident that I could do this.

It hit me like an ice pick to the spine while I was locking the door, but afterwards I walked down the stairs calmly and nimbly.

In the front garden, full of weeds and muck and broken stones, it became very bad, a crescendo so intense I could hardly remain standing. The rain fell, and with the pain my world flashed into reverse, the garden resembling a solarized negative: the moon and the streetlights flipped black, the fence, so far away, shone white; the crouching cat in the far corner was revealed in striking silver with glinting jet eyes among the weeds and the rain, dark and bright simultaneously. For a moment I had a mad thought it was the neighbour crouching there at the bottom of the front garden. The contraction passed, and I staggered towards the gate, battled with the latch and the rain-swollen wood, and stumbled out. Tom was waving both arms at a taxi.

A cab heading for the motorway twisted into an illegal U-turn.

I became suddenly extremely talkative in the taxi, outlining my plans in some detail to Tom and the driver, saying that I'd been worried about how bad it would get, but I was filled with a tremendous confidence, and I hoped the birthing pool room would be available, because I'd read that labouring in water reduced the need for pain relief, after which I'd gone down a rabbit hole watching videos of dolphins giving birth and yes, I felt that was the way forwards; it sounded a lot more comfortable than lying in a bed hooked up to all sorts of things, being poked and prodded. Yes, I would like to get the pool. Then I shouted into my clenched fist for a few moments, while Tom said in some puzzlement that he thought I was against all that yoga-style, tantric natural birth stuff, that I'd come home often enough moaning about it, mocking women who insisted that pain could be sensual.

I told him I was planning to have a natural birth in honour of my mother, who had always wanted to experience childbirth but never could.

We were paying the taxi driver at the hospital entrance by this point, and Tom was saying "keep the change," and "that's completely crazy" in the same breath, then turning to help me along, but I was so incensed at this criticism that I pushed past him, powered forwards by my own glorious confidence; my mother hadn't done it, but Nan had, and her mother and all the women stretching back in childbirth history ad infinitum. The automatic glass doors closed gently, lovingly, like a trap. We had to wait a quarter of an hour to see a midwife, and I periodically gasped in pain and clutched my back throughout, but in fact I was pleased, pleased with every passing moment that reduced the time remaining, pleased with every contraction that I quelled by breathing deeply and focusing on the middle distance and walking around the waiting room, and sipping water, pleased until the midwife appeared, shook her head ever so slightly at the sight of me, and said that she could tell I wasn't in real labour yet by the look on my face, but nonetheless told me to lie down and she would examine me.

With a couple of fingers inserted inside of me she said, "Just two centimetres out of ten, I'm afraid."

I felt a sweaty clench of fear at her words, and the next time the pain came, it came magnified and treacherous, it came with the promise of more, it came laughing, caressing, humming to me that it had hours and hours more to offer, it came in a wall of panic so that I hardly heard Tom arguing quietly with the midwife that we weren't going back home, we couldn't be taking taxis back and forth all night, and could they not see about a birthing room, and the midwife assenting, disappearing for ages and coming back to usher us into a much smaller birthing room than the ones I'd seen on the tour, a room that was almost all bed, with a comically small toilet whose door opened on such a sharp angle that it was nearly impossible for a pregnant woman to fit around it. I paused on the threshold, taking in the four walls, the antiseptic beige cabinetry, reminiscent of the funeral home I had visited twice last summer. I tried to reach inside myself to that joy and optimism I had felt in the early hours, tried to reach for the curiosity to see the baby's face, but felt only jagged fear and a wet trail running down between my legs.

"Oh, good, your waters have broken," the midwife said. "Everything is progressing nice and normally. Let's see how it develops."

I lost the rhythm of breathing and began to fixate on things: the cabinetry, the foxes, the neighbour. Snatches of conversation I'd heard earlier in the week jolted around my head like crazed mantras. The midwife left us alone, and I rocked back and forth on the bed. Tom told me I was as white as a sheet, and I said that might be true but I was still having a better day than the pigeon, which he didn't understand, so I had to go into it, the darling baby foxes, how they had surely eaten the pigeon by now, and to think that at first sight I had thought it was some kind of magical bird, survived from the distant past, but it was just one of nature's throwaway creatures, of no value in its own right, and so I was reflecting that it wasn't a very good omen to see it on the day I would give birth. Tom rolled his eyes a little here and said I shouldn't go reading so much into a creature it had taken me a full five minutes to identify, by my own admission, even though it was the city's most common form of wildlife. I laughed a good while about that, though in truth I had lost the thread of what made it all so funny, especially as the pain came harder and faster, though it only made me laugh more, laugh and laugh and lapse into sulky silences, and then talk again when the peak of the pain was over, talk about anything that came into my head, think up names for the little foxes (Beckett, Mirrlees, Yeats, and Woolf, or was Woolf too much like wolf and therefore a stupid name for a fox cub? Virginia? But I hated that important men were always referred to by their surname but women half the time by their first name: "noted, Brodeur," Tom said), ask Tom if he was sure, at the end of the day, about our own name choices, tell him that I was worried growing up in Splinters might make the baby turn out like the downstairs neighbour, deny fiercely that I wanted to move elsewhere. It was getting late, and Tom had a stunned sort of look on his face; I remembered that he had worked all day.

A midwife appeared after half an hour and felt around inside me again. "Two and a half—let's say three," she amended, seeing the despair on my face.

I felt hot tears leak out from under my glasses and I took them off and put them on again, bit my fingernails, snapped at Tom that I was perfectly in control, thank you, because he'd asked the midwife at what point I could have an epidural on the off chance that I changed my mind and wanted one after all. I slumped despondently when the midwife told me enough sitting around, I was possibly slowing things down, I should walk around the room to see if I could get things moving again, but though I rebelled in spirit I did what she said, shuffling around the bed in circles, hissing that this was ridiculous (Tom agreed), trailing amniotic fluid and streaks of bright red blood and purple clumps like a horrible yoghurt with berries I'd eaten months ago back when I had the terrible morning sickness, shuddering and clinging to the bed, reaching back to knead my own back, twitching away from Tom's attempted back massages, pathetically light and gentle, like trying to attack the wolf with nothing but a blunt pencil, apologizing for being horrible, explaining that I would never eat yoghurt again, being sorry to hear that he didn't think he'd be able to stomach it again either, telling him to not mind me, I was just losing my mind but I'd be all right when I was done being made a sacrificial pigeon out of, screaming, apologizing for screaming, reasserting that I would do this all naturally, for my mother, telling Tom to fine, be like that, when he said that this mother-daughter thing was a bit mad, his mother had told him about labour too and said she'd wanted to have half her body amputated, which didn't seem to be the kind of thing you should go through feeling just for the sake of it; so as to what, exactly? live the experience for someone else, who might well have taken an epidural herself if it had come to that? I said I was sorry if my screaming was bothering him but he said to go right ahead and if I wanted him, he'd be over by the toilet having dental surgery with no anaesthesia just to prove he could, like.

"I wish I could help," he said afterwards, stroking my sweaty hair away from my eyes.

In between, it was silent, it was boring, as Auntie Angharad had said, it was just a pool of light holding Tom and me, except for a series of bumps from the hallway, probably the midwives dragging a body out by her heels, someone else defeated by nature, someone else whose time had come. What did it mean for a person's time to have come, in any case? Was a good outcome Nan's eighty-six years, even if the death was sudden, unexpected, caused by a random flu? She seemed so strong and full of life, and it all came as a terrible shock. It was a terrible shock, a terrible shock. It was impossible to say anything without sliding into cliché. Labour was becoming a terrible shock; I had spouted clichés last summer when I made it up to Nan and Grandy's house and joined the family, and Grandy shuffling around in confusion unable to respond to any of my clichés . . . He's the one we'd all thought would go first; in the end he lasted less than a month after her. A bad summer, last year. And Nan's funeral was full of clichés too: all platitudes about Nan being a good woman, and she wasn't a bad woman, but she was a formidable character, full of beans or full of ire, depending how you caught her, the original of the Angela types in my life. The whole thing was dismal, I told Tom, remembering the funeral; and he said yes, he also remembered my dad remarking as we arrived at the restaurant for a family do afterwards that if this had been his side of the family, if this were the Brodeurs, there would have been a party for a send-off; they were all dead by then but they'd been a very musical family who had always responded to any life event with French-Canadian Knees-up-Mother-Brown kinds of parties at wakes, or so he said. Actually, I told Tom, gritting my teeth through pain, bucking against it like a fish with a hook sunk deep in its guts, that comment of my father's had annoyed me, even though he was right: the problem with the event was that there was no sense of celebration. But that was the day he started talking my ear off about his genealogy research, and here I paused in pain to roar my terrible roars and gnash my terrible teeth, and, and, and my father hadn't stopped since, and while I wasn't usually oversensitive I thought that a) it was the kind of thing you could reasonably anticipate your adopted daughter might be not terribly excited about and b) particularly not at the funeral of her beloved, not blood-related, grandmother; you might envisage that the implication that blood was thicker than water might send *her* blood pressure spiking.

"I've seen you get annoyed whenever the topic comes up, but I didn't know you felt that strongly about it—you should tell people how you feel, Queenie."

It was very bad now, it felt like the climax, surely a person couldn't endure more than this, and yet I knew that I, Madeleine, Maddie, Mads, Queen Mab, Queenie, Madeleine F. Brodeur, was still somewhere in the middle of act 2, still had all the real drama ahead of me, damn the similes, why had I thought that labour could be compared to dramatic structure or the Fibonacci sequence? I cowered before my fear and pain. Tom had gone to the vending machine as we were both famished, and in his absence I glared at the cabinets, and I recalled the funeral and its aftermath. There was my father boring everyone stupid with his names and dates, and I was trying to listen to a story Nan's oldest friend, Sarah Clifton, was telling, about how when she was a girl Nan had come to live with her for several months. We asked why but Sarah didn't know, she'd been younger than Nan and no one ever talked about it after, and so we asked Grandy but he was frail and confused and I'm not sure he even knew he was at his wife's funeral, and I looked across to the sideboard where someone had put up a photo of Nan, who had always described herself matter-of-factly as having a face like a hatchet, and I stared at her, gone forever now, and thought here was a story, and the last person who might have told it was dead, and we had never thought to ask her. Think of it! I wailed through a contraction, and tried to spit it out, what I meant, to the empty room. Think of it, what was a list of dead relatives compared to a real story, an almost-living story, dead through negligence. Stories were what we wanted, not blood. Sarah knew plenty of other stories and told them well, about Nan's sharpness and determination, her withering wit, how she couldn't be doing with people feeling sorry for themselves but would throw herself into a cause for others, abandoned children and whatnot, maybe that's why *I* couldn't be doing with Marie's feminism-by-experience; it only focused on helping those who'd been in the same situation as you, and Nan had been so generous to everyone. Losing Nan had been a terrible shock. She always introduced me to everyone as "my granddaughter Madeleine," and she'd glare black spite at the ones who asked "Is this the little adopted girl then?" I did stand out in that tiny village of hers, with my curious always-part-something appearance. Nan would tighten her lips and reply, "That's what I said, my granddaughter Madeleine." I cried from the pain, and the funeral having been what it was, and my subsequent decision to bring the moth into the world, the decision that had brought me here, pitching like a minnow on the end of a line, of lineage.

"Did I miss anything?" Tom said, slipping back into the room while I lay spent between contractions.

Back at the funeral, Dad said again that Nan deserved a more colourful send-off, and he wished he'd thought to pack his fiddle; when his own father died, he had serenaded the forest beyond our house with an old French air in farewell; this is the kind of comment my father loves to make, and it is more or less true but it also misrepresents. It makes it seem like my parents lived in a forest, but well Tom, you've been to the suburb where I grew up; the "forest" at the time was a few undeveloped plots of lands beyond, which were finally built upon when I was eight, erasing those patches of bush and tangled trees and replacing them with another set of identical houses. Not rural. Not urban. When he told these kinds of half-lies, it depressed me; it seemed to come from the same impulse as the genealogy research, which he was still blathering on about, with the difficulties of not knowing your grandparents on one side and tracing things back to the people who had come over in whatever year and had to hack up the backwoods all by themselves and bah! Oh god, oh god, what was hacking up the backwoods compared with this? I felt my own back was being hacked up. The backbreaking work of the dead relatives was nothing to my travail now, Papa. My father just liked to collect the dead relatives with their past struggles and tragedies and surviving the Canadian winter and blah blah blah to validate living in the boring and unromantic landscape we actually inhabited: the not-not land. For my father was not the roaming gypsy musician he had fancied becoming, and not even really the French Canadian he pretended to be—as only one parent, his father, had been a French speaker. But all this, Papa, what had this done to me, who was even more not-not than he? Not French, despite my name, not British, despite my mother. Not my parents' child. History not certified. A stable future not yet secured. Potential, potential, but the outcome still not known.

I paused, exhausted from saying everything I had not spoken before, even to Tom.

It was just depressing to see all this in my father, whom I had indeed adored before *all this*. I couldn't even remember why I was talking about this, and increasingly, I was losing the power to string sentences together, indeed I don't believe I said all of these things aloud, and if I did, Tom was not there for all of it, and mostly I was merely panting and crying out and saving my breath in between. And so, was Nan's death in her eighties the tragedy it seemed to me, and more when I looked on my mother's devastated face; she too had arrived too late to undo the constant low-level friction of their relationship by saying a proper good-bye (always missing the parenthetical moments); or was it just nature? and was the real tragedy the baby pigeon, barely begun on life's journey? or was that just nature too, and was it all going to be fine, ultimately, because a baby would be born today, replacing one or both of them? That was just nature too. And my brute suffering was just nature; the hours I had spent by this point, lying awkwardly on the bed, sweating, screaming, attempting to focus and breathe, tearing away the monitors they had strapped around me and then having to lie still when they came to put them back. At some point I progressed to four, then five centimetres, with an hour between each one, with the sensation of a knife being twisted in my lower back every five minutes, and the numbers on the monitor that measured the strength of contractions growing and growing, surpassing all the limits that had previously seemed unbearable to me, until those limits were the stepping stones to peaks that seemed never to end. I pitched around the bed like an animal and then huddled and wept. Didn't I maybe want to try walking around again, Tom asked. I did not. Wasn't it supposed to help speed things along? Did. it. look. to. him. as. though. things. were. speeding. along? Then a tentative foot on the floor despite myself, only to be slapped by a pain so staggering I climbed up to the top of the bed, trying to climb out of myself, anything to get away from the feeling that I would break and my hips go clattering off to either side of the room like a pair of scuttling ragged claws. I was consumed by terrible shock. I was outraged by the breathing exercises in those prenatal yoga classes and my frantic gulps now. I was appalled by the articles I had read about women's bodies being made for this, about the woman's pain being good pain because it heralded the baby and therefore the happiest day of her life. I was furious to discover this sinister force, the uterine muscle, hiding within my own body. It did not feel natural; it made me wonder what other hidden destructive forces were within me, what cancers might be growing, what tendrils were reaching out to overwhelm me. Nature was red in tooth and claw—I saw the little foxes in the underbrush, licking their lips. I might, after all, have broken a minor law yesterday and trespassed; it hadn't occurred to me because I was too dominated and cowed by social niceties, but I might have followed the pigeon into the neighbour's yard and protected it, interfered with the more drastic laws of nature, plucked it from the fox's open, smiling mouth. I screamed and clawed at all the wires and monitors and the mess of blood, and vomited onto the sheets. I clung to the edge of the bed, feeling myself grow white with humiliation. I looked up at the cabinetry. I could no longer speak, no longer formulate words, no longer remember language. At around one o'clock there was a spate of contractions so strong I thought I would break in two, and that the baby, if there was anything left alive in there, would be born from the bleeding stump of my torso. I implored the forces of civilization to make it stop.

Relieved, Tom helped me lie still through a contraction when the anaesthetist told me I risked piercing the spinal cord by jerking the needle. A drowsy numbness spread, and I closed my eyes.

They were back. A sagely nodding cluster at the foot of the bed. I was summarily told that it was all going wrong, that I would need a caesarean and that they would be back in five minutes to prepare me.

"Can't we try a little more?" I whispered.

"That would be extremely dangerous." A doctor had appeared alongside the midwives.

"It's my fault," I wept. "It's like what they said at yoga. I accepted one intervention and it leads to another and another."

"It doesn't matter," said Tom, red-eyed, gripping my hand. "Who cares about all that? It's not the nineteenth century."

"Yoga!" said the doctor impatiently. "If this were the nineteenth century, you and the baby would both die."

They came to prepare me. Everything was damp with sweat, tears, amniotic fluid, blood. They took my glasses away, and abruptly the world disappeared. I was surrounded by people I couldn't see, blurry figures fiddling with machines, whose quiet talk belonged to a different world. Nan would have seen something like this, before the end. Death would be like this one day. Stillness on a table, vagueness and plastic tubes and the dim, moving shapes of the living. Childbirth and life both drew towards an inevitable conclusion, and in both cases I would be alone. I called for Tom but he didn't answer. I called again, and a face swam closer. Don't worry. He's coming. He was changing into scrubs to enter the operating theatre with me. The operating theatre. The red room. My teeth chattered. I sobbed that I wished it were not like this, wished that I could have faced the end of labour, this prelude to death, with the violence of everything that had preceded it, screaming into death's bloodied maw and bringing forth life.

Instead I felt no pain, just pressure and a remote brutality. Machines and cyborgs and the alienation of the modern landscape. I kept my eyes tightly closed. The surgeon was ripping and banging at me so that my etherized body shook upon the table. I had imagined them lifting the baby out, but no. My struggle had been converted into another's; a man was fumbling around amongst my internal organs and straining within my body.

When I opened my eyes there was a new blur being held towards me, a fuming hole in a smudged head, wailing in disbelief.

"It's a girl," Tom was saying. He was crying, and his voice was full of wonder. I, abruptly, had stopped crying. I wanted to tell him to give her to me, forgetting I was immobile, and cut open. Instead I vomited again. A nurse dabbed my lips with a Kleenex. I watched his hazy form step aside, holding the baby, and quiet, otherworldly shapes came forwards to sew me back together.

O love, how did you get here?

—"Nick and the Candlestick," SYLVIA PLATH

A mother and child in a quiet room. Though in actual fact, it was rather a noisy room: a ward, with people coming and going, machines bleeping, newly formed families getting ready to leave, visitors arriving. The noise didn't matter. The quiet, finally, was within her.

It was a first morning, *the* first morning, and it was bright and calm like a beach when the waves have receded after high tide, when the sand is smooth and mirrorlike seen from afar, though full of minute textures and imperfections and wonderments up close. Wonderments especially. Miraculous details. The curve and crease of the new eyes, slightly swollen from the birth. The tiny closed fists, the paperlike nails, the down of hair on the shoulders, the surprising dimple behind each ear. She touched the backs of her own ears and marvelled. She wanted to sing.

The storm had passed. The landscape of her life was licked clean and new. The child was eight hours old, and her eyes fluttered closed under a great weight of ocean swells. But they opened again, onto the first morning, the first daylight, the first face. The first face was a mother's face, as it should be, as was natural. The mother herself had experienced no such thing. All the participants at her own birth had disappeared from her life afterwards. But she would be here forever, she would be here to hold and protect this child. This was her first morning too. She wanted to laugh.

The newborn baby was such a small, crumpled form, with all the gravity of the great, bright world bearing down. The mother whispered a poem. Some Yeats, for herself, because there was time enough to find a poem for the little one:

It had become a glimmering girl
With apple blossom in her hair
Who called me by my name and ran
And faded through the brightening air.

She would follow this child anywhere.

"Let them weigh her," said Tom gently, half asleep on the chair next to her. "You haven't touched your breakfast yet." They carried the baby across the room, and she fell upon the food. She needed to keep up her strength, to feed the baby, and spend the rest of the day observing the baby. She was scalded by love, and wanted to catch every flicker of new consciousness, memorize the curve of the cockleshell ear, hear the faint lapping of the brand-new heartbeat.

Later that day, both mother and child developed high fevers and were whisked off to different corners of the hospital.

Time passed.

PART II

La Belle Dame sans Merci

Ineffable effable
Effanineffable

—"The Naming of Cats," T. S. ELIOT

On the eighth day, Madeleine, Maddie, Mads, Queen Mab, Queenie, Madeleine F. Brodeur, twenty-three-year-old promising doctoral student sat upon her hospital bed, holding the infant on her lap, staring into the small face as though searching for something.

"Time passes," she was thinking. The famous middle section of *To the Lighthouse*, after pages and pages of minutiae about a dinner party, in which suddenly the war sweeps in, and the old times are past, and characters die, three of them (in parentheses, no less). It was one of the texts that had made her want to expand her studies in the non-human. Telling of the catastrophe of humanity through descriptions of fallen plaster and the matriarch's moth-eaten clothes. Well, she felt as though time had passed. Woolf squeezed a decade into a few pages; Madeleine's week felt like a decade. Little had happened. Yet everything was changed. Her body. Her dreams. Even the baby looked different. Everyone said they changed so fast, but it had startled her this morning when they had brought the baby back to her.

Tom was once more on the uncomfortable plastic chair at the foot of the bed, flipping through pictures of the baby on his camera. He was deciding which met his standards of composition and delicate newborn beauty, and he was frowning, because newborn beauty proved elusive. Every so often he looked up, his eyes met Madeleine's, and they smiled, though they were looking at one another across a great distance, the distance of days spent sleeping apart, on different rhythms, in different worlds. Madeleine had been hospitalized all week, in a vague and drugged state after further surgery to drain an infection in the C-section cut. Just this morning, she had suddenly been made responsible for the baby again. Tom had spent the week as a child, playing host to his own mother who was meant to be helping with a grandchild—absent, also hospitalized, declared complication free on the same day as Madeleine. Tom's mother had returned home to Wales yesterday. She would be back when she had holidays in July. And Tom's precious parental leave was half over.

The baby was the brick-red colour of most newborns, and when awake had tenebrous grey eyes. Madeleine kept a cotton cap pulled down over the baby's hair, which was black and shocking and flyaway, like an '80s music star or a Troll Doll. It made the baby look unfamiliar, though unfamiliar compared to what? Perhaps simply to her preconception of what a baby looked like. She tucked a stray tendril under, and reached towards a book.

The baby stirred, and Madeleine looked down into the little pursed face. The baby's features clouded, with pain or anger or some malevolent force. A small wail, gaining in pitch and intensity, was emitted. Tom glanced up and clucked soothingly. Madeleine unhooked her nursing bra and lifted the baby. The doctors had suggested there might be difficulties establishing breastfeeding after a week of tubes, but the baby had emerged from her incubator ravenous, with her tiny mouth opening and closing onto nothing until Madeleine was able to organize herself.

Tom stretched. "They're taking ages. Whenever they say

they'll be back in ten minutes, you can be sure you won't see them all morning. They said we would be discharged today, but I'll believe it when I see it."

Madeleine's thoughts were scattered. She stared at the wall until the words penetrated.

"Do you think you could give me my book?"

Tom picked up the book, opened it, and placed it in her cocked and waiting left hand, taking the opportunity to run a gentle finger over the baby's forehead. "Let me know when you want a page turned," he said. He had his laptop out and was editing photos. "Which of these do you prefer?" He turned the computer to scan between three similar baby portraits. "Your mom and dad sent me an email last night asking for more pictures."

"Of course." She smiled. They were coming next week. Her mother had been messaging obsessively. Through Tom, she had already made a first gift: a playlist of folk songs and lullabies, some classics, some very obscure, and a couple that her mother had even recorded herself singing.

"And your dad wrote back after to add that he wants all the details so he can enter her properly into his fancy family tree."

Madeleine's smile faded. "As long as he's not buying her a DNA test."

Tom giggled. It was one of many endearing features, that his laugh was so joyful and so unmasculine, and that he never tried to curb it. "I did wonder if we should add a few middle names so she'd look impressive on his scroll or whatever," he said. "I wouldn't get in a huff about it. He's a man with lots of interests. He'll find something else to focus on. He'll either hit a wall, or learn the relatives are all boring and leave it be. Unless he discovers he can trace the family back to William the Conqueror, that is. Even a whiff of that and you'll never hear the end of it."

"And even if he discovered he's a direct descendant of Marie Antoinette, and even if I were shallow enough to want to bask in that, I couldn't because it wouldn't be *me* related to Marie Antoinette," Madeleine said. "I'm not being funny, but . . ."

"I know," Tom said. "*Not* being related to Marie Antoinette can only be a good thing though. Oh, look who's been lurking around the house all the time while you've been away," he said, turning the laptop again.

She frowned. "A cat?"

"It's the immortal cat that ran under the night bus last year and lived to tell the tale. I'm calling it Greymalkin."

"That's . . . from something I've read."

"*The Midnight Folk*. John somebody."

"Hmmm."

"He or she is a tough customer. Look at the ear on it."

"Or almost off it."

"Exactly. It fits right into the neighbourhood. Though I found the downstairs neighbour railing at it in the middle of the road yesterday, so it has some enemies."

"Is there anyone who hasn't been railed at by the downstairs neighbour?"

"True. I was going to murder him when he had one of his nights of passing out with the music full blast literally the day after you gave birth, but he's been quiet as a mouse since then. I was even wondering if he'd gone and died, until I found him shouting at Greymalkin." Tom returned to his editing.

Madeleine gazed at the book. Her spine was slumped and aching. The book was heavily theoretical. She must have had delusions of grandeur when she packed this for a hospital stay. The baby awoke slightly and suckled. Nothing was visible of her face but needled, angry brows.

Even if they were discharged today, they would have only a week together before Tom had to go back to work. And then she would have two days absolutely alone before her mother came. Two days not alone. Two days alone with the baby. She should stop calling the baby "the baby" and start calling her by her name. The name was surely the window to the soul. But it was difficult to imagine the baby having a soul, and difficult even to imagine her having a name. Her name was Maud.

"Tom," she said, after a few minutes of silence in which she stared vacantly at the book. It was difficult to talk to Tom, suddenly. Something about all the hours spent apart this week. So many hours. The hours he had needed to spend in the NICU, feeding the baby from bottles of Madeleine's expressed milk, cooing and stroking Maud's nose and temples. The hours she had not been well enough to go there herself, and the stilted visits they had made together, when Tom was businesslike and efficient and Madeleine felt like some kind of disaster tourist. She had held the baby when allowed, and attempted to hum one of the songs from her mother's playlist. It did not seem very baby appropriate: the tune was light, but the lyrics were about a prince shooting the white duck of innocence. They were drowned out by the roar of all the machines anyway. The moments in the NICU always had a veneer of unreality. She had looked at her baby and wanted so much to see her again in natural daylight, like the first morning, not under the hectic lights. But today, the unreality lingered.

Tom was looking up at her.

"I thought maybe you could take a few days' holiday," she said quickly. "Just two days, really. To tide me over until my mother arrives." She expected him to nod, eagerly or at least sensibly. He was chewing the corner of his lip slightly.

"I'd love to, Maddie. It's rubbish how it's gone on . . . this. But, um, alright, I wasn't going to tell you because it might not happen, but there was mention of a promotion maybe coming up." She looked at him. He looked at her.

"You weren't going to tell me?"

"Just because it's one of those unsure things. They just mentioned it to me a few days before you gave birth. It would be more money. Not so much more money, just so we're clear. Don't go buying a flat. But obviously every little bit helps. And I just feel I should make a good showing. Give the appearance that fatherhood hasn't derailed my dedication or whatever. But it might not happen. Don't get too excited about it."

"That's wonderful," she said, though there was a traitorous clench in her belly. She wished Tom had never found this job. She hated the distance it put between them. "Tom? I've always regretted that you haven't been able to pursue your photography properly, or some other interest."

"It's a hard field," he said. "Perhaps it's better to have a hobby that I don't try to make money from. Something unsullied."

"But if there were something you wanted to do," she said. "It wouldn't matter to me if it made less money. I can pick up the slack. Not right this moment, of course, but I'm sure we can work it out."

"Let's see where we are in a year." Tom had something of the project manager about him, since starting his job. His hands made chopping movements, dividing time into manageable chunks. "Meanwhile it would be a good thing if we could earn a little more." He looked apologetic then and still chewed his lower lip. "Maybe move somewhere a little bigger, once you're back to work. Somewhere Maud can have a bedroom."

She went back to looking at the baby. Maud Anna, born on April Fool's Day.

"Did I ever tell you that my mother wanted to call me April?"

"Really? I don't think you could have studied Modernist poetry if she had." Tom's laugh was a happy-to-move-on laugh. "It would be a bit like Doctor Bird the ornithologist. Or Doctor Darling the sexologist."

"Ha."

"Doctor Hausmann of the Architectural Studies department."

"Or Doctor . . . no, actually, I'm too tired, I can't think."

"Though come to think of it, Madeleine demands a Modernist joke or two."

She looked at him blankly. She almost needed to mouth the words, "Modernism, madeleine," before she got it.

"I would blame the hormones," she said. "But you know, I've never thought of that. Anyway, my mother said it was April when she learned my adoption had gone through. My parents had gone to Vancouver on holiday so they wouldn't have to wait by the phone. The cherry blossoms were late and weighed down all the branches like piles of snow, and my parents just walked around in a daze saying 'how beautiful, how beautiful,' but they weren't really paying attention. They were waiting by the phone at a distance of four thousand kilometres. When they called through to their answering machine from the hotel, they had been approved, and they looked out the window and realized it really was as beautiful as they'd been saying it was."

"That's a nice story."

"Yes, but my dad wanted something to reflect our French heritage, which is mostly all in his own head, so it was Madeleine in the end. Anyway, probably for the best." Madeleine blinked down at the baby, as though she had just remembered she was there.

"Tilt your head a little," said Tom, and when she looked up there was the digital whirr of his camera. "You with a baby and a book. You can send it to your friends and prove it's possible to write your thesis with the pram in the hall or whatever." He looked down at it. "I'm such a genius photographer."

"Oh?"

"I've framed it so you can't even tell we're in the hospital. Behind your head are just leaves from the bushes outside."

She turned her head to look outside and began to cry fiercely. Tom stared.

The pediatrician and nurse who had just entered together with the discharge paperwork also stared, until Tom heaved himself up onto the hospital bed and began to rub her back. "I just said something about the bushes," he told them defensively.

She could see the nurse looking at her like she wouldn't be allowed to take the baby home after all, and so she said angrily, "It's just that I opened the window the first night, and I'm sure that's how she got sick and had to go into the NICU."

The nurse came and stood by the bed. She was a brisk girl with a throaty voice who called all the women on the ward "mummy" and had taught a humiliated Madeleine to change a nappy the first day.

"You, opened a window? That first night—hours after a section?"

Madeleine nodded. It was after Tom had gone home. Late, maybe 4:00 a.m. She had deviously disconnected the drip and staggered to the window through shooting pains. She had just wanted some air. There had been a chill breeze, and in the end she had gladly hobbled back to the warm baby.

The nurse gave her a very strange look, but said with game cheeriness, "It's nothing you did, mummy. The baby caught a virus. She didn't catch it from an open window."

Madeleine palmed her tears away, humiliated again.

"It's true that we don't allow the window to be open," said the nurse. "In general it's not a good idea to have temperature extremes. But even in summer we don't let the mummies have the windows open. Do you know why? Funny story, actually. There were foxes in those bushes last year, and there was some worry they might come in. It's not very likely, but hospital management thought it a risk. The city was going to cull them, but the public didn't like that. And fair enough, really, poor things. Though they are pests. So you didn't make the baby ill by opening the window, mummy. We just need to make sure the foxes stay out."

"Don't call me mummy," Madeleine looked down at the sheet for the remainder of the time it took to arrange the paperwork. Sometimes she looked at the baby and adjusted her cap. Tom's mother had asked if Maud looked like Madeleine as a newborn, and Madeleine wasn't sure. She had been ten months when she was adopted. If there were baby pictures, she hadn't seen them. In photos, Tom and his brother were both bald as coots.

"The health visitor will be calling in next week," the pediatrician was saying to Tom. "In principle there shouldn't be any problems; the baby is feeding better than we expected, given the early interruption, but if you have any worries you can call this number. And the health visitor also makes sure the mother is feeling well," she added brightly.

Madeleine glanced up sharply from the baby. The nurse and the pediatrician were both smiling supportively. And both watching her closely. So that she would not have to look at them, she picked up Tom's heavy camera, lying on the bed, and looked at the picture. He did take wonderful portraits; it was true that but for the blurred lip of the window behind her she might almost have been outside, in among the bushes, reading a book with a baby accessory on the crook of her arm. She was surprised to see a peachy bloom of health and happiness in her cheeks. Her hair looked artfully tousled. The hand holding the book wore chipped red nail polish, which she had applied before going into labour. The baby was tranquil and perfect.

"I will send this one to my friends," she agreed, smiling up at them all.

I met a lady in the meads

—"La Belle Dame sans Merci," JOHN KEATS

She still had her pyjama shirt on, under her anorak, under the cloth sling bound across her chest with the baby in it. She was at the bus stop. Tom stood next to her freshly shaved, freshly pressed, with a freshly made sandwich in his old, university-era rucksack.

"You don't have to be obsessive. Obviously you should get a cup of tea here and there. Just try to eat at home. Can't quite believe what we've spent on bits of this and that, coffee here, cake there, lunch, after the last few days, and me of course all week you were in hospital eating at that vile canteen."

"Got it."

"It's just that we never had buckets of disposable income to begin with."

"I know I know. Operation-save-a-penny-here."

"I know I'm annoying, but my parents fought constantly about not having money. I hated it and just don't want to end up there."

"Mmm."

"But you should get out as you need to, of course."

"Right."

"Sorry to leave so early. Research suggests that men who are new fathers often get promoted, so."

"Is that the same research that says mothers' careers stall?"

Tom grimaced as the bus pulled up. "Bye now, Queen Mab. I'll be back as soon as I can, without looking like I'm ducking out on the stroke of five o'clock."

The bus hauled away. Her destiny was severed from Tom's. She suspected he was glad to get back to work. The first days at home with Maud had been claustrophobic, punctuated by unexplained bouts of crying and wild attempts to provide food, nappies, or sleep on demand. When they went out, the baby slept, so finally they had gone out as much as possible. Now she faced morning in the flat. She had been awake for three hours already, as well as most of the night.

On one side of the road were small-windowed eighties builds, and on the other crumbling blocks of Victorian flats set back from the street behind towering hedges. If she turned left, she could be in a warm café on the high street in ten minutes. She turned the other way, back to their home behind a high wooden gate, just before the road rejoined a strip of motorway.

Splinters was generally considered dilapidated and ugly, but she had fallen for it hard when they moved in almost two years back, at the start of her PhD. It was vibrant and alive. For some reason, the impulse that made her nervous around Dorrie and all her care-system dramas had the inverse effect here. She felt drawn to the neighbourhood, maybe because she could float along the surface, observing, and for the most part she could choose to interact, or not.

She loved the march and flux of urban history all around. There were guided graffiti tours that came up the high street, Hartley Road, to see the bright murals that covered dead-end corners and even whole decaying buildings. The real Splinters lurked beneath the paint, and down the side streets and alleys.

The tours never came out the way Madeleine and Tom lived. But local architecture students had created a kind of informal museum on interesting corners, installing ad hoc plaques to explain the area's history. The city had been a major port and a nexus point of the slave trade, and the original houses had been built with its wealth. They were now as dilapidated as the nineteenth-century tenements that had once housed garment workers. The whole area had been heavily bombed during the war, and afterwards migration brought the descendants of the slave trade back to fill some empty spaces. Discriminatory employment policies and urban rot, widespread neglect, heavy-handed policing . . . The district first earned the nickname Splinters in the 1960s, as activists organized strikes and protests and the community rallied itself into thousands of individuals jabbing away at the established fabric of the city. But then another great wave of change had swept through. A famous riot, crack epidemics in the eighties, and now Splinters meant something quite different. Madeleine, in a fairy-tale-esque mood, had nicknamed the street below theirs the Path of Needles, and theirs was only marginally better. And then, the students' plaques declared, came the rise of the street artist, to paint over the neighbourhood's open wounds, and then the usual churn of gentrification began: the arrival of artists as residents in the early twenty-first century; then students and so, Madeleine and Tom. And Madeleine loved the neighbourhood, its scrawniness and crumbled glamour, even the eternal wind tunnel outside the chip shop on the high street.

Tom said it was a great place, yes, with some real characters and an undeniable buzz in the air; but to be perfectly frank, she and he were part of the problem. It had gone beyond underground music and some nice cafés. There were two tapas bars going in opposite each other on Hartley Road, for fuck's sake.

But Madeleine raised her face to the brisk morning wind. Good morning, Splinters. Change was intrinsic to life. Once upon a time, before all that, the neighbourhood had been a hamlet; and before that, the heath. The wiry ugly road had once been a gurgling stream.

She jerked open her water-swollen gate and stepped into the front garden. There he was. Stopped on the path, mid-harangue, the neighbour from downstairs was staring straight into her. She avoided his yellowed eyes with their burst blood vessels, and crossed her arms over her chest to shield the baby.

His eyes narrowed. "You're the one who stole from me at the shop." Enunciating too well, too carefully, keeping the slur out, just.

Two steps back, out the gate again. The shop thing had all been a mistake but one that was going to haunt her. They had both been at the checkout, he taking ages to pack his bags with shaking hands. Kamal at the shop was just trying to keep the queue moving. She had come through after him and had grabbed one of his bags by accident, and she'd realized almost immediately, but not before he'd darted at her like a snake and clutched it back. And that was her done for. The man's memory was in pieces; he didn't know what day of the week it was, but her face was imprinted somewhere deep within, and so she had to skulk across roads at the sight of him, or listen to make sure he wasn't coming around the side of the house when she left by the front door.

"You stole from me at the shop. Fucking thieving students, taking my bag, taking my things."

Another two steps back, and he followed her. He was weaving. Up early today. She might step around him once he came further out, dash past, jam her key in the door, take the stairs two at a time. He was fast though. It took him all day to cross the front garden, but he wasn't old, that was just the state of him. The stream of curses continued, unbroken but unfocused. When she moved, his eyes snapped up again.

And back in the flat, what? He could stand there for hours in the garden, ranting.

She turned and walked the other way, towards the motorway entrance and the traffic light. There were still people at the bus shelter by the entrance to the park. He wouldn't follow, and if he did, appearances were against him. Appearances were in her favour. He hadn't seen the baby. Somehow that seemed important, to keep the worst of the neighbourhood from the pristine baby. Apart from the neighbour it was all right. Cheerful, greasy-spoon fry-up joints and Jamaican takeaways, good slang, accents, nice cafés a little further afield. Vibrant streets. Things she'd missed out on, growing up in a suburb. But there were less predictable elements: dogs that barked but were never walked, junkies screaming at each other in the night, a house that was set on fire three times. The neighbour's shouts faded against the roar of cars accelerating on the ramp to the motorway.

She ate a jacket potato in a café around the corner.

Me: You won't begrudge me that will you? I'm hiding from the neighbour

Tom: Ah, Maddie, head high, just walk past him

Me: No chance

Me: Easy for you to say

Tom: Madeleine Brodeur: "I love Splinters, it makes me feel alive after the bland identikit housing of my Canadian childhood." Also Madeleine Brodeur: "I can't talk to the neighbour for five seconds."

Me: You. Were. Not. There.

After, back in the flat, the silence doubled down upon itself while outdoors the day marched onwards. She'd got stuck feeding the baby on the couch. The baby was asleep now, but Madeleine couldn't reach the pile of books on the coffee table. They might as well be on the moon. If she reached for them, she would wake the baby, and if she woke the baby, there was no point having the books. There was one book on the arm of the couch, the delusions-of-grandeur one she had taken to the hospital. No possibility of reading that, but there was a small square of folded paper tucked into it, and a pencil. She could write down her thoughts and feelings. The pencil hovered. What to say? *This baby eats too much. This is so much more boring than I imagined. Why does she never sleep alone?*

It was a weekday. Office workers were opening emails, bus drivers were mid-shift, baristas were steaming milk, hairdressers were getting their kit in order. The night shifters were having a bite to eat and going to bed. Tom could not leave work for at least another seven hours. She wondered if the unemployed, and there were many in the neighbourhood, were being asphyxiated by their silent flats, as she was.

The baby opened her eyes, stretched, and looked up at the ceiling. She did not cry, and she did not try to suckle. The silence lay heavy over them both. The baby closed her eyes again. Madeleine shifted, irritable. If the baby went back to sleep in the same position, she would have to sit here longer, potentially all morning. She leaned for a book. The baby's eyes opened again, and she began to cry a quiet, nerve-shredding mewl.

As Madeleine fed the baby again, she stood at the front window and looked down at the busy street, the bus shelter, the triangle of park, the neighbour shuffling back home through it, his bags all laden with cartons and cans.

She did not want to be here, and she did not want to tiptoe about all day thinking of the neighbour downstairs, of the traffic, of the rhythms of useful urban life. "Let's go and be in nature today, baby," she said, and she hurried down the hall, laid the baby on the bed while she wrapped the sling around herself, and shoved the baby through the straps. The baby wailed, and ricocheted against Madeleine's chest with her mouth gaping. Hungry to the point of nausea herself, Madeleine felt a grim pleasure at frustrating the baby.

The last few days she was so ravenous she could think only of food. She would buy a bacon roll on the way to the bus, though they were meant to be economizing.

The neighbour had reached the edge of the park but not yet crossed the road. She would not take the pram, because she would miss her window of opportunity if she had to unchain it and bang it along the garden path.

On the bus she joggled gently from side to side while the baby slumbered in the carrier, head thrown back and mouth open. Madeleine was thirsty from the bacon roll. She should have got a tea while she was at it, even if her maternity pay was less than the old stipend and set to decrease over time. But then she would need the toilet later, and how was that to be managed in a park, by herself, wearing a baby sling?

A woman in her fifties smiled broadly every time Madeleine's jolting brought the baby's head into view. She had the rhapsodic look of reliving a happy time.

"Sit down," said a woman kindly, indicating an empty seat.

"Better I stand," said Madeleine. "She'll wake up if I sit, and then it's all over for me." She gave the cheeky smile that Tom had already perfected for talking about the baby in public, but the woman frowned and toyed with her necklace.

"It's not about you," the woman said. "What if you fell, because the bus lurched and you landed on the baby? Mothers, you know," she said apologetically, "sometimes we have to sacrifice our own comfort. It's tempting never to wake a sleeping baby, but think of how it would be if something happened."

Madeleine's mouth had gone dry and scratchy during this speech. She never could take criticism coolly, which was why teaching seminars was always so fraught. She sat but stared at the woman, imagining a litany of things she would do to her if she could make a getaway on public transportation, carrying a baby. She would kneecap her; she would take a small hammer and knock her teeth out one by one.

The woman twitched under her glance, and looked away.

She would push her sharply from behind when disembarking so the woman would sprawl off the bus and crack her head. But she saw herself falling instead, and the baby's head bursting like a tomato upon impact, or nothing so dramatic, her head merely bruising, internal bleeding setting in until the baby opened her eyes and they spilled over with blood. She clung to the pole beside her. She might trip; a dog might run in front of her. Would she be able to break the fall before she hurt the baby?

It was noon when the bus drew up to the park. She descended carefully, clinging to the handrail and placing her foot full on the ground.

In the park the smells were deep and green, and the signs of spring were partly stunted, partly overblown, as microclimates established themselves in open fields and sunken hollows. Spotless primroses were tucked neatly into a wall; daffodils were spent and browning. A few more pushes through the shrubbery, and she was out into a meadow hemmed with trees. There was a small lake lined with rushes, a conservatory tearoom at the far end.

It was Wednesday. In another life Madeleine would be teaching, which was always nerve-racking but gave her a sense of accomplishment when it was over. Instead, she stood alone in a field, looking at an artificial lake, deciding if it was extravagant to have a cup of tea and if she had the energy to circle the lake to the tearoom. What separated one Wednesday from the other was this small, warm cluster of life at her chest. A woman's greatest accomplishment, people said.

Maud's head fell sideways in the sling, revealing pursed lips and the apple-sweet curve of a cheek. Madeleine looked on her and felt nothing. She tried to remember how she had felt the first morning. The adoration. More: the *kinship*, the perfect equilibrium of Maud's weight in the crook of Madeleine's arm. The tiny hand that closed in a fist around Madeleine's finger. But then confusion, blood, machines, strong drugs. And when she surfaced, the connection was gone.

At the edge of the lake she looked back. The field sloped slightly, giving the impression of an empty mound. In the distance, at the conservatory, she could see some tranquil heads enjoying the weak sunshine, but here in the meads, a cold hill was at her back.

She was startled to find the baby gaping up at her. Haggard and woebegone, Madeleine thought, though she knew Maud was merely trying and failing to focus her eyes.

The baby began to squirm, and Madeleine sat on a bench to feed her. She had a sudden misgiving that it would be difficult to get her back into the carrier again, alone, without laying the baby on the cold ground.

She watched as the eyes closed again in spite of themselves, lulled asleep by milk, a force stronger than the baby's control. People and dogs came and went on the far shore of the unruffled lake. There was a silence that wasn't natural, a hush before a storm. No birds sang.

How much could a cup of tea cost at the conservatory? A pound fifty? It was a small price for company, to see other people and not just be alone and palely loitering here in the reeds.

The baby did have to be laid on the ground, briefly, while she readjusted the sling. But no one was watching, and the baby didn't seem to mind. She was fascinated by the diverging patterns of rushes that rose above her head. She was such a small, pretty baby, Madeleine thought as she tightened the sling over her hips. Full beautiful—a faery's child, as Keats had it. Empty words. She felt nothing.

As they set out along the path again, the baby squirmed. Perhaps she had tightened the sling too much, or not enough. Madeleine bounced from foot to foot, but the baby grunted, moaned, and finally let out a long, agonized shriek.

Madeleine ran wild-eyed, light-footed along the path. But where could she go? She could not go into the conservatory with the baby like this. She did not want to see the faces swivelling towards her, the lunches disturbed, herself helpless before the crying. She wanted another bench, but she went on and on and didn't find one. The lake looked less artificial as she ran through the rushes; with every gasping breath she took the ripples slapped sharply against the shore. In her classes she would draw attention to this. The inanimate world takes on the inner state. Pathetic fallacy. Meanwhile the baby screamed and writhed and squinted in anguish moist and fever-dew. She seemed to be having an existential crisis. They moved along the marshy path, and the baby sobbed and wailed, sobbed and wailed, and the rushes parted before them like waves.

A bench came into sight, and Madeleine dashed to it, tugging at the sling again, shrugging off her anorak. She pressed the baby to her breast with a sigh of relief. But the baby howled and twisted, stretching her skinny legs, her mouth an *O* of horror, her tearless eyes rolled back in her head. Madeleine again tried to crush the baby forcibly to her breast, and the baby recoiled in fury. Madeleine stared at her, helpless and frozen, clutching the tiny body as it pitched and contorted in her hands.

And then it was all over. The baby cast a martyred expression to the sky above, and then her face became cunning, and an explosive roar came from her nappy. A pause, another roar, and Madeleine sat on the bench, helpless with laughter. The waves subsided back to sunlight and calm. A duck floated by.

When she turned back to the baby, she noticed a mustard-coloured line seeping along the curve of one thigh. And she didn't have the changing bag. How could she not have it? It was the only thing she needed, apart from her own breasts. A frantic rummage, and she found a single nappy tucked into a side pocket of her bag, no doubt by Tom. But no wet wipes, no change of clothes. And now, of course, people were coming around the bend from the conservatory—retirees, pale warriors with newspapers under their arms who clucked at the baby. Madeleine scuttled to a patch of bushes, and the baby was changed in a hedgerow, cleaned as best she could with a handful of grass and a dock leaf.

"This cannot be my life," Madeleine muttered. She felt chilled. She was kneeling in a bush with a stained baby. The park was an exhausting place and merely a distraction from her solitude. The conservatory tearoom beckoned. She should go home, and buy nappies on the way, another six pounds. But she could not resist the call. She did not want to linger here or make the return journey yet.

By the time they got to the tearoom, Maud was sleeping.

Delicate breaths fluted against Madeleine's collarbone. Looking around, she wondered why she had hesitated to bring a crying baby here. Most people in the place were mothers with babies or toddlers. Two babies were crying at that very moment. A toddler was screaming among upended crayons for his mother to draw him something. The mother ignored him, speaking with staccato intensity to a friend.

Madeleine ordered tea, and the man at the counter tried to upsell her a sandwich. "Not today," she said. She was starving from all the breastfeeding, but the tea was almost double what she had thought it would be.

She shuffled over to the table with her tray. She didn't dare remove the baby or even move much herself. She poured the tea at arm's length, beset by waves of hunger, and found herself staring fixedly at an uneaten corner of cake on a nearby table. There was a bowl of sugar cubes on the table, and she slid one into her mouth. The day was passing, slowly. The day after tomorrow her mother would come. They would go around together; her mother would feed her and help her.

The toddler with the crayons clutched at his mother's arm. "You draw, you draw." Without taking her eyes from her friend, the mother took a black crayon and drew a hasty outline of a cat. "Colour."

"No! No cat! Mummy. Draw mummy!" With a squeak of impatience, the mother reached for the crayon again and made a vague stick figure with shoulder length hair. "There you are, darling. Now you. Colour me in."

Madeleine watched the child colour. It was more of a strong scribble, first with one crayon, then another. His mother turned blue and scribbly, overlaid with red and scribbly. He spent extra time making her face green and scribbly. He coloured until she blended with the cat sketch further along the page.

The cat flicked its tail.

Madeleine blinked. When she looked again, he had coloured so much that no lines remained.

Through the steam rising from her teacup, she watched the faces of the mothers around her. Mothers and more mothers, overlapping, overlaid, tired faces, death-pale faces, puffy faces, bodies that drooped and bent, bodies distorted with excess weight or shrunken as though they had lost more than they'd gained. Expressions of tedium or bland impatience, wavering smiles, terribly tender kisses planted on babies' flossy hair. They turned their heads simultaneously, to look at her, and their mouths opened all together, twisted, deformed, their starved lips gaping wide in warning. Their eyes receded; they were only mouths, chanting as one: she had fallen, she was one of them, caught in an age-old enchantment.

An infant crying in the night

—"In Memoriam A.H.H.; 54," ALFRED, LORD TENNYSON

Madeleine stumbled along the hallway one dark morning, terribly hungry for buttered toast, torn between sleep and food, foiled in both by the baby in her arms. She sank onto the nearby sofa, feeding and feeding and feeding. Feeding, one of those tricksy words. She wished to be feeding, but she was too busy feeding. She liked words like this. Half of what they called promising in her was just her knowledge of strange odds and ends. She lived in fear that they would realize this. She *had lived* in fear. It all started to feel very past tense, not least her wonderful memory. Facts and stories and ideas scattered away from her now. She lived from one bodily moment to the next. But she still liked those words: the odd, out-of-favour ones that had a subtly different meaning from what was commonly accepted. Words like gossip, which once meant midwife, or companion in childbirth, back when childbirth had been a social event full of women talking and helping. Master and mistress, once both denoting power and respect, now hopelessly diverged into authority and scandal. Words that were their own antonyms, like weather; words that sounded like they should mean one thing, but actually meant something else, like noisome. Or just old words, outdated words. She had written an essay about the word "puckish" three years ago that had won a scholarship. After returning home for her final degree year after the exchange program, she had been able to return to the UK for her master's with the proceeds of that essay. "Puckish" had brought her back to Tom. Actually, it had been the first instance of fairies in her studies too.

The night reeled above her; she was hallucinatory in her lack of sleep and her hunger and pestered by pains in her muscles and her scar, and under all of that, full of nervous energy.

"'I am—yet what I am none cares or knows,'" she said experimentally in the dim room, the rasp of her voice like sandpaper to smooth away the night. With no one for company, she would recite to herself awhile, train her mind. "'My friends forsake me like a memory lost.'" And then that odd turn of phrase: "'I am the self-consumer of my woes.'" It was this line that had always called to her about the poem. What did it mean, precisely? It tended to peter out for her after this whiny ironic high in the third stanza. Clare was like that, starting strong, and then what? What was the other one of his that she liked?

The Old Year's gone away
To nothingness and night:
We cannot find him all the day
Nor hear him in the night.

She laughed as she recited those lines. These days, she would hear a penny drop in the night three streets away. But here she was, reciting poetry aloud, and Tom was sleeping deeply in the other room. Tom felt more distant from her than at any time since they had met, including the year they had mostly been apart when she went home to compose puckish essays. Tom slept oblivious, and she was alone on the sofa.

She had always been a very heavy sleeper, actually. It was rare to find her pacing about after she'd gone to bed, though not unheard of.

She and Tom were inseparable, and they were going to share every duty. But she couldn't blame him. Society dictated he must return to work. Somebody had to keep them afloat. But it did feel like the old year had gone away. You could only describe this living room as nothingness and night. Perhaps she should turn on a light.

Would she find Tom in the day?

How tiring were her own thoughts at this time of the night.

Perhaps quoting Clare should have been relegated to her time as a moody adolescent. After the event she always thought of as the "Great Nondiscovery," she had sworn off anything that smacked of self-pity, of consuming one's own woes. Even so, Clare stayed on the respectable side of self-pity; she always had time for Clare.

All this insomnia and staring into nothing and feeling sorry for herself was, actually, reminiscent of the Great Nondiscovery. Another period of turmoil. The days leading up to her nineteenth birthday, and then the days after it.

The days before: she had felt so grown-up. She was preparing herself to *know*, to be in an enlightened state. Back then she had put stock in *knowing* things, like Marie. What mundane or tragic history would swim forth from the murky past? She was finished with her second year of university, already applied for the exchange program that would bring her to England. A safe jump, one that would take her away from her parents but deposit her near to Nan and Grandy. It seemed an appropriate time, with her life on track and her head full of a million lives and circumstances from studying literature, to take a measured, clear-eyed, deliberate look at her own backstory.

She realized she was murmuring to herself, out loud, in the black living room. The baby gnawed away restlessly. It felt like someone pushing hard on a bruise. But at least while the baby was eating, she wasn't crying. She was crying the rest of the time, unless Madeleine was walking with her in the sling.

"Funny story, baby," she said conversationally. It was nice to hear an adult voice, something that wasn't an inarticulate mewl, even if she was just talking to herself. "To you it seems natural enough to suckle away at your mother's breast, but I had to be legally an adult before I could go and even learn who mine was. Those were the terms of the closed adoption. When I was growing up, it was just an element of mystery. At about ten, I made up a story in which it was discovered that I was actually the long-lost heiress to the castle that's a few hours' drive from Nan's. I would receive a letter informing me I'd inherited, and we would all go live in the castle, and it would be very Dodie Smith. Apart from these fantasies, I never thought I'd know anything, but then I learned they'd been passing new laws to make it easier for adoptees to access their parental records, to facilitate reunions and knowledge of medical history. The concept of illegitimate birth had become less stigmatized." She had taken on a droning, bureaucratic tone, and then lapsed into silence. She sounded like Madeleine F. Brodeur writing a paper.

God, she was hungry. She leaned her head back against the sofa. In the dimness, she could see the outline of a bare light bulb. She must get a lampshade. But she shouldn't spend the money. And though she couldn't see it now, she knew from sitting in the same position by day that there was a large cobweb hanging down. She must dust. Cleanliness was next to godliness. And, Nan would say, it was also free.

“I didn’t tell my parents about it, because my mother’s feelings would be hurt. I just gathered all the documents together, and the day after my nineteenth birthday I sent them in and waited for a response. I wasn’t expecting to be an heiress by then of course. More likely the daughter of a drug addict. I thought I could handle that information. It was pleasingly Victorian, in a way. And I was safe. I had my loving family; I was getting my education. I’d done a bit of teenage rebellion, with heavily smudged black eyeliner and music that my parents found obnoxious. But it was all very innocent: I’d been careful never to truly go off the rails, never to try anything too dangerous, because there was probably a dark, dark story behind me, and I didn’t want to be a self-fulfilling prophecy. We no longer believe the Victorian notions of superiority of birth, Maudie, that idea that a chimney sweep who is really the son of a duke will be a little gentleman whatever his circumstances, but they *do* say addiction and trauma can imprint in your blood, or your DNA, or whatever. There is some scientific basis to the idea that man hands on misery to man whether or not you actually know your parents.

“My mother, by which I mean my real mother, by which I mean my adoptive mother . . .

“Sorry, lost my train of thought there. My mother Carol. Your grandma. Or should we call her Nan? Somehow it seems wrong because Nan was Nan and Carol is nothing like Nan; that’s something we will probably all agree on. Nana maybe. It sounds softer and my mother is soft; she bruises easily in more ways than one.

"My mother is the woman who spent nineteen years packing my lunches, French-braiding my hair, listening to me ramble about everything from invisible friends to high-school intrigues. I could talk the hind leg off a donkey when I was younger. She would say so, when she could get a word in edgewise: 'Maddie. You could talk the hind leg off a donkey.' When I was little, I would reply, 'No! A kangaroo!' She listened to all my enthusiasm and drama. She would remember it long after I'd forgotten all about it. Well. That's Carol. That's your grandmother.

"Anyway, shortly after my nineteenth birthday she found me lying on my bed, a flat smear of misery and, frankly, drunk as a skunk for the first time. Or well, not the first time, but the first time she'd seen me. I knew you were supposed to react to news like this by obliterating yourself, so I'd gotten into the liquor cupboard, and brandy seemed the kind of thing, and, uff, I don't recommend that particular medicine, should such a day ever come for you, baby. I was all limp and green, and the ceiling was rocking above my head, and I couldn't even reply to her questions, which were full of panic, and her voice quivering more than mine even. Couldn't or refused to, and I just lay there with tears leaking everywhere. It was a shameful scene, Maud. I'm ashamed to remember that I couldn't hide my self-pity long enough to keep from her that I'd gone looking for knowledge of my birth mother, and that I'd failed, because, to paraphrase the letter I received from Library and Archives Canada, the birth parent can file a veto to prevent the child from finding them. Very few do so. It requires knowing the law; it requires action, Maud. It prevents any information from being released until two years after the birth parent's death. The parent can choose to leave an explanation. They can choose to disclose medical information that may be of interest to the child. The woman who is by birth my mother did neither. She left a sealed door barring me from knowing, for her lifetime anyway."

Madeleine swallowed. "That's not the important bit, though, Maud. Although I think it's worth saying I disapprove of going looking for missing ancestors. But the important thing that day was the state of me. I wondered later if I inherited wallowing in self-pity from my birth mother, or being a weepy drunk. Or hurting people. Because the worst thing about that day was letting my mother find me like that. She was so hurt that I had gone looking for the other one. She had never hidden my origins from me; she had done everything well. She was a model mother, but jealous. Doing things perfectly was supposed to be enough. Ironically, by driving a wedge between us, I made our relationship real. But my mother and I have never quite been able to look one another in the eye since then."

The baby's eyes were closed, but she was not truly asleep. She was asleep enough not to be awake, but she was not asleep enough to be put in her cot. The only one asleep enough to be in bed was Tom.

"My mother and I have never spoken of the Great Nondiscovery. She tried, in the beginning. All her questions had a stench of pity, and self-pity. I wouldn't say anything. She continued to be exemplary. She continued to mother me. She took me shopping for new clothes. She helped me apply for grants for my exchange year. We cultivated closeness. It was a performance. We spent the summer going for coffee as though we were friends, and watching British soap operas to get me into the spirit of my year abroad. We did all this before; we used to have *fun*, but after the Great Nondiscovery it was an act. Even now, I text her most days. But it's not real. Or too real. She looks after me, but I'm always having to look after her. When I do something nice for her, she's terribly happy about it. Too terribly happy."

Some shouting from the street rose to a brief pitch of rage and violence. Just as quickly, it faded away.

"But I still want to make it up to her. I heard her crying in bed herself that first night. Self-pity, self-pity. Crying because she wasn't enough."

Madeleine rested her head on the back of the couch. What was she doing? Surely reciting all this in the night was just her own self-pity rearing up. She must nip it in the bud. But she was so tired.

She and Tom had initially taken turns on night waking, she feeding and he changing nappies. But since he had returned to work, he needed his sleep. She was fully committed to this. He had never unvolunteered, but she leapt up at the first grunts from the baby. Sometimes she just lay awake and waited for the crying to start; it was easier than falling asleep and getting up again.

"So," she said, "to sum up: I find her too stressful to be around, and I made sure I left her. In a way, seeking out the other one was the end. I think my mother always dreaded that, and I can't deny that she was right to."

Nothing punctuated the end of the story, just some more twitchy half-sleepiness from the baby. Madeleine returned to staring at the light bulb. She considered taking her glasses off to make it recede. Well, never mind.

All this past year she could have bought a lampshade, a cheap one, but now was when she was fixated on needing one, with all her spare cash being piddled away on cups of tea and scones and sandwiches and biscuits when the hunger struck, or the thirst, or just the boredom. You couldn't sit in the house all day, and you couldn't stay out all day in a wet spring in a wet country. You couldn't just wander directionless for hours; you had to sit down and warm up sometimes and eavesdrop on another human being.

Tomorrow her mother would come and stay for three days, and then they would go north together to meet her father at her grandparents' house, which needed to be organized, and then they would decide with her Uncle Julian what to do with it.

Her brain ran in little distracted spurts.

Should have bought . . .

There was nothing original worth thinking about. She refused to spend a minute more on that lampshade.

The ceiling was rocking a little, like it had when she stared at it drunkenly on the day of the Great Nondiscovery.

Why did no one learn poetry anymore? You were never really alone with your dead authors clustered about you. How about some Yeats. There was something for most occasions; for this, maybe the one about civilization being hooped together by collective and tacit illusion. That had some of her favourite lines, about man coming "ravening through century after century, *ravening, raging and uprooting* . . ." She loved that bit.

She remembered reciting Yeats to Maud the first morning. The words had flamed in her mind. She would try again:

Though I am old with wandering
Through hollow lands and hilly lands,
I will find out where she has gone,
And kiss her lips and take her hands

It was useless. There wasn't the same feeling. In all honesty, she hadn't felt anything like that first-morning happiness in any moment since. Hadn't felt much of anything, really. She'd spoken "the silver apples of the moon, the golden apples of the sun" one morning, and her life had subsequently fallen off a cliff.

Best not to dwell on it, or wallow.

So, Yeats. Sometimes she wished she had studied someone else. She liked the early bits, before he got old and all new-agey and tried to marry teenage Iseult Gonne, after trying to marry her *mother*, the creep. Tom wasn't wrong when he fondly called Yeats "that reactionary old git." But the man did have a knack with a good line. She liked that "ravening, raging and uprooting."

God, she was so hungry. She would like to go ravening, raging and uprooting a bit. Once the baby was sleeping properly, she would make toast. But toast was like air, like chocolate biscuits; it entered her and evaporated, seeming hardly to have been there at all. She dreamed of other things, sumptuous feasts. Lemon chicken from the Chinese restaurant. Densely seeded buns and slices of sharp farm cheddar spread with ancient grain mustard. Fried eggs and crispy bacon. Devilled eggs—she didn't really know what a devilled egg was but she had read about it somewhere, and the name had stayed with her—she would eat those too. And cups of tea and cups of unsweetened cocoa, and wedges of brie, and toast laden down with baked beans and avocado slices and curls of fresh parmesan, Tom's post-dancing breakfast of champions. Only not with toast; she would have it in a jacket potato. And perhaps breaded scampi. And a falafel in a wrap, where the falafel was crispy, oily. And porridge. And tourtière, a concession to her surname, and to her father and his hobbies. And smoked salmon, and fresh Greek yoghurt—or no, not anymore. But oh, roasted vegetables covered with béchamel sauce and a lamb chop and roast potatoes. And raspberry cranachan. And fruit, heavy fruit, heavy in the weight of its juice. She wanted it all. Her lips were open to receive it.

When she awoke, her neck was bent like an accordion. Her throat was dry. She had been sleeping with her mouth open, the kind of pose in which the soul might fly out of your body. The room had the chill of those hours when morning is still distant.

Her footsteps were heavy going back down the hall. She placed the baby in the cot and stood at the window looking into the garden. She wanted to go to the toilet, another stagger down the hall. But the toilet . . . In the dark in recent days, she had been consumed by the idea that something would leap out and bite her. What, precisely? Perhaps a cockroach or a mouse. It hardly mattered. She couldn't face the thought of going there and not knowing, and she couldn't face the thought of turning on the light to see. Electric lights were violence in these midnight hours. They forced her to confront her own white and staring face, tangled hair, undetermined shape. It could not be done.

So she accepted her unmet needs and collapsed into the bed. Oh, the pleasure of lying on her back, of stretching her legs and her feet to the tips of her toes, of sinking into the pillow, deeper, deeper.

All was silent. Madeleine lay wakeful. She was on her feet before the screams tore through the night. Tom mustn't be disturbed. She staggered to the cot, seized the baby, and collapsed onto the armchair near the window, fumbling to hold her and raise her nightshirt. The baby attached to the breast with a force that sent a shockwave through her. Her leg was trapped beneath her and already numb. Her other breast spasmed milk onto her clothes. Madeleine hissed and stretched an arm towards the dresser to snare a facecloth, which she pressed against her soaking nightshirt. She managed to reach her glasses too. They clinked as she leaned her forehead against the window.

She heard voices, calling all together.

"Come into the garden, Maud!"

Outside, two shapes crept by through the tangle of untended rubbish belonging to the man downstairs. Maybe cats, maybe foxes. One of each. Greymalkin, and . . . Reynard the Fox, of course. What were they doing?

They paused in a clear patch by the light of the setting moon and the orange glow of urban light pollution, and both rose, with awkward grace, onto their hind legs. A line of smaller shapes followed, joined them in a rude circle, small hand joined with paw, and they all began a slow, stumbling dance.

She leaned her forehead against the window and watched, nodding slightly to the unheard music, shifting when her breath fogged up the glass to keep the little people in sight. Chiming voices sang.

She is coming, my dove, my dear;
She is coming, my life, my fate;
The red rose cries, "She is near, she is near;"
And the white rose weeps, "She is late"

Why were they calling Maud to join them?

When Madeleine finally glanced back at the baby, she saw an empty, headless doll.

"Maud!" she cried. There was a scuffle in the garden, running feet.

Her eyes adjusted and the baby's face returned. It was just the facecloth, which had fallen from her breast onto the sleeping face.

Madeleine clung to the baby as though she might break or run away, while her thudding heartbeat returned to normal. When she plucked the cloth away, she found Maud to be purely, deeply asleep. She turned back to the window, but the black-bat night had flown, and the dancers were gone.

They are beyond me, are fishes.
I stand at the pale of my being
And look beyond, and see
Fish, in the outerwards,
As one stands on a bank and looks in.

—"Fish," D. H. LAWRENCE

"Sing to her," Carol suggested.

She had arrived just that morning, bearing gifts. A bouncy chair for the baby leaned in the corner, waiting to be assembled. A hodgepodge of very useful items—things like absorbent breast pads, which Madeleine had never thought to buy—was piled on the coffee table.

"I don't know any baby songs," Madeleine said firmly. She had tried to sing to Maud in the empty flat, but the words came out cracked. She was so exhausted from the night before that singing seemed physically impossible.

"I sent you some; didn't Tom pass them on?" Her mother was delicate and dreamlike, perched on the edge of the couch.

"He did, yes, thank you for those. I've been playing the playlist to the baby." Madeleine in fact found the playlist rather horrifying. It was full of old folk songs about cruel mothers, and eerie French ballads.

"I had great fun looking for them," Carol said. "I always liked the spooky ones best when you were a baby, and with the

Internet now I was able to find so many more. I can't be doing with the kind of baby songs they put on children's albums. They're all so namby-pamby. I like a bit of menace."

"There's *quite* a bit of menace," said Madeleine. "One of them tells the baby to sleep or a crab will come and eat it."

"I thought that might be relatable," said Carol with a laugh. "Anyway, it's the crab that ends up in the pot, so crisis averted. But this one might be my favourite. She sang in her rich, warbly voice:

I left my baby lying here
Lying here, lying here
I left my baby lying here
To go and gather blaeberries

Hovan, Hovan Gorry og O
Gorry og O, Gorry og O
Hovan, Hovan Gorry og O
I've lost my darling baby, O!

"That's cheerful," Madeleine said. Carol always had a song, and Madeleine's childhood had been full of her father playing the fiddle and her mother warbling along. They had met at an after-hours session at a live music bar in Glasgow.

I found the wee brown otter's track
Otter's track, otter's track
I found the wee brown otter's track
But ne'er a trace o' my baby, O!

Madeleine hoped this would be an end to it, and they could move on to nonmusical entertainment, although the baby did seem to enjoy being sung to, more than she had enjoyed Madeleine's attempt at reading an old picture book. Carol continued singing, full-throated and passionate, and Madeleine wandered over to the window. There was scaffolding on the building next door, and with a lurch she saw Greymalkin sitting there, neck aswivel, looking in on them.

Hovan, Hovan Gorry og O
Gorry og O, Gorry og O
Hovan, Hovan Gorry og O

She stared out at Greymalkin. The cat was framed against the wider sweep of the neighbourhood. It was Splinters peering in. Madeleine saw her own outline reflected, overlaid with Greymalkin's narrow face, and the bright room behind, a woman leaning over and singing to a baby. Outside, a man was going through the bin in the park, next to the statue of Splinters's one well-known writer, whom Madeleine had never read.

I've lost my darling baby, O!

She had waited for her mother in pent-up nervous energy, practically feral from her late night. When her mother finally rang the bell, however, all Madeleine's hope and trepidation had given way at once to the feeling that the flat was cold and dim and messy. She had hurried around turning lights on.

"Another chocolate biscuit?" she said, turning back to her mother. But the box lay empty on the coffee table. "Oh, there are no more. The health visitor had a raging hunger on her this morning."

The health visitor had weighed the baby but otherwise had

mostly shown interest in the tea and biscuits Madeleine offered. She was pleased to hear that Madeleine's mother would arrive soon: "Oh, that will give you a nice bit of a rest, then. A chance to take a bit of time just for you." Madeleine had steadfastly matched her, chocolate biscuit for chocolate biscuit, and the health visitor had left with a sigh; she had approximately a million appointments.

Carol was trailing a soft finger down the baby's cheek. "I have something for you, Maud, for when you're older." She reached across to her handbag on the coffee table and extracted a small cardboard box. In it, Madeleine found an amethyst pendant nestled in a bed of cotton.

"She's too young but I couldn't resist. Your first amethyst was your first present too." Carol smiled through the mists of time. As a child, Madeleine had always found her mother enchanting, eternal, different from other mothers. She always wore purple, but unobtrusively: dusky violet shades that suited her, both in the flaxen youth of photographs and the premature silver Madeleine had always known. She steered clear of the more eccentric signifiers of the woman in purple: velvet, hats, ankle skirts, cloaks. But she always had small amethysts dangling from her delicate ears. Madeleine sometimes wore her amethyst earrings for luck, but she had not worn them during labour. Perhaps that was why it had all gone wrong.

"My little fairy," Carol said, dangling the pendant above Maud so that it caught the light.

Her mother knew all about fairies. Fairies had been part of Madeleine's childhood, her gateway drug to the Victorians. Carol drew them; she was talented at drawing in a self-deprecating kind of way. She owned beautifully illustrated books of Victorian-style fairies sitting on mushrooms, or perched in blackberry bushes, and also that attractive but disturbingly sexual pressed fairy book from the '90s, which Madeleine had loved and hated in equal measure. And on windowsills there had been fairy decorations: polystone figurines of winged girls with trailing hair and striped stockings, reading books or bathing in teacups. Madeleine had gone through a fairy-drawing phase, and her mother always sat and drew alongside her. Carol had bought her some intriguing but ultimately disappointing Wiccan texts—disappointing on a literary level. She had left those behind in favour of classic literature, and now she and her mother saw things very differently: for her mother, fairies and their paraphernalia were collectors' items and an uncomplicated pleasure; for Madeleine, they were something to dissect, to make a career from, if academia was a career anymore. To Carol the word "fairy" conjured gossamer wings; for Madeleine it might mean a sly sprite, an ugly brownie, a selkie bride, a changeling child, séances and photographic trickery, a justification of empire, a repudiation of empire, a problematization of childhood and femininity. Her guilty pleasure reads, hidden on the bottom shelf of the shared bookcase, were still lush fantasies in which women were as beautiful as the moon and could speak to magical beasts. But insofar as she believed in magic, it was the older, darker kind. Her mother, of course, didn't believe in magic at all. She probably believed in the universe; Madeleine didn't want to ask.

Carol rose from the sofa, brushed her hands down her narrow hips, and looked around. Madeleine followed her mother's eyes around the cold room, the damp patch on the wall, and peeling paint near the table.

"Let's go out," she said harshly.

"Is that a good idea for Maud?" Carol asked, eyebrows

raised. They both looked out the window. It was not raining, but threatened.

"There's a plastic sheet for the pram." Better for her mother to get a feel for the flat later, when Tom was home, the lights were on, and the heat of supper cooking warmed the common area more than the radiators ever did.

In the street, Madeleine saw all the latent threats anew: sharp bits of rubbish, too-narrow sidewalks, the poverty that sidled along the street and waited to gobble up anyone who lived here. The man she'd seen earlier was slumped against the bin in the park with his head sunk to one side. There were so many junkies around; she hadn't noticed them before because she'd never been home much in the daytime. Madeleine hustled Carol the other way, and tried to point out the good things. "The old man in sandals at that door there is waiting for his grandsons to come home for lunch. When Tom was job hunting, he said he was there every day. And do you see that flag in the window, and those windows over there, and the one across the windy meadow—that's what we call the park. It's the flag from last summer's fair, which is such a big event in Saint Peter's Wood." She used the correct name for the neighbourhood.

Carol pushed the pram and continued to look around with that bland gaze she had turned on the front room.

"Let's do some sightseeing," Madeleine said. "We'll go to the harbour." She was already checking bus routes.

"Maybe we should just go have some more tea somewhere?" Carol looked doubtfully at the lowering sky.

"There's a seventeenth-century ship in the harbour," said Madeleine. "It was used in naval campaigns or something. Or maybe it's eighteenth century. Anyway."

"Have you been before? Is it worth visiting?"

"Tom and I decided it was a bit too much of a Ship of Theseus, actually."

"What's that when it's at home?" Carol said, slipping into the northern speech of her younger self, and smiling complicitly at Madeleine.

"It's been remade and had bits replaced so many times there might be nothing original left in it, so is it really a seventeenth-century ship? Can you say something is what it once was if it's all been replaced? That's the idea."

"Hmmm."

"Anyway," said Madeleine. "We should do some tourism now you're here."

"There's really no need for that, sweetling. It can wait for another time. You must be so tired. Wouldn't you rather go sit somewhere warm and catch up a little?"

But Madeleine did not wish to see the way her mother looked at the baby, a look so pregnant with emotion that it could only highlight the frightening absence of feeling in herself. She shook her head sharply, and Carol pursed her lips.

She had wanted her mother to come so desperately, but she had not wanted this. Not wanted all conversation to linger on the baby, not wanted to sing to the baby, not wanted to look into the baby's face and speculate on whom she resembled. She couldn't bear the diagnosis of features. The baby did not look like anyone. Perhaps this threw into question Madeleine's ability to love something outside of herself. She looked over at Carol, who had so expertly and with such confidence loved a child she had not birthed. Madeleine stood at her side, mother to her own biological child. But—and though it had not occurred to her until just then, the truth came suddenly—she did not love the baby.

What kind of person didn't love her own child? She didn't want to answer that question.

The bus arrived.

They had to stand squashed together; it was too crowded to talk much. Though, "this would be a nice place to live," Carol commented as they passed the outskirts of Angela's leafy area, home to dog grooming parlours and estate agents.

"The rents are crazy out here. And it's full of bankers and advertising executives and so on."

"Is that worse than the junkies in needle park out your way?"

"We call it the *meadow*," Madeleine said lightly, to try and add some levity. "The windy meadow in Splinters Wood. The corner shop is the crossroads; everyone passes through there. The block of tenements is the Crooked House."

"They all looked crooked to me," said Carol, tucking the blanket more firmly around Maud in the pram.

The bus passed remodelled warehouses, gastro pubs, then cobbled streets and pubs on houseboats and cavernous industrial galleries. The waterside district.

They pushed the pram through an ominous afternoon. The quayside was full of flustered pigeons and watchful gulls. There were occasional splashes of rain. The ship loomed ahead, creating an extreme sense of unreality; it was like walking through a historical film with continuity errors and half the crew tinkering on the set. The thrusting prow was crowned by a gold-painted mermaid, and by clusters of visitors in rain jackets. Mothers in pairs or small groups went by in loungewear with expensive-looking prams. Madeleine steered Carol towards the ship.

In the ticket office they looked at postcards and coasters shaped like ships' wheels before moving to buy tickets.

"You can't take the pram on board," said the woman behind the counter as she rang them in.

"Oh, don't be so bloody awkward," Madeleine snapped. "We'll just push it up the gangway."

Her mother and the ticket seller both stared at her, then looked away. There was a pause, during which the red mist that had risen before her eyes subsided, and then the ticket seller said "health and safety regulations—" and the mist swept back in.

"Perhaps we could—" began Carol diplomatically, but Madeleine was not to be condescended to.

"No, no, just no. You go aboard, Mom. I will wait for you on the quay."

"Madeleine, this wasn't even my idea."

"No. Just."

Carol shrugged, an expressive shrug encompassing defeat, criticism, and solidarity-against-health-and-safety-zealotry. "Just the one ticket, then."

"And give her the senior's rate," Madeleine added, pleased to speak that second too late, so that the order would need to be cancelled and rung in again.

After her mother had passed the gate and headed towards the ship, Madeleine turned a look of disdain on the cashier. The woman held her gaze nervously, then dropped it. Madeleine turned, wrestled the door back open, and held it with her foot while she rammed the pram over the threshold.

"And don't bother being accessible to people in wheelchairs," she shouted over her shoulder.

She moved off along the water. She was jubilant, relished the kind of words the ticket seller would use to describe her, words like lunatic, hellcat, vixen, harridan, demented, evil, or well probably just bitch and psycho, really. She hoped the woman had been scared; had wondered, however briefly, if Madeleine might leap across the counter to stab her in the neck with a reproduction letter opener.

The water lapped the quayside. An elderly couple on a bench smiled and leaned over to get a look at the baby. The woman in particular was frail, and Madeleine watched in fascination as she reached arthritic fingers towards the baby's cheek. The fingers trembled; they were like twisted branches with a thin veneer of skin and nail. They didn't stop, as most old ladies' did, before touching; they carried straight on into the pram and felt for the baby a little too hard, dry and crusty and grasping. The man started forwards and pulled her hands back. "Now then, Hilda." Madeleine supposed she should have stepped in first. Like everything with the baby, there seemed to be a lag in her actions, while she processed what the correct response should be. She pushed the pram on.

There was beauty down here by the water, in the stillness of the day. She broke into a light jog, unbothered by the spectacle she must present, an ungainly, poorly dressed young mother jogging with a pram that wasn't made for it. But this was freedom, defying the other mothers who went by in pairs, talking, holding takeaway coffee cups. And the jolting on the cobblestones had rocked the baby back to sleep.

She slipped abruptly on a wet patch. The pram leapt forwards and rolled several feet, and Madeleine fell heavily onto her hands behind it. Her head jerked up, for they were by the edge of the water, and if the pram should tip in . . . but it had rolled the other way, and it was she who lay very close to the edge of the wall.

She looked down into the water below. A large fish swam out

from the murk of a moored boat and circled under a rainbow of oil. It flicked its tail and turned a frozen opal eye upon her. Madeleine remained unmoving, staring down at it. Primeval-dumb creature. It looked up from its world into hers, and she looked down.

She wanted to reach down, through the membrane of water, and take the fish in her arms and sob into its cold flesh. Its eye had seen all, knew all. It was as cold as prehistory, and so there was room there for all her lost emotions, which she could feel thawing within her now. It was emotion she had been missing these past weeks. She was hemmed in by the city when her thoughts and needs were wild. This creature, and not the baby, was her kin.

The tail flicked again and carried the fish away under the shadow of a canal boat. She sat up, dazed. The palms of her hands were scratched and smarting. A man bent at her side to help her up. His girlfriend stood sheepish guard over the pram. Madeleine thanked them, muttered something about her ankle giving out. The couple looked embarrassed. When they moved off, she could tell by the angles of their heads that they were talking about her. She stood next to the pram on the edge of the water that spread, smooth as glass, unassailable, before her.

Belatedly, she remembered to look at the baby. Her eyes were open and placid as the canal, yet there was a severe line between them that deepened as Madeleine watched.

"Do not cry," Madeleine hissed, bending over the pram. The line remained, but the baby did not cry.

Deep within the baby's dark eyes was another eye, a cold fish eye, spinning lazily there at the bottom of the baby's soul. She wavered before a greater truth, one she had battled since the baby had been returned to her at the hospital. She could remember that first morning after the birth, the evenness of the light upon her daughter's newly hatched face. Feelings of peace, of well-being, of expansiveness, of love. Wanting to sing, wanting to laugh. It seemed another life. It was another life. And also—a great reluctant tug in her mind. It seemed another baby.

"I don't know who you are," she said, staring into the pram. Nothing about the face was familiar. There was nothing of Tom. There was nothing of Madeleine either.

The line deepened once again, the small face clouded, and the scream came, a scream unlike any human sound. It twisted in her brain and hijacked her body, caused milk to gush spontaneously from her. Heads turned, even the couple halfway down the quay looked back, but these things she noticed only in passing. She had eyes only for the red, furious mouth, and its rage and despair. She reached towards the baby, repelled but needing to offer herself.

All moments since the hospital were like this, a frantic yo-yoing between need and satiety, between Madeleine as goddess of warmth, food, comfort and Madeleine as criminal and blackguard who withheld and failed to understand and moved too slowly.

Eyes near and far watched. The canal dusked and shivered against the wall. She rushed to the nearest bench. Once the baby was quiet, she gloomily watched the abandoned pram and thought how easy it would be for anyone passing to steal the nappy bag with all her possessions, while she could do nothing but shout from the sidelines.

"But really," she said aloud. "What does it matter? What do I have that's worth stealing?"

I don't know who you are. What had she meant by it? She had meant that she saw cunning in the baby's eyes, something old and dour, and the baby had responded with that inhuman shriek. Now she suckled and occasionally let out a sniffle of outrage or bereavement. The small chest heaved tragically. Madeleine was flooded with remorse. She hummed.

I left my baby lying there, lying there, lying there.

And then it came. Of course. Of course. In plain view, in Yeats's most famous poem.

Come away, o human child!
To the waters and the wild

No, no, no. Things were slipping and sliding away from her, thoughts, memories, belief systems. She tried to hold them. She saw small people dancing in the garden. This wasn't the way. She would need to do proper research.

David Bowie was singing "Changes" snidely in her mind as she tried to cram various runaway thoughts back where they belonged.

"I opened the window," she said.

La belle dame sans merci, thee hath in thrall.

And the belle dame is a . . . is a fairy.

Once there was a sweet baby a few hours old, and that baby had been her own little Maud, unknown and unknowable, but her own. And then she had changed, and this mad, sucking, needing creature with her preternatural understanding and her evil screeching voice was here in her stead.

The baby jerked up, away from the breast, and regarded her with hollow, grey eyes, inhuman eyes.

In the legends, the fairies came and took a human child to be their servant or their plaything, and left one of their own.

Madeleine stared numbly into the face. It was not full beautiful, as she had thought in the park; it was gnarled and needled. It scrutinized her coldly.

She looked away. The changeling returned to the breast, triumphant. Madeleine felt her body and her life emptying. Every suckle emptied her further, milk flowed out and left her a dry, starving husk. Her mind rattled around, demanding how, and when. The week in the hospital? The following week at home with Tom, spending too much, out too much? The two days absolutely alone, waiting for her mother? And who, and how?

"Shall we go get some cake somewhere?"

Madeleine stirred. She had not noticed her mother come down the gangway or along the quay.

"I can't speak to whether it's a real seventeenth-century ship or not," said Carol. "Chilly, certainly. Overpriced, indubitably. Still, according to the audio guide, it's much less smelly than it would have been back in the day. That's something, I suppose. Anyway, you've done your duty by your visiting mother. Let me do my duty as a grandmother. Let's go warm up somewhere."

Madeleine nodded.

"I'll carry the baby," Carol said, leaning Maud over her shoulder and patting her back. As Madeleine hobbled along to get the pram, stitches, nipples, skinned palms aching, she heard a great, roaring belch leave the baby. A small head on somebody else's shoulder, the baby looked briefly human again, briefly vulnerable, but then her unfocused eyes flashed dark and cunning, and old, very old.

Your children all, your children for ever;
But I, so wild,
Your disgrace, with the queer brown face, was never,
Never, I know, but half your child!

—"The Changeling," CHARLOTTE MARY MEW

In the tea shop, Madeleine had immediately barricaded herself in the toilet with her phone. Various universities had helpfully compiled dozens of changeling stories from Ireland, from the British Isles, and from mainland Europe. They had been written down throughout the nineteenth century of course, during the folklore craze, but as oral records they stretched much further back. She read with a dry mouth and darting eyes. They were all very similar.

> A woman gave birth to a fine, healthy baby. But within a few days of the birth, she was called across the valley on an errand. Having no one to watch the baby, she wrapped him tightly and left him in his cradle.
>
> It was evening before she returned, and night was falling. On the last stretch of the road home, men in blue cloaks passed her on the road, with a bundle she could not make out. A little ways on, she came upon a tailor in search of a meal and a bed for the night.

"You should be wary to be abroad at this time," said he. "The good folk are about; I passed them on the road."

When he asked if he might stay the night, she agreed, and they entered the house together, to the sound of the baby crying lustily in the cradle. The woman caught up her son and fed him, but though he fed and fed, he was insatiable, and cried the more. Over the coming days, he ate ravenously, and yet he grew thinner and lost the rosy glow in his cheeks. The tailor watched the child often.

One day, the woman was called away again, and asked the tailor to watch over her son. Once the woman had gone, the tailor began to prepare a meal, but brought neither pot nor pan to the fire. Instead, he broke an egg and prepared to cook in the shell. The baby in the cradle watched, and then spoke.

"What are you doing?"

"Cooking," replied the tailor.

The baby burst out laughing. "I'm as old as the fields and as the oak, but never have I seen a dinner cooked in eggshells."

The tailor leapt forwards, seized the child, and threw him into the fire. There was a loud bang, and a little old fairy stood among the flames a moment before bounding up the chimney and disappearing.

Instinctively, she knew. It all clicked. She was not unsuitable, incapable, unforgivable. It was the fairies parading in the garden. It was Greymalkin and Reynard.

But she would have to do more research. She tucked her

phone away with cold, shaking hands. She would have to talk to Tom.

She emerged to find Carol cradling the baby. They had holed up in the kind of place her mother always found. Just off the main walk, pink chintz and teacups with baby animals painted inside them. They were in a small room on the second floor (the pram politely folded near the entrance) overlooking the cobbles, and they sat next to an unlit fireplace painted buttercream yellow and filled with artificial flowers. It was freezing. Madeleine had her arms wrapped around herself for warmth as she took a seat opposite her mother.

"You haven't told me about the birth yet," Carol said, a little shyly.

"Oh, the birth."

"Yes, I've been meaning to ask you. If you feel like sharing, of course." There was a note of wistfulness in Carol's voice that cut through her distraction. The experience Carol had never been able to have. The ultimate treachery of her body, refusing to do what she felt it was meant to.

Well, Madeleine's body had refused too, ultimately. And the third, her other mother, the unspoken presence between them? Had she managed all right? All she really knew was that the other mother had survived, lived on, lived on to thwart Madeleine. Had Madeleine's botched attempt at birth been a symptom of the endless tug-of-war between these two women? A delivery, but mechanized; an acceptance of the bonds of responsibility, but not the bonds of love? A baby that was not hers.

"I had a C-section in the end," Madeleine said. She recalled the blurry figures, the faceless baby carried away. Perhaps Greymalkin and Reynard were not involved. She had not been able to see clearly; perhaps the baby had been taken as soon as she'd come. But no, the first morning Maud was Maud, she was sure. She had felt something then, whispers of eternity and legacy, great airy joy. The first morning she had been a mother who loved her baby.

"I do know that," said Carol eagerly. "Tom called and told us the basics. How horrible for you. But they say it's common these days. Maybe the doctor just wanted to go off shift."

"They said I would have died otherwise," said Madeleine. But was that true? Was the doctor in on it too? "Maybe you're right, and they just said that to get me to agree. Surely people weren't all dropping like flies before, having them at home, with a grandmother sitting there to watch that no one took the baby when it was born."

"Au contraire," Carol said a touch severely. "Your Nan was born at home, and I believe it was touch and go for her mother. The maternal mortality rate used to be shocking."

She knew that of course. Women in novels died in childbirth all the time. Cathy Earnshaw. Prue Ramsay. Fanny Robin. What's her name from *A Farewell to Arms*. Snow White's mother. Although maybe that was just to conveniently get mothers out of the way of the main plot, because nothing killed drama like a mother. But their real counterparts had died too. Exit Charlotte Brontë. Exit Mary Wollstonecraft. Exit the real Amy March.

Tom had been there to hold the baby. So Maud couldn't have been taken then. And she was getting ahead of herself. She still needed to read about it, really read about it.

"Still," Carol said. "It was all worth it in the end, wasn't it? A healthy baby is the most important thing. Were you very long in labour though?"

Madeleine was looking at the baby, and it was looking at her, rather too closely for a baby with limited vision, she thought. She would have to be careful what she said out loud.

"I'd rather forget about it, to be honest," she said. She saw her mother's face drop, chastised, excluded still, and hated herself. The waitress brought tea and a large slice of cake for Madeleine. Carol poured silently.

"Sorry," Madeleine said at last, reaching for the milk.

"Don't be silly."

No, it must surely be related to the cat and the fox. The fairy rade. A cat and a fox together could never be up to any good. And they had danced in the garden with the little people—so it had not been a dream—and one of those little people must have been her Maud. A Maud who had already been stolen. Gone since the hospital. Madeleine had lapsed in her responsibilities by leaving the baby's side. Well, she had needed surgery. She had been spirited away. But even before then she had lapsed, by opening the window.

Time passed differently in the fairy world. Would Maud be an old woman if she got her back, as old as Nan?

"Now, what else is new?" The silence had become too much for Carol. "Ah, your father is on holiday already, but he won't come to meet us up north for another week."

"Oh. Why not?"

"He decided to go to Quebec, to do some of his genealogy research."

"Is he still faffing about with that nonsense?"

"That was rather sharp, Maddie."

Madeleine filled her mouth with cake to avoid answering. But her mother's look was challenging, and perhaps it was better to air this grievance than to have to talk about *it*, the baby, which was pretending to sleep.

"I find it very boring. What does he expect to learn from all this? Don't answer that; I know what he wants, but I think it can't be learned. Where do we come from? How can birth and death notices in parish registries really answer that question?"

"I remember a time when you were interested in birth notices," Carol replied.

She had to swallow her fury with the cake. "I got over that, didn't I?" Civilization is hooped together, indeed. She and her mother, both sitting there with the mental image of the Great Nondiscovery, neither willing to mention it directly. "I consider myself all the better for leaving bygones to be bygones," she said.

Carol inclined her head delicately. "It's just a hobby for your father. We're reaching an age when there's more behind than ahead, and a person gets curious. Or nostalgic. I don't see why you should mind."

"I don't see why I shouldn't mind. It's insensitive to me, that he's poking about after some long-mouldering blood relations instead of coming to see his nonblood daughter, who is actually alive and had surgery two weeks ago. It's insulting to his newborn granddaughter." Never mind that it wasn't a granddaughter, that it was an *interloper*.

Carol, perhaps irritated by her exile to a chilly reproduction sailing ship, would not bend or understand.

"Long-mouldering relatives are of some interest to you anyway, since Maud's middle name is after my mother."

"She isn't long-mouldering."

"She will be by the time Maud is old enough to know about her."

"Thank you for bringing up this painful subject."

"We should consider it a blessing really, that she went before she began losing her marbles. My mother was always adamant, and you know she could be very adamant, that this was her great fear. 'I don't mind feeding the worms, Carol, but I don't want to lose my marbles.'" Carol sighed. "It was practically her refrain; she was obsessed with losing her marbles. I remember her twenty years ago, already worrying that she couldn't remember where she'd put something, and I always said it happens to everyone but only older people worry about it. But she was getting a little vague in the last year or so, and depressed probably, from watching your grandad's decline. So yes, as painful as it was last summer, I count our blessings."

"Only because we've got Maud to balance out the family."

"That was a wonderful surprise, of course."

"Not entirely a surprise, surely."

"Of course it was. You're in the middle of a long degree program, and so young, with so many other things to be doing. I wasn't expecting grandchildren for many years yet."

"I thought," said Madeleine, "that you wanted a third generation."

"What's that?" said Carol.

"You were the one at Nan's funeral who was going on about how all real families have three generations."

"Did I?" Carol drew a gentle line along the sleeping baby's eyebrow, and afterwards drank tea again, and seemed not to follow the thought through to its logical conclusion.

"You said," Madeleine nearly shouted, "that it was heartbreaking when the old died out of the family and there were no young to replace them. You said that death in one area should be balanced out by birth in another. You said what was a family without children? You said that anything less than three generations was cack-handed, broken."

"I surely didn't say *cack-handed*."

"That's exactly what you said."

"I think your uncle had started me into the scotch," Carol replied. "Of course a family should include children, everyone thinks that. But as you know, it takes all sorts. I didn't manage a child myself until I was over forty, and the world didn't end. A time to every purpose under heaven, you know."

In the light of a table lamp, Carol and Maud had something of the lustre of an oil painting. Madeleine shivered. She felt damp to her bones, as though dew were forming on her as she sat. She longed to eject the—to eject *it* from her mother's warm, encircling arm and climb in there herself. She had a memory of being a child in her mother's lap, age three or four maybe, and Carol murmuring in her ear, "You're like a daddy long-legs. Shall we call you *Maddie long-legs?*" And then singing a made-up ditty, which had then passed into family lore.

Maddie long-legs tall and thin
big brown eyes and cheeky grin
night-time creeping down the hall
dances on the ceiling, tip-toes down the wall.

Her mother *had* always liked the spooky ones.

And she had wanted to make her mother happy, to make up for the Great Nondiscovery. She wanted to scream that she had done this for Carol, but she was too furious even to speak.

She looked out the window. A gust of rain had blown through, leaving the cobbles slick and slippery.

Why should a family have three generations? Why have any? Why be? She was affronted that her father was chasing his ancestors instead of coming to see her, but if he wished to reject her, so be it, she could also reject him. Him and her ungrateful mother. She had no blood relatives; she could be her own family, with Tom, her own single-generation family.

She was forgetting Maud. She could never be a single generation again. For she shared blood with Maud. With poor, missing Maud of the tiny, perfect features and the dimples behind each ear, that first day in the hospital. This was the tragedy of children, then. Until you had them, the generations simply stretched away behind you, fading into the distance. You were their culmination point, as though all ancestors had mated with one another, and raised their children, simply to produce you. You were the best they could manage. And more than that, you were the end point. The whole point, really. The effect to their cause, the climax of their story.

And then you had a child, and all that you were faded to irrelevance. You were no longer a shining figure who represented the sum of all evolution and progress. You were just a cog in a generational wheel, grinding on, your only importance the fact that you had kept the drama unfolding.

And it was worse having a girl. A boy could escape from this pitiless wheel, as Tom was escaping, going to work by day, playing father by night, or as her own father was escaping, keeping up his own interests despite the family bonds that should be pulling him to the site of this birth. But a girl, what? She might grow up to be something. She might be promising, brilliant even, but unless she rejected maternity—which could not fail to reflect upon your own mothering—she too would come to this. Another cog in the wheel.

She could not undo it, could not return to being the centre of the universe, and meanwhile the cats and the foxes had gotten in, and the only thing emptier, really, than being a mother was to play mother to a false baby. Where was Maud? How was she to recover her? One thing was knowing that she was missing and what had happened, and another thing was knowing what to do about it.

"A penny for your thoughts?" said Carol.

It was funny how just yesterday she had believed having a baby would cement her relationship with her mother. But funny haha or funny peculiar? She shook her head.

Suddenly as Little B. watched the sparrows on the grey frozen grass, they grew, they changed, still flapping and squeaking. They turned into tiny little boys, in brown coats, dancing, jigging outside, up and down outside the window squeaking, "Want something to eat, want something to eat!"

—"A Suburban Fairy Tale," KATHERINE MANSFIELD

The symptoms of changeling children were all there, in the stories, running like a line of silver through all the many variations. It was a relief to see them written out. The insatiable hunger, the crying and irritability.

Madeleine had the square of folded paper from the same book of theory she had taken to the hospital and not read since. She took surreptitious notes. *Changed at birth. Always hungry. Always irritable. Cooking in eggshells. Throw in the fire. Or beat with a poker. Or leave by the shore/a fairy mound (where?). First need proof anyway.*

It was the original folk sources that made the most sense, though Google Scholar had plenty of other things from disability studies—changelings standing in for children with developmental delays. She had taken a long, hard look at the changeling. No, she didn't think that was the problem.

"Tom?" she said. Her mother was off in the bedroom at the other end of the flat, rocking and singing to the changeling, so she could risk a talk with Tom. He was making his special dish. He looked bone-tired when he turned to face her.

"Do you not sometimes think." Difficult to go on. Impossible to just come out with it. "That there's something off about the baby?"

"Off?"

"Something not right about her."

"Not *right*? Has the health visitor said something?"

"No, I don't mean that. Something not . . . babyish then?"

"Like she's an old soul?"

"Or has no soul at all."

He was giving her a peculiar look. "I guess a soul is arguable for any of us. I've been having a little read-up on babies at work," he confessed. "She's coming along wonderfully. In as much as you'd expect someone two weeks old to be coming along, obviously. I'm not saying she's Mozart or anything. Do you know, Maddie, it just wasn't real until the birth. I expect that's normal with fathers. Women have the pregnancy to get used to the idea, and the hormones. And I was excited before, and frankly scared, but I wasn't sure how I'd react when actually faced with it. And then, she's just perfect, isn't she? It's such a little miracle. I know I'm not saying anything profoundly new here, but to look on her and see it all . . . the little feet. The *nails*. A little person who wasn't there before." He stood before her, flushed and glowing, holding a wooden spoon and wearing Nan's old apron.

Madeleine returned to the computer and surfed around, reminding herself of fairy characteristics in general. She knew all this already, of course. Fairies were thought to be child-sized, until the Victorians decided they were flower-sized. That was the first thing you learned about fairies. Though sometimes they manifest as a swarm of flies. Some believe the fairies are the dead. Sometimes they are thought to be invisible. If you see fairies but a fairy blows on your eyes, you will cease to see them (she hadn't known that). Those who visit fairyland sometimes return to find that many years have passed, that they have danced their feet clear away—yes, a classic finale to fairy stories.

"Dinner's ready," said Tom, approaching. Madeleine hastily switched to a news tab. The news was all bad, the news was terrible. Wages were stagnant, living costs were rising, and children were drowning in the Mediterranean trying to reach Europe. The horror of it all. Tom was standing before her, homecoming and companion, and for a moment the house felt warm; inside was good even if outside was bad. Then she remembered that inside was bad too; the rot had infiltrated. She closed the laptop and slid the paper back into the book.

Carol had succeeded in singing Maud to sleep, so they took their places at the table in an imitation of a normal family dinner of their past holidays together. Carol was pleasantly pink from a first glass of red, and the cooking had warmed the room.

According to various endings, the real child either miraculously appeared in the cradle once more, or the mother and father went in search of him at the fairy hill nearby and found him healthy and whole, lying upon a rock.

Except, of course, for the variants in which the original baby was not returned, and it seemed that everyone was simply happy to be rid of the changeling.

Usually it was the cooking in eggshells that broke the spell.

But sometimes the tailor took out a fiddle and played a tune. Then the changeling leapt around, unable to control itself, and danced on the ceiling.

If her father had come, he could have brought his fiddle and put all that pseudo-nostalgia of his to work for once. He could have played and made the changeling dance. It would be logistically easier than cooking in eggshells. She glanced back towards her book. She would have to note these things down, and hatch a plan.

Carol was criticizing the flat and the neighbourhood again.

"Love alone was enough to keep us warm when we took the flat, Carol." Tom's cheeky delivery told her he was trying to take the teeth out of her mother.

"Of course, Tom," Carol replied in kind. "We have all lived in these places. It's not enough to keep the baby warm though, is it?" Earlier the heating meter had beeped a warning, again, and Madeleine had switched it off.

"It's such a racket," Tom admitted. "It would definitely cost less if we just had an account and paid monthly bills, but this is the way it's been set up."

"It's maybe time to look for a better place—in a better area."

"I can't believe you said to the woman out the back that this was no place for a baby," said Madeleine. "Did you not notice that she lives here herself, and has children?"

"Actually, Maddie, she was the one who brought it up. Her children are teenagers, and Saint Peter's Wood might have been quite different when they were young."

"It wasn't though. If anything it was worse."

"Eh," said Tom. "I wouldn't say it was worse. It had problems but at least it was affordable. People who grew up here are all really proud of it. I actually do think we should move elsewhere, but not because the flat is cold or the park is dangerous. I hate contributing to what's happening to Splinters, pushing the locals out, diluting the neighbourhood."

"In any case, all she meant was she wouldn't fancy living above the man downstairs."

"She's not wrong, is she?" said Carol.

Tom looked cautiously from one to the other. "What woman out back?"

"The family with the foxes. The mother works next to the petrol station where the neighbour works. She says he hasn't been fired yet."

"Yet." Tom took a sip of wine. "It's definitely going to happen one day. I didn't know you were chatty with the neighbour," he said to Madeleine.

"Today was the first time we spoke, actually."

"Yes," Carol said lightly but significantly. "Part of Maddie's new tourism initiative. The local murals, and other people's gardens."

The bad blood between them was palpable. Carol was leaving the next day to sort out Nan and Grandy's house up north. Madeleine had announced earlier that she would not, as planned, go with her mother. She needed to rest, she said. She needed a chance to get to know the baby better. She would see her parents when they came back to town for two days at the end of their trip.

She needed time. She needed to figure out when and how the change had occurred. She needed to find out where Maud was, and how to recover her.

"Other people's gardens?" said Tom. He likewise spoke lightly, treading a line between politeness to his mother-in-law and support of his wife. "Can I trouble you for the bread, Carol?"

"Yes, we had a tour of the fox family's garden. Madeleine insisted on being taken to see the cubs."

"It wasn't like that. It wasn't me who started chatting with her. You were gushing about the hydrangea."

"Such a beautiful colour. I'd love to see it in full bloom. But that was out the front of her house. I certainly didn't invite myself into the back garden."

"Explain," said Tom, lifting the wine bottle. "Anyone want a top-up?"

"Yes, please."

"Me too, please."

"Should you, Maddie, when you're breastfeeding?"

"Yes."

"Right, so."

"Oh, it was nothing. I just mentioned we loved to watch the baby foxes from the bedroom window."

"And then you asked if we could go into their back garden and peer through the shed door."

"Well, why not? I've been seeing the family in the garden out my window for months; I know they aren't serial killers."

"You can't just go barging into other people's yards."

"She said it was fine."

"What else could she say? The teenage daughter didn't think it was a good idea though, did she? Kept trying to dissuade you from opening the shed door. Pointing out, very sensibly, that wild things don't like to be backed into corners. And the mother fox did snarl at you. Did you even see the cubs?"

"Just squirming away." Yes, it all sounded bad, repeated that way by her mother. She needed her mother to go, so she could get on with her search without needing to invent stupid reasons to stay in Splinters, the tourism of murals as her mother called it, dragging them down one grey road after another in search of Reynard and Greymalkin. They were her prime suspects in the disappearance of Maud, and she hadn't seen so much as a whisker of either in two days. Probably she had been stupid to imagine such an easy solution: bursting in upon the vixen, demanding to be taken to her leader, leaving the changeling, and scooping up her own baby to emerge, newly whole again, back into the world.

"The teenage daughter was reading *The Tempest*," she told the table. "For A levels, but still, she said she liked it. And she said she'd be happy to babysit any time."

"It will be years before Maud is old enough to be babysat," said Carol.

"Years? She'll be in nursery before the year is out."

"That's unfortunate," said Carol. "Such a pity you can't afford to take more time away to be with her. Babies need their mothers in these early days. It's hard to be needed so much, but you can always get back to your work after. At *least* give her a year."

A year. She counted the days remaining in a year. Three hundred and fifty-ish days like the days she had now. And her mother didn't know of her special circumstances. A year would make no difference because fairy children failed to thrive or develop. A great welling up of despair threatened to overwhelm the table, drown Tom's spicy prawn pasta, flood the wine glasses, carry them away, out the window, the same despair that led her to cry at news headlines although she never had before.

"They're resilient though, aren't they?" said Tom diplomatically. "And they change so fast. Maud seems vulnerable to us today, but compared with a mere two weeks ago . . . Actually, Maddie, I have a favour to ask. When you go out to top up the heat tomorrow, could you take a detour down to the photo place? I sent some of the photos of Maud from the last week or two to be printed, but getting down there at rush hour makes me a full half hour later getting home."

"Sure."

"I ordered extra copies for you and Paul, Carol."

"Thank you, Tom. Since Madeleine isn't joining me tomorrow, I suppose we'll pick them up a few weeks from now."

If only it were tomorrow, and her mother gone, and Tom at work, and the changeling asleep, and she could forget the dreary task of participating in conversations, or pretending that everything was normal, and get on with what needed to be done.

World is crazier and more of it than we think,
Incorrigibly plural

—"Snow," LOUIS MACNEICE

It was tomorrow, her mother was gone, Tom was at work, and the changeling was uncomplaining in the baby carrier. Madeleine was skulking down one of the aisles of the corner shop, holding a box of eggs. She had a plan for the morning, but was unable to go to the till until the neighbour had made his purchases and left. He was shambling today; he was barely keeping it together. He surely didn't go to work in this state or he would have been fired long since.

There were only a few aisles in the corner shop, and he seemed to have purchases to make in all of them, so she crept stealthily from one to the other. It was busy in the crossroads today. There was even another mother with a baby blocking the end of the row with an armoured tank of a pram. She was talking to the teenage daughter from the fox house, and the couple whose grandchildren came home for lunch every day, in an easy, rolling lilt. They were shouting with laughter about something, and the baby was kicking fat legs up towards the ceiling. Madeleine wished she could stop too, that she knew how to talk to people as Tom did, that she might have something in common with this Splinters mother who looked only slightly older than herself.

She looked warily around the end of the candy aisle. The neighbour was too bleary to really notice people, but a sudden movement might catch his eye. He always seemed to have a sixth sense. Though she would have a few things to tell him, if it came to words. The music on full blast until two or three in the morning again. It always happened when he went on a bender and passed out. In the early days Tom had tried to go downstairs or knock on the floor, but you couldn't communicate with him in that state. So the neighbour, drinking himself into oblivion, left them shattered; even more than the baby feedings. It was a hangover kind of feeling, but without the party, as Tom had remarked sourly at the breakfast table. Carol, holding a mug of tea for support in the early-morning chill, had commented that even in the kitchen, on the other side of the house, you could feel the vibrations coming through the floor. Damn the neighbour, showing the place up in front of her mother. And now that Carol was gone in a rental car, Madeleine was gripped by terror that her mother had slept badly on the sofa and would fall asleep at the wheel and be in an accident. It would be Madeleine's fault, for living here, for being intimidated by the neighbour, for not having gone north.

He was among the tins now. She might sneak up to the counter and pay and get out. But she had to top up the heat, and sometimes there was a delay in the system, so she risked him emerging at any time, right behind her in the queue, where he could shout at her for stealing his bag.

She hovered among the chocolates and industrial baked goods, joggling the carrier so the changeling would drop off. Galaxy, Bounty, Crunchie, KitKat, Snickers, Starbar, chocolate Digestives, Mr Kipling pies. She wasn't to spend money. Not on these things. Soon she would make an omelette. You couldn't make an omelette without . . .

Her phone vibrated.

Marie: Hey! First day teaching your class. I think I'm really going to love teaching, love these girls (they all say congrats by the way, and better you than them, but you do you, hahaha). Anyway, thanks again for this opportunity. Hope you're having fun with the baby!

Madeleine's resolve evaporated; she began to grab one of each of the chocolate bars. The brightest, brashest, and most supersized. She would eat them all.

The neighbour was going towards the till now, annoyingly slowly, with his bits and pieces, his one tin of food and his various cartons of cheap wine, and in his endless crossing of the floor.

She began furiously typing a message to Tom.

Me: As predicted, Marie got given my seminars and is just excelling SO MUCH and they all love her

Me: This is to follow up on her coming along to Angela's to steal my project

Me: And the time I told her I was sending a paper for that edited volume and she sent one too without telling me and got in and I didn't

Me: (I guess I just need some validation that I'm not terrible at everything here)

When the neighbour had finally picked through his change and packed his bags and looked around for the bag snatcher and made it out the door, Madeleine had already begun to eat a Crunchie bar. It was one of those unspeakably delicious ones, where the toffee was sticky rather than shattery-hard in the very centre. She handed the eggs and the chocolate bars to Kamal at the till, passed him the key for the heat and asked to top up ten pounds, and was so lost in her thoughts that it took her a moment to realize he was saying her card was declined.

How could she not have eighteen pounds? Was it not today her maternity pay was meant to clear? Perhaps it was sent today but would take a day or two to show up in her account. She felt herself grow hot, startled, stumbled out apologies. Kamal had heard it all before. He was kind, which made it worse. She'd never been declined anywhere. But the payments from maternity took a while to kick in, what with the filing of the paperwork and such. Of course, love. She rummaged in her purse. She had ten pounds after all, for the heat. Or rather . . .

She put seven pounds on the heat so as to pay for the half-eaten Crunchie bar and the eggs, which were essential, and gathered all the other chocolate bars to return to their places on the shelf. "I'll do that, love," he said. "You've enough to carry," nodding to the changeling, who was doing that trick of sleeping and looking vulnerable and sweet and human.

She stepped blindly outdoors, and made her way to the triangle of ratty park that separated the shop from her building. The windy meadow. It looked especially derelict and cold today. The neighbour was still shuffling through it with his bags. Of course he was. She could get ahead of him, cut across the grass rather than the path, but his seeing her and screaming after her was still a risk, and she felt bruised from the shop; she didn't think she could bear it. What else, then? Wait for him to shuffle home—including, of course, the crossing of the front garden once he was within the gate? Or take a long way around, hurrying, and hopefully arrive at the gate before he did? The long way around was much longer.

In the end she paced back and forth and ate the rest of the chocolate while he made his long journey, paused unsteadily at the traffic light, and crossed and fought with the front gate as she had done so often herself. She looked up at the house; her own flat was visible over the gate. The two front windows of the sitting room glared down on her, watching Madeleine in the neighbourhood. Madeleine, who, today, belonged to the neighbourhood and wasn't just passing through. Madeleine buffeted by the sharp gusts coming off the windy meadow, filled with worries for the present and the future. It was so easy to teeter on the edge of a great fall. She wasn't so buttressed against the wider world as she thought. She might be safe from her precarious past, as she had thought all those years ago, but you could always be swept under. Only eighteen pounds had stood between one reality and another. And she had a vision of a little girl skipping through the park, going with Tom to top up the electricity just when it was about to run out, with odd bits of change.

The neighbour made it through the gate, and she hesitated a minute longer, then crossed and entered. He had left the gate ajar, as usual.

Home to the cold, silent flat. She looked out the windows. The consciousness had returned to the empty eyes. The ghost had returned to the house. And the street was empty.

She pressed the heating key into its slot and waited for the numbers to update. Done. Immediately, the electricity meter beeped at her. It had only sixty pence remaining. Stupid thing, it was supposed to give more warning than that. Well, it would have to be enough.

The changeling woke screaming, and she considered its angry little head, its ugly face, its rage and need, with an appalled weariness. "You and I have been up all night," she said, not raising her voice. The changeling didn't so much as pause for breath.

Everything was déjà-vu. She could see each moment coming just before it arrived. The defeated puff of the sofa as she sat, the irritation of trying to tuck her oversized T-shirt into her bra, her exact knowledge of the weight of a baby, the reverse echo in the room when the crying stopped as its small lips clamped onto her nipple, the shiver of pain. Directly opposite her across the room were her books on their shelves. They had always given her a sense of life's unfolding infiniteness. A pleasure that had been with her since childhood.

There were no babies in any of them. There were no answers in any of them.

On her phone, she looked at one of the texts she'd selected to guide her. A magical recipe of sorts:

> There are different ways, dearest, to get the baby back. Our gossip advised breaking many eggs and having a pot boiling on a good fire with the poker in it red hot and then brewing the shells there. The child will lie, for a wonder, quite quiet in the cradle and watch closely. At last he will ask, in the voice of an old man, what you are doing. Then you must say, "I am brewing in eggshells." "Oh," he will say, shrieking with wild laughter and clapping his hands, "I'm eight hundred years old and odd, and never have I seen a brewery in eggshells." Then you must seize the red-hot poker and thrust it down the imp's throat, and there will be a great bang. When you approach

> the cradle once more, you will see your own child in sweet, peaceful sleep, plump and rosy and with a mouth as delicate as a flower, softly breathing.

The woman in that particular story had not followed through. And Madeleine did not have a red-hot poker, and would not have used one if she did. More than anything she needed the knowledge. Once she had confirmation, she would come up with a better plan. It was the twenty-first century, after all.

She found the changeling's pinched face and black eyes gazing suspiciously up at her.

"You're finished, are you? Well, let's get to it . . . *Maudie*," she said, like it was a joke they were in on together. The changeling was silent. She stood, and placed it in the bouncy chair. For once, there was no crying at being put down. The eyes followed her to the counter.

She turned on the electric stove and waited. The changeling remained quiet, and she avoided looking at it. It was anticlimactic waiting for the stove to heat up, certainly nothing like stoking up a decent fire, but you had to use the tools available. She hated this electric hob; it took eons to get decently hot.

She broke the eggs over a bowl, letting the whites and yolks slither out, and risked a sidelong glance at the baby, who was reclined in the bouncy chair and still strangely quiet.

She rinsed an emptied eggshell under the tap, filled it with a little bit of water, and awkwardly held it in place over the hot element with a pair of kitchen tongs. Attempting to cook in eggshells was every bit as ridiculous as it sounded. She sloppily spooned some of the egg mixture in, so as to actually be cooking something.

The water in the eggshell boiled, and the kitchen began to

smell burned. At this point, the changeling should be shrieking about being as old as the hills. Madeleine slipped another quick glance in its direction.

The small chin had collapsed into the neck, and the head lolled sideways. The changeling had fallen asleep.

Madeleine remained holding a burning eggshell, cooking the world's smallest scrambled egg.

Her own laughter surfaced, and bubbled on and on until tears streamed down her face and mixed with the rising steam, and she wiped her eyes and asked aloud, "And how old am I anyway, to be cooking in eggshells? Aren't I old enough to know better?" She laughed and laughed and cried. She accidentally burned her little finger, and then the stove and the lights both went out.

Sleep when the baby sleeps, the health visitor had told her. But the light was too aggressive, so Madeleine stood at the window watching the baby foxes play in the deserted garden. The family didn't seem to be at home. It would be a good time to break into the shed, but she was discouraged by the cooking. She hadn't proven anything. Perhaps she hadn't done it correctly. Reading the paragraph again, maybe she should have thrown the eggshells into a boiling pot of water. But she couldn't shake the new feeling the eggshell was meant to be a metaphor for something else. What had she missed? Oh, it was all so much more complicated than it needed to be.

Eggshells a bust, she wrote on her slip of paper. *Now what?*

Now what, now what? For the first time since the quayside, she felt doubt. Had she got hold of the wrong answer somehow? She tossed the paper down.

She was putting together a cold lunch when she got a message that her maternity payment had come through. She walked over to the window and looked out onto Splinters and felt a stab of guilt. She had been pardoned. She would no longer even have to tell Tom how close she had come to a whole new way of existing. He would have saved her of course, or her parents would have saved her. But what a feeling it had been, to need saving. Now she could go top up the electricity if she wanted, say to Kamal "so sorry about that, just a mix-up at the bank." And he would believe her. She could even, if she wanted, take herself down to the café on the high street for an hour or two. It was pure hypocrisy, watching Splinters rearrange into something friendlier before her eyes. Still, she couldn't help but feel almost jubilant as she turned her back on the Path of Needles.

But the changeling was screaming again. So she sat on the bed, and fed it, again. More drooping eyelids, more drifting off, then starting awake the moment Madeleine deposited her gently, gently. Manoeuvring her fingers out. A choking wail. Twenty minutes more of feeding before the face went slack enough to be authentically sleeping. She looked at the face carefully and tried to evaluate all the many things she had seen in it: helplessness and cunning, an ethereal being, a beast. With the eyes closed, it was just a sleeping baby, but not hers.

Another ten minutes humming over the cot, lowering the body with gravity-defying slowness. As she wriggled her last two fingers out, she knew it wouldn't work. The changeling gave a defeated sigh and threw its arms out in sleep. A moment passed. Two moments. And then it began crying, still with its eyes closed. Madeleine looked malevolently down. The changeling opened its eyes and cried harder, that tearless, red-rimmed cry. Madeleine watched. The cries grew to a fever pitch, and

Madeleine leaned over and seized the changeling, sat down on the bed again, offered her breast again. Time passed. Her back ached. She eyed a book and her phone on the dresser. But, as usual, movement could unsettle this fine balance. She sat and stared into space.

She could see the window and through it the sky, but nothing of the outside world, no Greymalkin or Reynard. She was thinking too much about making the baby—changeling—sleep. When you thought about it too much it never happened. She must distract herself. Any other thought would do, if it let her mind roam away from these four walls. Reynard, then, and Greymalkin. Although really, was it Reynard she had seen in the yard, or Reynardette? Why assume a masculine fox, a masculine magic? She didn't know Greymalkin's sex either, now she thought about it. The name might serve for either. Or did it? It was a strange word. Reynard had a straightforward etymology. Or, well, probably not, but its connection to the French *renard* was clear enough.

But the naming of cats was a difficult matter. Greymalkin, as a word, was quite mysterious. Tom had said a children's book, John Somebody, but hadn't she seen it in Yeats too, spelled differently? It must come from some older source.

"This bears looking into, Maud," she said. She was careful not to call the baby changeling to its face. Better not to let the baby know that she knew. Better if it just went to sleep.

Her phone buzzed and buzzed again. She decided that the vibrations on the dresser were disturbing the changeling as much as her moving would.

Tom: Ah, sorry Marie's message got you agitated. You know she always self-promotes though.

Tom: It doesn't mean your students like her better than you.

Tom: You know the edited volume thing was just that she had that particularly relevant paper. That one was always a long shot for you.
Tom: Have you checked out the mummy and baby groups like we talked about?
Tom: I was thinking, you should get a bit of time to yourself.
Tom: How about this evening for an hour or so? Just to get a break.

She should probably feel grateful to Tom. For thinking of her, for taking time out of his busy, baby-less day. For being willing to be left alone with the baby. A sacrifice, but one worth making for his beleaguered wife. "Brave boy," she muttered.

Me: Don't worry about it.

A small delay, during which she fumed.

Tom: I think you should. I know you're exhausted but a change of scene would be good.
Me: Oh. And where do you suggest I go? And with who?
Me: *Whom?

Minutes stretched by without a response, although he had seen her message. Finally, enraged, Madeleine opened a tab on her phone. It was probably stupid, but she wanted to know about that cat. She typed in "Greymalkin, etymology." Wikipedia was the first result. It would have to do.

> A **grimalkin** (also called a **greymalkin**) is an archaic term for a cat. The term stems from "grey"

> (the colour) plus "malkin," an archaic term with several meanings (a low-class woman, a weakling, a mop, or a name) derived from a hypocoristic form of the female name Maud. Scottish legend makes reference to the grimalkin as a faery cat that dwells in the highlands.

She stared at the phone, unmoving, unblinking until Tom texted back and the message blocked the screen.

Tom: Sorry, my boss came by.
Tom: Well you might ask, you know, your **friends**. Not sure why you're avoiding them.
Tom: Tell Marie, "great, thrilled to give you this opportunity. You owe me a drink!"
Tom: Make them come to the high street so you don't need to spend an hour on a bus. But you should get out.

The messages appeared and disappeared on the screen, leaving her staring at an illustration of a small girl and a large cat. She fished out her little paper again and wrote, "corner the cat." Then turned back to her phone:

Me: Yes, I would like a little time alone.

Without doubt scissors and razors are weapons

—**"Razor,"** VLADIMIR NABOKOV

She told Tom her friends were all busy. It was probably true. There had been a first flurry of congratulations, but no one had proposed coming to meet the baby. She was startled when he suggested rescheduling for a night they were free.

No, no, she said. Tonight was the perfect opportunity to get her hair cut. Self-care. So important for new mothers, said the parenting manuals. Make sure you take some time for you. To have a hot bath, or go to a yoga class, or get your nails done. The manuals all suffered from a chronic lack of imagination when it came to guessing what might constitute self-care. Well you are looking a little shaggy, Tom had said, and curses, she realized too late she would actually have to make time to have her hair cut as well.

So she walked towards the high street alone that evening, and kept her eyes open for clues. *Corner the cat.* But it proved impossible, when searching for wild things in Splinters, to find them. No silvery fish slipped through the long-dried streambed that was their road, only silver speeding cars, one after the other, headlights beaming through the gloom like fishy, gleaming eyes.

It had rained all afternoon and grown dark early, and she was expecting the streets to be deserted, and yet when she checked it was only seven o'clock. People were still returning from work; others were headed to the shops. She had expected the whisper of the trees in conference, the rats and foxes in the shadows, and skinny Greymalkin waiting to dart across the traffic-snarled street. Instead the human animals were still filling their habitat, rushing by with umbrellas or with collars shrugged up around the shoulders, stalking head down with heavy bags, and music of all kinds poured out of windows that were cracked open despite the rain. She paused at the entrance to the Victorian tenements. She could go in. There were many flats; it was unlikely anyone knew all the neighbours. And yet, what would she do? Walk across the sodden lawn and prowl its edges, peering under bushes? Had there been a fairy mound where the tenements stood? With the landscape smoothed and urbanized, nobody could ever know. If there *had* been a fairy mound, it could be anywhere; on the high street, or the motorway off-ramp, or outside her own front door. And surely she was not going to find baby Maud so easily. In the changeling stories, there was always some confrontation, some drama, first. You had to oust the changeling, then recover the baby.

Another reason not to enter the tenement grounds: she was frightened of the neighbourhood, something she could only admit to herself. And more so since the incident with her maternity payment. She lived in it as an observer; maybe Marie would even call her a vampire, observing the suffering, celebrating the resilience that bubbled along underneath, but avoiding the drama. Splinters Wood, human and non-human, represented a version of Madeleine that hadn't been successfully adopted, one that had fallen through the cracks of the foster system and ended up somewhere like here. Even now, another junkie shuffled along the opposite pavement. A woman this time, lurching practically on tiptoe. Madeleine leaned back against the gate and watched her pass.

Such ideas were speculation of course. The Great Nondiscovery meant that she could never know what kind of life she might have had. It might not have been so Dickensian. But children didn't end up in care for no reason at all. She always wondered.

People were jostling by her as she wavered by the tenement gates. A mix of students and new professionals. There were rumours of an express train to London coming within a few years. What would happen to Splinters then? A woman pushed past with an enormous pram. Well. She would go hide in the hairdresser for a bit. She knew she was being cowardly.

The hairdresser was a clean and well-lighted place. It was further up the high street than she usually went, where all the Tom and Madeleine kind of signifiers were: the café, the gift shop, the bars with dance nights and cheap beer, and her usual hairstylist, who was already closed at this time.

There were people having their hair cut but no one else waiting. "I'll be with you in five minutes," a young woman told her when she came in. Madeleine warmed to her immediately; she was a chubby woman in enormous earrings and turquoise trainers, topped off with the branded smock coat they all wore. She was much more stylish than the bland girls at the more upmarket place. Madeleine sat, and settled into listening to the roll and lilt of the hairdresser's words, warm and unthreatening, as she chatted to her current client.

But in the very comfort of the place, the plastic chair, the words, the prosaic swish of scissors, there was a budding dread.

Madeleine looked at the second hairdresser. She was not cutting hair but was plucking a woman's eyebrows, her tiny silver tweezers making sharp lapping movements against the face while the client sat immobile, her stoic head thrown back, her eyes closed. And Madeleine, watching, saw every dart of the tweezers, and saw how simple it would be for them to slip, by accident or design, and be driven into the woman's closed, unsuspecting eye.

The conversation flowed around her like a river while she sat motionless, and then she finally dared turn her gaze to the first hairdresser, the one who would be with her in five minutes. She was trimming her client's fringe with large scissors that moved with a delicate rustling sound.

The tweezers would blind a person, wedged into the eye, but the scissors might kill. Madeleine raised her fingers to her own eye sockets, and felt hot, surprisingly thin red blood well up spontaneously, but when she pulled her fingers away again, they were clean. She looked again at the clients. Either one of them could be herself, seen from without, with a pair of glinting silver scissors thrust through the eye socket into the brain, and the hairdresser bending over her with a look of concentration, thrusting them further, getting stuck on bone or gristle, jerking them out and stabbing down again. Not cruelly, not maliciously, but methodically, purposefully, fatally.

The scissors clicked closed.

It was so easy for it all to be over. The fragility of life had never been so immediate. So much was made of guns in America, knives in London, but tools of death and people to wield them were everywhere. Vehicles, of course, were notorious now, but what of scissors and shears, what of bottles of wine with the bottoms smashed off, what of hands that would push you in front of a train or into an intersection, or set your house on fire, or what of accidents, electrical fires, malfunctioning ventilation ducts, what of tripping on the street and falling into traffic, what of poison accidental or deliberate, what of mauling dogs, what of poor quality control on food products, what of engine failure on flights, what of accidental combinations of genes that caused you to have an aneurysm or a heart attack with no warning, develop cancer, or for your baby to be found dead in its cot in the morning, what then? What of epidemics spreading from the developing world to your supposedly safe country? What of climate change, what of war? What of murder, rape, torture, dismemberment? What of paramilitary groups who would execute your family before your eyes before turning to you? At what point would you even want to remain alive yourself? What of pain, pain, pain, pain? It was so easy to wield it, so easy to yield to it.

"All ready for you now." The smiling young hairdresser stood before her. The scissors glinted familiarly from the belt around her waist. Madeleine had been staring into nothing, nothing.

The woman emanated warmth, safety, and control. She would have perfect control when driving the scissors into Madeleine's eye.

But Madeleine was a rational person. The hairdresser *could* drive the scissors into her eye. That did not mean she would. It would be an extraordinary thing for her to do. In all her years of reading the newspaper, she had never heard of such a thing happening.

She rose to her feet with hesitation. The hairdresser beckoned to her.

Madeleine forced herself to sit down in the chair.

"What can I do for you?" the hairdresser asked.

"Just a trim," she said in a voice jagged with fear.

"Come along to the back then and we'll give it a quick wash."

Again she let herself be guided. Into the reclining chair,

leaning backwards, with her neck exposed, and her head hanging backwards over the porcelain curve of the sink. She watched the hairdresser closely, her eyes darting after the placement of her hands, waiting for them to drop to her belt.

The hairdresser seemed to sense her discomfort. "You have lovely, thick hair," she said mildly as she turned on the tap.

"I don't really," said Madeleine. The hairdresser was silent above her, so she added, "I was pregnant. That is, the baby is only a month old. So my hair did that thing of getting all lush, but I'll probably lose it all again in a few months."

"Ah," said the hairdresser with a smile in her voice. "Sure, that happened to me, to pretty much everyone. How lucky to have a newborn baby to snuggle. My son is nine now, and he's huge. Doesn't want any cuddles from me anymore."

"Oh," said Madeleine. "Cuddles" belonged to another vocabulary, for people whose children weren't changelings.

They went back to the chair, and her hair was combed out into a heavy black curtain. "So you have just the one son?"

"Just the one, yes. Do you want more?"

"No."

"They are a lot of work, at the beginning."

"They destroy your body and then destroy your mind."

"Hmmm." The hairdresser was noncommittal. "You look amazing though. As though you had never given birth."

"Oh, I don't mean destroy your body that way," said Madeleine quickly. "I meant the birth itself."

"It's that moment of your life when you have to be strongest, but nothing really prepares you," said the hairdresser. "I had a home birth. Not so much a planned one. I just couldn't make it to the hospital in time. If there had been a next time you can bet I'd be camping out there days before, first in line for the drugs. You?"

"I was at the hospital." It came out in a burst, a gush. "I was determined to have a natural birth because my mother had been infertile and unable to have children, and she says she's missed all the parenthesis moments in life—she means the first days with a baby and the last days with parents because they both died suddenly and anyway, never mind—somehow I thought I could make up for it by experiencing everything in its rawest form. Only it was horrible. Horrible. I had read so much, prepared so much. I always prepare so much for everything, and read everything I can get my hands on. I tried to breathe, like they say. I tried all the techniques I had read about, and I couldn't do any of them when the time came, or I couldn't remember them. And yet I didn't take the drugs, because of my mother, because I owed it to her to experience what she couldn't, and in the end I needed a C-section so I was drugged anyway and cut open, and that wasn't like anything I'd read either, though it was true there was no pain; I could feel them shifting bits of me around; it was a feeling of being delivered of the baby rather than delivering her." She was not crying. She spoke quickly, earnestly, eyes wide and trained on the hairdresser in the mirror, focused imploringly; she could not make herself stop talking. "I couldn't do it properly, and I can't forget it, any of it. Sometimes when I can't sleep at night it comes back to me. It was like a ritual . . . humiliation."

"Well," said the hairdresser. "My sister is a nurse. She worked on the maternity ward for a while. You're a student, are you? She tells me it's the brainy women who can't wrap their heads around childbirth. They can't think with their bodies; they can only think with their minds. Whereas if you can really use your body there's a lot of power and strength to be found in the experience." She pulled her scissors out of her apron, and reached forwards to straighten Madeleine's head.

The scissors opened with a gentle croak, but they closed on nothing, for Madeleine had leapt up. Her face was reflected in the mirror, staring out from a cloud of dark hair, blood pouring out from her punctured head, leaking out of her eyes and nose and from between her teeth. The hairdresser had a warped, twisted fairy face, and the blades of the scissors were twisting outwards, growing like fronds of untamed ivy, jolting and curving towards her again.

She ran out into the street. She had left her coat. She would never be able to go back. She would never be able to go to any hairdresser again. How could she have blindly trusted in these people throughout her life?

She slunk back along the spiky artery leading home. She saw a narrow shadow hurrying along half a block in front of her and quickened her pace. Greymalkin. But the cat was gone again, just a quick twist of smoke curling through the streets, one among many.

There was crying coming from the bedroom, but Tom didn't call out; he hadn't heard her come in. She ducked into the bathroom. The mirror, her own staring face, her tangled hair. Tom would know she had not done what she set out to. She would cut her own hair in as straight a line as possible, so he would think she had been to the hairdresser.

She opened the cabinet. The scissors were kept in a jar with Tom's razors, and they all gleamed dully and malignantly. She reached a hand towards them, and watched the blades twist towards her. They wanted to reach out and bite her. She could not touch them; she could not trust herself not to stab her own eyes out if she held them.

She began breaking little ends off her long hair and throwing them into the toilet, until her arms burned with the effort of holding them up. She let them fall. Her hair was the same as ever, just picked-over looking. The house still ricocheted with changeling screams. She breathed, looked at herself closely, and braided her hair back tight. Her face, revealed, was narrow like a cat's.

There was no scene of recognition. The animals gazed calmly at each other with their animal eyes, and obviously accepted their reciprocal existence as a divine fact.

—"A Crossbreed," FRANZ KAFKA

There were whispers in the forest. There was a spectral light, and a twist of smoke drifting between the leaves, and a chitter of voices behind it. The smoke drifted along rising ground, leaving the forest, corkscrewing through the heavy honey-and-rot scent of hawthorn to the crest of a hill on a moonless night. The city glimmered beneath. A jingling of bridles, whispering, chortling, cackling. Indistinct figures took their place, and then, with the crack of a whip, the fairy rade began.

Madeleine dreamed she was stalking alongside a curl of smoke moving from below the overpass bridge up onto the motorway. A late car hummed past, and then, in the stillness, the smoke solidified, took on a litany of old aches and pains, and became a cat that ran on ahead of a host of fairies, cutting a path down into Splinters Wood, always on the verge of being swallowed by the night, always just visible. Aha, dreamed Madeleine. It *was* the cat. She would corner the cat. She hurried behind. In bed, her feet kicked against the blankets.

Greymalkin trotted along the road. The forest was gone, or rather the forest spread out in the cat's wake, the forest was always two steps behind, gliding through the neighbourhood and overlaying the human wild with the wilder wild. Carousers weaving home were stunned by the sudden damp closeness of well-known streets, the green smells, the loss of the sound of their own footfalls. The oncoming rade moved among them like ghosts. There was a girl with them, long-legged, long-haired, dark-eyed.

Madeleine's heart sank. The girl was so much older. Time passed differently in the fairy world. So much of Maud's time was already lost. The girl ran ahead on tiptoe, dancing to a music Madeleine couldn't hear, clambered astride the fairy cat, and threw her arms around its neck.

Greymalkin flounced along the street and paused before Madeleine's own high wall, crouched, and leapt to the top. An astonishing jump, even for a cat, and all the fairies swept up in its wake. From there the group moved on, ran along the edge of the wall, and scrambled up into the scaffolding of the building next door. Greymalkin, carrying the girl, set foot on the branch of a beech tree that reached almost to her front window.

Madeleine awoke. The downstairs neighbour's music was swirling and pumping around the edges of the night, and she could hear him singing. The changeling often slept better with all the rhythmic background noise, but Madeleine could not. She stood and hurried away from the sound, down the long corridor to the front of the house. The creak of the beech swaying on a windy night, cunning footfalls in the meadow, singing from below and from the scaffolding. Greymalkin was bringing her Maud.

The outermost branches tapped against the window. She threw up the sash, and a great gasp of forest air poured in. She reached out to receive her child.

In the watery starlight, she looked into a face: narrow, large-eyed, expressionless. Her own cat face, looking back. There was no one else. With a cry, she shook the branches, and Greymalkin, alone, tumbled out of the tree and twisted, smoke again, to the ground.

Whom the gods wish to destroy, they first call promising.

—Enemies of Promise, CYRIL CONNOLLY

There were messages in the group chat she shared with Marie, Bronwen, and Ollie. Madeleine turned to them with relief. Her morning had been fraught so far. She had gone to the baby weigh-in at the doctor's surgery. The room was full of other local mothers, most of them looking as tired and defeated as Madeleine felt. But she found herself incapable of speaking to them. There was a woman next to her, and they exchanged smiles, but that was all. A blond woman was arguing with reception that no, *that* address wasn't good anymore, she was living in her mother's front room now. Bureaucratic arguments ensued and the woman shouted, then wept.

When Madeleine had gone to weigh the changeling, the nurse had insisted that, while not growing by leaps and bounds, it was within the acceptable limits for a baby her age.

"She's scrawny," Madeleine insisted. And when the nurse replied in a soothing tone, she responded, "I think they weighed her wrong the other day." And after, "She doesn't look like she's thriving to me."

"She's just wonderful," snapped the nurse finally. "If you could see the low birth weights of some of the babies we see around here, you'd change your tune. She isn't scrawny, she's just long—as are you." Madeleine left in a rage.

Since then she had been sitting for ages with her scrap of paper trying to think of a new strategy for finding Maud, but the changeling had been alternately squirming or wailing in her ear all morning, and thinking was impossible.

Ollie: Coffee later?
Bronwen: Usual time and place?
Marie: Yes!
Marie: I'll be a bit late tho, have to see Angela quickly first

They were not really writing to her, but it was the old way of being, and she was still there. She didn't allow herself to hesitate.

Me: I think I'll come too. Hope the baby is invited. ;-)
Bronwen: Really? Wheeeee!
Bronwen: We were just saying how we had to come see you when things had calmed down a bit!
Marie: ☺

Even the bus could do nothing to dampen her excitement. She might pop up and see Angela, after Marie was finished with her. She could ask her about changelings. She might ask the others too. Get some clarity. Strategize. It was a day of muggy grandeur. She had put her contact lenses in; that alone felt like an accomplishment. The neighbour, the cat, the foxes, and the stolen child all became unreal, folded in upon themselves into another compartment of her mind. There was a break in the relentless clouds. Her life and work remained, she could go and visit now and it would be a first step to recovering everything. Splinters fell away behind her as she passed the new Tesco under construction. She changed buses. The old university buildings came into view. Maud slept obligingly on the walk through campus, vexed to slumber by Madeleine's eager, rocking footsteps. At the university bookshop, the same new releases were in the window. Only a month had passed since she had last been here.

She turned and headed through the denser part of campus towards the usual café. It was relatively quiet, between classes, the first week back after Easter. As she walked, a few curious heads turned her way.

The café was busy, however. This was where everyone was. There was no sign of her friends yet, so she lurked outside. If it was too noisy in there it would wake the baby.

Bronwen was coming. The same as always; blunt fringe and a Studio Ghibli T-shirt (always on brand with the Japanese studies) tucked into tight jeans, strident makeup.

"So cute!" Bronwen peeked into the baby carrier. She was glad Bronwen had come first; she'd known she could be trusted to gush a little and be less awkward than the others.

"You can't really think that," she replied lightly. "All babies are hideous."

"Cute hideous," Bronwen conceded. "Can I be like an auntie though? I'm always hoping my sister will make me an auntie. Is it heavy carrying her like that? Can I hold her?"

"Yeah, but not until she wakes up, sorry. I have to take advantage of every second she's sleeping to, you know—have a conversation and stuff."

"Yeah, I bet. Let's go in."

It had always been a noisy, jovial kind of place, but entering now, all the shouted greetings and squeals of steam were like descending into an underground train station. Madeleine wrapped her arms around the carrier to block the world out further. All that was visible of the changeling was its hair. "It's so noisy in here."

"Yeah, I guess."

"Maybe I'll go hold down that seat by the window."

"Sure. Cappuccino as usual?"

"Just a tea, thanks." She handed Bronwen some change. The relief of being solvent again. She mustn't squander it.

The table by the window was just as noisy as everywhere else, so she didn't sit but stood next to it joggling. Ollie came.

"Hiya."

"Yeah, hi."

"This the baby then?"

"She's sleeping. I hope it stays that way."

"Do you . . ." Ollie was clearly casting around, ". . . not get much sleep then?"

"Not a lot."

"I guess it comes with the territory. Nice baby, anyway."

"Yep."

Bronwen came, placed the cups on the table, snorting with laughter. "It's not like you sleep much these days, Ollie. Got any tips for Mads?"

Ollie grinned broadly.

"Oh?" said Madeleine. "Ooh la la?"

"Ollie's got a new woman in his life. He met her at the protest."

That sounded like something she was expected to know about, know what the protest was for.

"That's great, Ollie."

"So double espresso for you, then?"

"Ah, give it a rest, Bronwen."

"I'm just jealous." Bronwen sat and pulled herself forwards with a scrape of the chair. There was a stirring and wriggling from within the baby carrier. Madeleine breathed out, and bounced as if she were on an exercise ball.

If only Marie would come before the baby awoke.

"Read anything lately?" she asked the table at large.

"Nope," said Ollie, grinning again, and left to get his coffee.

"Me? No, you know. Probably should have done more reading over Easter. Went up to London to see a friend though. We were both meant to get some work done but one thing and another."

"Right." Maud squawked and Madeleine bounced fiercely.

"You'll hit the table behind," said Bronwen, making a sorry-to-mention-it face. "Have you read much?"

"Er, no." The squeaks and grumbles sounded angry now, and Madeleine peered into the sling to see the now-familiar poo grimace. "Damn."

She changed the baby on the floor of the bathroom stall. Back at the table, Ollie and Bronwen were arguing about the upcoming local elections. "He's just a disaster though, isn't he? It's not like anyone takes him seriously?"

"I'd vote for him."

"You and who else though?"

"What has your supposed most-pragmatic option done for the city anyway? Selling it out piecemeal to developers. They've even decided to give the management of the mural program to some Danish design firm, did you hear? I mean, first of all, the street art that was fucking illegal when it started, and now it's like some nice window dressing to drive up property prices, but it can't even be homegrown anymore."

"There's so many out where I live," Madeleine said. "They're going up all the time."

"Sure, you're the epicentre. They're putting one up on a

deadline next week; gotta be done and dusted in three days. They want to make it sound spontaneous, but the American artist probably just wants to get home to Berlin in time for Friday night." Ollie always got worked up about urban design issues. Bronwen didn't care about street art one way or the other; she was still incensed that he wouldn't vote tactically in the local election.

"Nah," Ollie said. "I'm sick of being tactical because other people are cowards or just fucking stupid."

"Saying people are stupid is a sure way to make them vote for you."

"He didn't actually say that though, did he? If you actually read what he said. That's just what I'm saying. Everything is twisted around by the press. And it's not like your lot don't think the electorate is stupid. They treat us like children."

"In a perfect world, Ollie, I probably would be in favour of some of what you say. But we don't live in a perfect world, do we? You've got to go with the lesser of two evils."

"No, that's exactly the problem. That's how everything gets chipped away and then nobody, justifiably, trusts political institutions anymore."

"Let Mads be the deciding vote. She's our top scholar. Yea or nay, Mads?"

"Um, I'm a bit out of the loop. But the first one to mention Hitler loses." She smiled at being called the top scholar.

"Haha, exactly. Let me hold this baby then. Isn't she gorgeous?"

Maud immediately contorted and wailed in Bronwen's arms, turning her head sideways and making darting motions with her lips. Madeleine sighed. Marie arrived once she was breastfeeding.

"I'd give you a hug, but," said Marie with a broad smile, indicating Madeleine's exposed breast with Maud gnawing away at it. She leaned in and gave the baby's head a delicate pat.

Madeleine tried to look brazen and unconcerned.

"Here's your keys back, Bron."

"Thanks again for looking after the place."

"Yep, it worked out beautifully for me. Total luxury, after sharing with four people. Just me and the plants. It sent me on a bit of a botanical loop with my reading."

"Lovely," said Madeleine.

"Oh, by the way, Mads, I told Angela you might pop up and see her. She seemed really excited to meet the baby. Something I've never understood. No offense."

"None taken." She struggled to keep offense out of her voice. "Did you have class with Angela this morning?"

"That's right. For your other seminar, actually, which is *great*, by the way. So I went along to the lecture this morning. I can't tell whether it's amazing when she puts Shakespeare to pop music or incredibly cringe."

"What are you saying, it's clearly amazing."

"I'm not sure all the first years would agree. And I'm not sure Angela's up on what undergraduates are listening to."

"You're practically an undergraduate. What are you listening to?"

"I never listen to music. I'd only ever heard those songs in shops."

"You've come dancing with me and Bronwen on Hartley Road."

"That's not listening to music though."

"What?" Bronwen was laughing. "What would you call it?"

"I mean, obviously it's music. But I wouldn't call it listening. You can never hear a word in that place, so that's all right."

"So are you anti-lyrics?" asked Ollie. "You, a literature major?"

"I've always been a bit anti-lyrics," Marie said. "Maybe I'd be more pro-music if there were no lyrics. Don't lyrics drive you mad? They're always so full of cliché and crap, if they're not actually outright misogynist. The same old stupid stories, I love him, he left me, ooooh. And I swear ninety percent of the time they don't scan, they always have to do little verbal tricks to make it fit on a line, or fill a pause with *oh oh oh* or whatever. I hate lyrics. And I basically hate pop music as a result. Doesn't the scansion drive you mad?"

"No."

"No."

"I never listen to the lyrics," Madeleine admitted. "Maybe if I did it would bother me. I just kind of tune everything out except the melody."

She felt so happy she could break out into singing *oh oh oh* herself. She was having a real conversation. It didn't matter that it was about a load of crap, or that Marie found her seminars less stressful than she had.

"God, teach me how *not* to listen to them. They totally ruin everything."

"You have the look of a lead singer though," Bronwen mused. "Such a waste." Nobody would say that of Madeleine. Second fiddle, always. Though maybe top scholar. In the past tense.

"No, gracias. But I suppose from that point of view I am in favour of Angela putting Shakespeare lyrics into Taylor Swift or whoever, I don't even know what most of these songs are. It makes them less inane. Though I'm not sure it really gets the students feeling Shakespeare in their bones like it's meant to. It's just a bit of performance, really."

"You win some, you lose some," said Bronwen. "In my BA I always appreciated the bits of performance you got from Angela. I still remember her dressed as a caveman and throwing large cardboard triangles across the room to illustrate something. Don't ask me what anymore. Something to do with Plato?"

"I heard she tried to rewrite a medieval romance about a unicorn as a pornography talent search for a virgin. Caused a bit of a scandal."

"That was long ago, but a brilliant approach. And hypocritical to be scandalized about it. That's why they have her, isn't it? To liven things up a bit."

"Definitely."

"So, how are you finding it all?" Bronwen asked Madeleine pointedly, as though to remind the rest of the table that there was more to discuss than all the usual gossip, although this was what Madeleine craved hearing.

"Oh fine." She lightened her voice several tones for a conspiratorial sound. She would joke her way in to test the waters. "I discovered the baby was switched at birth though. You know, such a thing would have to happen to me. Haha."

"Come again?"

"Sorry, I mean, changed at birth by a fairy. It's a changeling." Her friends looked at her like students asked to explain something they'd forgotten to read. "Like in folklore. Appropriate for me, studying Yeats and all."

"Back up," said Marie. "A changeling?"

"A fairy changeling, yes. Like in the old stories. A fairy steals a human baby and leaves one of its own. Never mind," she hurried on. "It was a bad joke."

"No, no, I know what you're talking about now," said Bronwen. "It just took me a while to get there. I thought you meant the baby had been actually changed at birth, like in the hospital, and I was going to say nice joke but you'll never get anyone to believe that. She looks just like you."

"No she doesn't." Madeleine shot the nursing head a quick glance of dislike. "And there were foxes in the hospital grounds, so it's more like one broke in and stole and replaced her, right."

"A fox did?" Marie and Bronwen were both grinning broadly.

"Sorry, I'm rambling. Sleep, what is it? Do they have changelings in Japanese folklore?"

"No, I don't think so," said Bronwen. "Lots of ghosts. And foxes are . . . like female shapeshifters though. So, um."

"I read an obscure Spanish story when I was having my botanical sabbatical last week," said Marie. "'The Tender History of the Plant Baby,'" Joan Perucho. It was awesome. A living plant crawled up a drainpipe and camped out in the baby's cot, and then when the mother came in to feed it, all bleary and sleep-deprived, it attached itself to her breast."

"What did it do with the real baby?" said Madeleine.

"Hmm, can't remember. Shoved it in the cupboard, maybe? But can you imagine, looking down at your breast right now and finding plant tendrils creeping along it?"

Madeleine did not look down at her breast.

"Anyway," said Marie. "What have you been reading?"

"I—uh, nothing. Too busy trying to figure out the changeling thing." She saw they were all looking uncomfortable now. This conversation was not going to yield results. Best to just beat a retreat, from the conversation and then from campus, get back to Splinters and her checklist. "I guess I just don't feel quite myself." She took a large sip of scalding tea.

"What you're doing is so important though," said Bronwen

soothingly. Madeleine smiled into her cup. Was there nobody who didn't have a platitude fit for the occasion of a baby?

"Right, I know. I need to raise the next generation so there will be someone to change *our* nappies when we're ancient. But why does it have to be at the cost of everything—everything!—that's mine?" She was almost shouting. Bronwen looked startled, and Madeleine forced her voice down, but all the words were coming out too fast. "I'm not going to even pretend otherwise. My own things—our things—it's like learning a language. Everything is, studies of course, and life. If you don't use it, you'll lose it. And the baby is just an endless time suck."

"But she's only, what? A month?" Bronwen said. "You won't be carrying her in a scarf when she's ten." Ollie threw back the remains of his coffee and tapped his fingers on the table.

"However," said Marie, with that combative tilt of the head that Madeleine adored when directed at others. "You did *want* a baby. At least that's what you told us." Marie laughed lightly.

"Yes, I *did* want a baby."

"Then really, the lack of sleep and everything goes with the territory." Marie lined up her coffee spoon and two sugar packets, then reached over and lined up Bronwen's spoon and sugar packets too. "I guess what I mean is, what did you expect?"

"There was that article, wasn't there?" Bronwen said. "Saying that most successful writers only have one child, if they have any. Most successful female writers, obviously. Though they've probably done studies on other professions. But it will probably be all right. Once she gets older, you can get back to work."

"So long as you don't have any more of course," Marie said.

"What a load of crap," Madeleine looked directly at Marie. She had sworn just that morning that the changeling would be her first, her last, her only. But who was Marie, who benefited by stealing all the classes and projects that Madeleine had worked for, to tell her how to live her life?

"Is it crap? Why?" Marie reached across the table and added Ollie's sugar packets to her lineup.

"Eh, let's just leave it," Bronwen suggested.

She knew never to rise to Marie when she was speaking in that calm voice, the one intended to rile people up while feigning politeness. Madeleine struggled to keep her eyes steady, to wear a smile as placid as a lake in July, never hinting at the depths of the black water. She tried to assemble the jigsaw pieces of an argument.

"Well, Dickens had about ten children, didn't he?"

"He was a man, of course."

"He also lived a century and a half ago. We have to hope things have changed since then."

"Is Tom going to stay home with the baby then?"

"Marie," said Bronwen. "Maybe she'll put Maud into childcare."

"I'll have to, yes, once my leave is up. Though it's like a second rent." Every time she thought about the numbers, she stopped thinking about them immediately. She'd believed, before, that she could look after the baby while working from home, and just pay a babysitter when she had to teach a class or go to meetings. But she knew now that it would be impossible. At this age, a baby was meant to sleep all the time, but the changeling only slept in motion, or on top of her. Already she couldn't get anything done, couldn't think, couldn't read or concentrate. She couldn't even do proper research on changelings. There had been one interesting-looking article but she didn't have access to it, had not been able to hack her way in, and had not had time yet to write to a friend from her master's who might be able to get it.

"Maybe I'll do a paper on that. A study on men *and* women writers who have had children, and how it affected their work."

"Ah," Marie said sagely. She reached for Madeleine's sugar packets. "You'll be going down that path. You've had a child now, so you'll only be interested in research relating to children from now on."

"It's normal that it's foremost in her mind at the moment," said Bronwen.

"Because nobody else lets their life circumstances influence their area of study," Madeleine said. "Certainly not you. You were sexually assaulted once, so now you're only interested in studying things relating to hating men."

From the distance came the roar of the coffee machine, and students laughing and grumbling and crumpling the tinfoil from their sandwiches.

Madeleine pushed her chair back, seized the baby more firmly, and walked away on shaking legs. A moment later she returned, kicked her bag out from underneath, and bent to lift it. Maud's head fell back with an angry mewl.

"Hey Madeleine," said Bronwen.

"No."

She left to the image, which would smart in her mind for months to come, of Marie's cramped, angry smile, her pink cheeks and averted eyes, and her hand laid elegantly, turned slightly upwards, helpless, alongside her coffee cup, and the neatly arranged spoons and packets of sugar.

She went back through the campus, the pavement seeming to evaporate beneath her feet, the buildings flashing by, the whole of it full to bursting with students but empty of everyone important.

"Madeleine," a voice called. She ignored it until a man jogged alongside her. "It's Madeleine, isn't it? I'm not the best with names."

She stopped and stared at him, for she was not the best with faces. But it resolved into someone known. Now goatee free, the novelist seemed milder, gentler. Or perhaps this was just how he was when he wasn't flirting.

"How are you?" he was saying. "I see you've had the baby. Isn't she lovely? It's a she, isn't it? How is motherhood treating you?"

His good cheer was a slap in the face after Marie.

"Oh, you know, not willing my own disappearance." She was quoting the novelist back to himself; all those months ago he'd criticized his ex-wife, who he said had birthed their son and immediately chosen self-effacement, prioritizing the child above everything until he felt he lived with a stranger. They had separated when the child was a year old.

"Those first days are hard and disorientating." He seemed to have forgotten all that.

His manner was kindly and real, looking her in the eyes, actually looking at her. "Are you on your way to see Angela? I was just popping by myself to borrow her library card. Shall we walk up together?"

"I can't," she said. "I was supposed to see Angela, but I've—come out without nappies. I think I should just go home."

"Are you all right?" he asked. "You look a little rattled. You've got a bit of a fixed glint in your eyes. I'm sure we've all looked that way as new parents, but still. Are you getting enough sleep?"

"Not really. Not with the foxes and the neighbour downstairs."

"And the baby, I imagine."

"And it. That."

"Why don't you come and sit in Angela's office a minute? We can have a chat. She can make you a cup of tea."

She could not go to Angela's office. Not now, maybe never again, after what she had said to Marie. The woman who had recast a medieval romance as pornography with a unicorn would take a dim view of Madeleine's work that day.

"Make my excuses," she said, turning away from the novelist and stumbling back towards the bus stop.

At home, she lay in a shadowy bedroom, feeding the baby. The hard little jaws sucked all goodness, common decency, and belief in herself away.

Because I seek an image not a book

—"Ego Dominus Tuus," W. B. YEATS

It was early May and not cold, but she had the unshakeable chill of exhaustion upon her, and the duvet pulled up to her neck. She liked being awake all the time; it meant she could fully enjoy the bodily sensation of lying down. She forced every vertebra to align against the mattress with a whimper of pleasure. She was not propped on her elbow to breastfeed without rolling onto the baby; nor twisted like a candy wrapper or the DNA sequence. She had no sides; she was like a woman in Flatland.

There was the soft brush and creak of the door opening over carpet.

"Sorry," Tom whispered. "I've got to go in five minutes. She's asleep for now, but I've left her surrounded by cushions on the sofa, and I don't think she should be left there alone."

"What time is it?"

"Half seven."

Tom had taken the baby at five and insisted she lie down, and she had surrendered. Had she been staring at the ceiling since then?

"How did you comfort her?"

"I just walked about. I think she wanted to be asleep, actually. She just doesn't know how to sleep for any length of time unless she's being moved around."

"You walked around for two hours? God, I'm sorry."

"It doesn't matter. That was a hard night for you. I'm sorry I have to leave."

"I just need a shower," she said, and scuttled by before he could argue.

"Mads, I don't really have time to wait." Tom followed her anxiously into the bathroom.

"I can't face another day of my hair lank and greasy around my head and being covered with sick before I'm even dressed."

"Well, hurry then. I shouldn't really be late, if it can possibly be helped. They still haven't assigned that promotion."

"Have you heard anything more about it?"

"No, so it could be one of those things that, you know, doesn't really exist. Like someone mentioned it once and then the budget wasn't approved and they've forgotten to update you. But I need to operate on the assumption that it does, and that it could come to me."

She mulled this over in the shower. Had Tom always talked like that? She thought, as she scrubbed fiercely at her scalp, that he hadn't. Or that when he had, it had been ironic, a send-up of others among their friends who moved to London and changed jobs dizzyingly often. Or perhaps he *had* talked like that before, sometimes, but so had she. They must have had some serious, professional conversations, when they were deciding to move here so she could study under Angela.

Well, the promotion would mean they could afford childcare, although probably still not full-time childcare, not if she wanted to take home any of her own salary.

She should hurry; she should relieve him of Maud so he could get to work. But the water was so intensely hot as to be painful, and it was bliss; she felt she could almost fall asleep in here, and she was sure she hadn't slept at all during the night. She let her hands glide over her body along with the water. She had shrunk dramatically, with the changeling sucking everything out of her. The hairdresser told her she looked as though she had never been pregnant. It wasn't true though. She had, like Alice, grown and shrunk and grown and shrunk with little warning, but her body was not the same. It was a stranger to her with its whitening scar; and it was as though, in removing the baby, the doctors had rearranged everything. Walking, sitting, everything was changed, and then there was the constant feeling of weight, the way her arms closed automatically as though holding something, because she was always holding something. Her ribs hurt, her shoulders slumped, her posture was ruined. The person in the shower was the body-horror version of herself.

She wrapped herself in her fluffy green dressing gown, a present from Tom's mother two Christmases ago. It was later than she thought. Tom shifted from foot to foot, but now that he could leave, he seemed to want to stay and talk to her. Last night she had cried and cried into two and a half glasses of wine, while Tom stroked her back and said maybe she could try apologizing to Marie once she'd had a chance to cool down, or maybe Marie hadn't taken it as badly as Madeleine suspected.

"She has, she has. She left the group chat we have, immediately after." She knew only too well that Marie was as uncompromising in anger as in most other areas. And she felt through her creeping guilt that she, too, was uncompromising in anger. Who was Marie to speak to her in that way? "Two years younger, not even capable of a functional relationship, not mother to a—a *thing*."

"Oh come on," Tom said. "She's twenty-two. We don't exactly have our lives sorted either. To be honest, my problem with

Marie was always that she's just a bit callous. Good fun but a bit mean. I never could see why you were so bothered with her. Just let her go." Madeleine snuffled while taking another sip of wine. "And what do you mean, mother to a *thing*?"

She should tell him. She should have told him before, and probably would have if Carol hadn't been staying. But she hesitated. She considered the faces of her friends earlier, how they had avoided her gaze. She wanted to present Tom with proof. But cooking in eggshells had not worked. She had nothing definitive. She had allowed yesterday, with its attempt to be Madeleine-from-before, to distract her.

"Nothing," she said. "I'm just tired of being with the baby all day. You can hardly consider it a person yet."

"She's only a few weeks old."

This morning he said, "I really think you should get out and see someone." He was rummaging around fiercely on the coat rack for his scarf.

"Right."

"I know it didn't go well yesterday. But write to Angela. Promise me you'll write to Angela."

"Yes, fine, yes."

"You'll need to top up the heat again."

"Again? I just did." Though now she remembered, she had not put the full amount on it. Tom was jamming his shoes on now.

"Well, it's running down again. To be expected with you home so much. And taking such a long shower, if I can say that without sounding passive aggressive. Can you pick up the photos while you're at it?"

"Yes."

"And check out some local mother and baby groups."

"No."

"Mab, seriously." He jerked the shoelace too hard and the knot slid out. "I think you should meet some other mums."

"I hate other mums."

"You don't know any other mums."

"I've seen them all in pregnant yoga class."

"They weren't mums then."

"One or two of them were."

"Don't be pedantic," said Tom, stuffing his phone and a book into his laptop bag.

So Tom was her antagonist now. He headed for the door and she turned angrily back into the bathroom and reached for her contact lenses, careful to avoid Tom's razor, which lay on the edge of the sink. As she was putting the second lens in, a shape stepped, fully visible, past the bathroom window. She screamed.

Tom ran back along the hall and into the room.

"There was somebody out there, standing on the ledge."

"What?" he burst past her and stood with his face pressed to the glass, craning his neck to see down to the garden.

"But it's impossible," he said. "How could someone get up here? And where would they go from here? They could only step out into empty space."

"I saw it."

"I think you're imagining things," he said. He was teasing her. She crossed her arms over her chest.

"Is it so hard to trust what I see with my own eyes?"

"In this case, yes. It would be suicide!" He placed an arm around her, damp, fuzzy, and ridiculous as she was, and said, in an echo of so many old jokes, "My madwoman in the attic."

She leaned close to him and laughed and laughed, past the point where laughing seemed an appropriate response, at which point she made herself stop because she felt a tension coming through him. He was checking his phone for the time.

"Please," Tom said, when Madeleine demurely followed him down the hall to bid him goodbye, "try and get out today. See some people. Write to Angela. Tell her you'd like her to be Maud's fairy godmother. Maybe she'll give the gift of sleep!"

She laughed, and he kissed her and sprinted down the stairs. At the click of the door, Madeleine heard a wakeful squawk from the changeling. She padded silently back along the hall to collect it, and then returned to the bedroom and slid into yesterday's clothes, abandoned on the dresser. The changeling was wakeful but unprotesting. Madeleine went directly to the window and looked down into the neighbour's patio, which technically was for the use of both apartments but in practice was an overgrown mess littered with everything the neighbour had accumulated over twenty years, everything from a defunct barbeque to an armchair that had once been brought out on a nice day and was left there to rot, all of it overgrown with weeds and soggy, abandoned cartons. Weaving amongst all this, and turning to look up, was Greymalkin.

"You," she said. She opened the window and leaned out. She could swear the cat looked smug. As though, yes, just as though it had been peering in at her while she was in the shower.

Music came up from the downstairs flat, but she picked up the changeling in the crook of her arm and headed for the door before she could overthink it. She had as much right to the patio as he did. She slid into the shoes she only used for taking the rubbish out. Down the stairs and then along the narrow path that ran by the entrance down the side of the building, then through the little gate and onto the patio into a day that was surprisingly warm and pleasant with a friendly, if low-hanging, sky.

The music was too loud, but it was all right. She didn't know the names, but she knew the sounds. He'd have been ahead of the curve, whenever he started listening, twenty or thirty years ago.

It was strange to see only the rooftops of the houses that backed onto theirs. The fox cubs lived just beyond that fence, but it was behind a dense bush and seemed worlds away. So too did her own flat when she looked up. The bedroom window was still open. It was too high for a person to have climbed up, but it looked vulnerable. A water pipe ran straight up between the bedroom and bathroom. She turned and pushed into the bushes with the music pulsing behind her.

Greymalkin looked up at her from a broken flagstone, a rat held between red claws, still twitching slightly. Madeleine drew to a halt. Greymalkin, with undignified speed, grasped the trophy by the neck and retreated through a gap in the wall with the garden next door. And so Madeleine was left alone, standing in a bush with a baby, almost touching the wall they shared with the fox garden. She glanced back up at her own flat, the wide ledge of the bathroom window. Could it have been the cat up there? Could it have been the rat? Perhaps Greymalkin was protecting her. Look at how she'd left the window open. If it were the rat, it could have got in. Open window, water pipe, trailing ivy, in a world so bright, so warm, so caressing, and yet full to bursting with all these threats and death. She had left the window open; it was the same window as in the hospital. You climbed through one and you came out the other. She had opened so many windows. She had left the baby lying there, lying there, at the hospital, and here by the fairy circle, the hitherto unnoticed magic of the neighbourhood fauna.

Another thing hitherto unnoticed. The neighbour was standing behind his own window, looking out at her. His square, unshaven face hung slack, and he wore the thick blue petrol-station jacket.

She approached and he opened the window, the lower twin of her own open window. He looked neither more nor less drunk than usual. His eyes were bloodshot and looked sore and for once did not narrow at the sight of her. She looked him fully in the face and suspected her own eyes were a mirror of his. She could match him capillary to capillary.

"I was just trying to find the cat," she said.

"That cat is a fucking ghoul," he replied. "Like I think it walks on its hind legs at night and does spells and things."

"Yes!" she said, so surprised that her voice soared into something like a scream. "It does!"

"Like, it's got a seriously evil look on its face." His eyes were wide, looking beyond her so that she looked over her shoulder, but the cat was not there.

"Yes!"

He turned to look at her properly then, and she had a sudden panic that he was going to start accusing her of stealing his bag again. But no.

"Is that a baby?" He was looking at it like he'd never seen one before.

She looked down at the changeling.

"I found a baby picture of me recently," he said, in a voice thick with some emotion. He wandered away, into the interior of the flat, and returned almost immediately with a small photograph, already bleaching orange from the passage of time. A pretty woman, impossibly young, sat on a sagging sofa with a large, laughing baby in her arms. She could scarcely credit it with being the neighbour.

"That's a nice picture," she said.

"My auntie found it and sent it round. My mom passed away two years back." To her horror, he seemed on the brink of wet, fuming tears. "Heart disease. She was sixty-five. I guess she'd had good innings, except for the last years when she wasn't well."

Madeleine paused. Carol was almost sixty-five, though the man downstairs was much older than she was. Life expectancy was shockingly low in this part of town, she remembered reading.

"Since she died," the neighbour said, "it's like every woman with a baby, it's like she's my mum, and I've gone and shrunk into a little child again. My mum was great when I was a little. We'd always be out, running errands, visiting her friends. She called me Spidey cos I had, like, unrealistically long legs. Later I just wanted to be with my mates. And she got into some sticky situations. When I see a baby, I think how lucky they are. Back to innocence, yeah?"

"I'm not sure babies are innocent," said Madeleine. "We just like to project that onto them. They're cunning in a way, and manipulative. They are just endless raw, unmeetable need. They are wild. And they never let you sleep." She felt she could fall into the neighbour's half-focused eyes; there was a whole universe in there among all the broken blood vessels.

"I never sleep anymore," he said. "Even years ago, I never needed much sleep. Like maybe four hours, like Maggie Thatcher."

"Have you always lived here?" she asked.

"More or less."

"It must have been different, back in the day."

The neighbour cast a depreciating look at the bush and patch of grey sky. "It's had its ups and downs. The landlord wants to kick me out, did you know that? He wants to raise the rent. He wants to raise the rent for all of us, and get some students in. I grew up just around the corner. There's one of those big, smiley fucking murals there now. Not by what's his name. Some second-rate poser with a spray can. Now they're building luxury flats though. Students."

"Students don't live in luxury flats."

"Maybe not. Students'll live here then. When they get me out."

"They're not all bad," she said.

"There's a young one upstairs who's all right," the neighbour said, startling her. "Knows how to talk to a person, and he's not one of these slummers. Don't think I don't know what they're like. Swanning around feeling some second-hand glamour at stepping over the tramp sleeping on their doorstep. Bit of street cred to tell their friends now and bore their grandkids with later. 'Ooh, I was that poor when I was young, but I came up in the world through my own hard graft.'" He practically fluttered his eyelashes at this bit of theatre. "Yeah, he's alright though, the one upstairs."

There was a volley of growling from the next garden over, a terrible hissing, and a few moments later a chorus of foxy barks.

"The landlord wants to raise my rent." The neighbour was dwelling on it, was entering into a loop. There was something more unstable about him by the minute. "Do you know how much he wants to charge me, starting this summer?" He told her, and started crying, an ugly, alcohol-fuelled whimper.

It was less than what she and Tom were paying.

She reached across the windowsill and touched his arm. He seemed indifferent.

"Students will be lining up to live here. Even though it's

a shithole. It's got a garden, right? Perfect for their parties. Fucking students. They're all over the place already. A student tried to steal my bag in the shop."

She shifted on her feet.

"The students steal and they steal. They come and take it all away."

"Something *has* been stolen from you," Madeleine said. "A bag though?" She was still clutching his arm; the changeling was growing heavy in the crook of her other elbow. "They steal and they steal."

"They despise me. They think they're better than me. And this one thought she could steal from me."

"I should go," she said. She pulled away, and stepped carefully back onto the rubbish-strewn patio.

"Keep away from that cat," he said in a sudden wheeze. "It would eat its own babies."

"You watch out for the students," she said. Ill-advised levity; she saw his eyes narrow, and then recognition dawned in them. She turned and bolted back around the side of the house.

Angela,

I meant to visit you on campus a couple of days ago—sorry that didn't happen, the baby was pretty nervy in the end and it didn't seem the best conditions for having a conversation. I hope you're well. Maybe we could meet somewhere to have a reconnaissance conversation sometime soon. I'm free whenever. There are a few ideas I'm toying with—when I have the time.

—Madeleine

That had taken all the rest of morning, but she had sent it. Promise kept. Tom could not say she wasn't making an effort.

And, in fact, she wanted to see Angela. With Angela she would be able to talk about the changeling. Angela would know things, without needing to research them. She would have interpretations, for the failure of the eggshells maybe. And Angela would be able to give her an answer: what to do with a fairy being, or a fairy cat. Where to find a fairy mound. Angela, who could find a unicorn in pornography, who could find the hidden pop song in Shakespeare, she would find an answer in Madeleine's half-knowledge. Yes, Angela was her last hope.

But what now? Nothing to do but wait for a reply. And try to be quiet. She didn't want the man downstairs to hear her walking about, now that he had recognized her again. She had heard him shouting incoherently into the garden for a while, and she didn't put it past him to come up the stairs and stand, rapping at the door, crying through the lock about students.

Her book of theory was sitting on the arm of the couch, and in it her little paper. While feeding the baby she tried to write left-handed:

> Still no luck with cat. It leads me on, like a game. Angela may know something. Need a place to abandon changeling. Fairy mound, but where? In the city? Up north? The moors near Nan and Grandy's?

Her scrawl was barely legible, and she closed the book again wearily.

Tom: I found a baby group happening this afternoon. You have to pay for it but that's fine, I think it's worth it

Me: Ugh

Tom: I'm not saying you have to become best friends with the high street yummy mummies, but what harm can it do to have a bit of a chat?

Me: I'm busy

Tom: Right

Tom: I don't know why you want to make these first days so difficult for yourself

Me: I thought you liked complexity

Tom: Soz, just starting a meeting

That would keep him off her back for a bit. But meanwhile, what was her next plan of attack? Her mind drifted off, and sentences twisted down forest paths, never-ending, producing nothing solid in her mind.

She heated a tin of soup for lunch, and then, still starving, finished off all the bread in the house. The changeling was tetchy, and she fed it into forced somnolence, feeling the food she had just eaten drain out of her before it was even fully digested. The bookshelf at the far end of the sofa loomed mockingly over the proceedings, and she let her eyes stray over the familiar shapes and colours and rest briefly, cynically, on the battered orange spine of a second-hand *Tess of the d'Urbervilles*. How romantic she had found those dairy scenes, Tess milking away with her cheek laid against the cow's flank, Angel watching through the golden summer air. And yet what was milking, but this? Well, perhaps that was a false equivalency; Tess had nursed a child and never made the connection. Or perhaps it was Hardy who had not made the connection.

In any case, she should go and buy some milk of an exploited and enslaved cow, or there wouldn't be enough to have tea later.

She left for the shop. It was mid-afternoon and Splinters was empty. There was a woman with a slightly older child, old enough to sit facing forwards in its pushchair, standing in the park and looking at her phone in confusion.

"Are you going to the mummy day group?" the woman asked, like some manifestation of Tom's psyche sent to intercept her. The woman wore bright colours and deliberately naïve patterns, and so did the baby.

"I don't know anything about it," Madeleine replied firmly.

"It says it's in Banner Mews," the mother said, inclining her phone towards Madeleine. Her baby watched with good-humoured blue eyes. Madeleine rocked back and forth on her feet and turned the phone around until she saw where it must be.

"Right, so it'll be back down that road and to the right. You've got to jog up a bit diagonally. Technically it's a different neighbourhood, though right around the corner. There'll be a thali restaurant, a couple more shops, and it's in like a cul-de-sac with a couple of bright painted houses."

"Thanks," the woman said, turning around. "I'll muddle along there, I expect. Or—would you like to come? It's an event for mothers, after all."

She opened her mouth automatically to say that no, she couldn't. But Tom's eyes were staring out of the woman's face at her. She blinked, rubbed her eyes. Still Tom, overlaid onto the mother. "I—why not?" she said finally. They walked along in silence for a few moments.

"How old is yours?" the other woman asked cheerily.

"One month, just."

"Oh, those are hard days. Mine is almost eleven months. Does she sleep much?"

"Not much."

"Yes, Diggory didn't sleep much at that age, did you, my darling? Aren't they little beasts?" Diggory laughed like one in on the joke.

"Does he sleep now though?" Madeleine wanted reassurance badly enough to unbend a little.

"More or less. Some nights all the night through, anyhow."

"And—was the birth all right?"

"Oh yes, yes. I can't complain. And it's funny how you forget all about it as soon as it's over, isn't it? Are you breastfeeding?"

"Yes."

"It's so tiring but so precious. Until they get teeth, hahaha. No but really, I just love the special bond it creates. I hope I'll be able to express enough to keep it going when I go back to work next month. I can't believe it's come around so soon. It seems wrong to leave the baby to strangers already and, well, I'm just not ready, I suppose."

There was a sheen of pleasure that coated the other woman's words. All her stories were tales from the trenches of an unquestionably worthwhile war. Yet Madeleine felt warmed by this. She wanted to believe it was so.

They had walked through the quieter streets, past the fox house, and by the next corner they were leaving Splinters Wood. It was so all-encompassing, the thicket she lived in, and yet a few short steps in another direction, and she was out. They cut upwards on an angle towards the high street. They reached a half square, where many of the shop fronts had been painted bright colours. There was a pop-up art space, and a café that gave onto Banner Mews, partially blocked off with large planters.

There were groups of women pouring out of a community centre Madeleine had never noticed before, just beyond the square. These were Splinters mothers, she divined immediately, loud and laughing and wearing tight clothes and a million miles from her new companion, who noticed it too.

"This can't be right," she was saying, consulting her phone again. "No, never mind, it's actually down this alley here, in a back room of the café. That must be one of the free groups." Madeleine cast a glance behind her and sighed as they entered Banner Mews proper, where two women with pushchairs and a man wearing a baby sling were just passing through the door. Different accents, different clothes, with even the toddlers wearing expensive-looking shoes. This lot must all live on the other side of Hartley Road.

The entire opposite wall of the mews was a mural, stretching from the ground to many feet above their heads. This one was in the usual startling, glaring colours: cyan, magenta, lilac, lemon, and appeared to show a woman, partially underwater, contorted and possibly sinking but strong in her writhing form, shoulders thrown back. Her long neck was stretched and straight and elegant. Her head was above the water and wore a carnivalesque mask of bright feathers that covered all but her eyes, which were green, with constricted, slit-like pupils. They were Greymalkin's eyes. And they were moving.

They were doing that involuntary drifting thing of cat's eyes; gliding in an unfocused way in one direction, then jerking the other way, right as Madeleine passed. It was this that drew her attention. She stopped, and the eyes snapped into focus, the pupils dilated. Madeleine looked around quickly over her shoulders, but no, the eyes could only be for her. No one else was even looking this way; other parents were stepping through the door, into a space that promised them respite and understanding. Even her new friend was gone, too busy trying to get her pushchair over the threshold to notice that Madeleine hadn't followed.

"Are you coming in?" asked a woman who seemed to be manning the door. Madeleine hesitated.

The masked woman in the mural opened her mouth, and inside she had cat's teeth, and a cat's tongue, and a long, elegant throat curving away into the unknown. She bared her teeth in an unmistakable snarl.

"No," Madeleine said, seeing her new friend peek her head back now too. "No, I . . . realized I'm meant to be picking up the photos." The door closed. The world receded. She stood in the empty alley. She had chosen the neighbourhood. The women from the other group had dispersed, but all the roads led back to Splinters.

She knew the mural would just be a mural again when she looked back, and it was.

No matter. She didn't regret it. She chose Greymalkin. She even chose the downstairs neighbour if it came to that. It was all the same at the end of the day.

Angela had replied, confirming a meeting the following day at a café on the high street, "No arguments, unless there's another one you prefer. I don't want you having to trek all the way here. My house isn't particularly child-friendly."

Madeleine mulled over the meaning of this as she strapped the irritated changeling into the baby carrier. Simple tutor meetings were almost always at Angela's house, if they weren't at her office. She wouldn't have minded trekking out to Angela's for a free cup of tea, somewhere quiet and comfortable and warm. What did it mean, anyway, that her house wasn't child-friendly? What were the special requirements of a month-old baby? She couldn't crawl; she couldn't break anything or accidentally stick her fingers into electrical sockets. The most the changeling could do was leave odours. What was Madeleine's own flat, if Angela's house wasn't suited for children?

Tom: She just doesn't know anything about children. My work is full of these people. Let's discuss when I'm home.

But she had lost confidence in Angela. Clearly Angela understood nothing; her intellectual rigor was no different than that of a mummy and baby group.

"I can't possibly see her," she said to Tom that night. "I'm going to cancel."

"Of course you have to see her." Tom ran his fingers through his hair. His voice was close to snappish.

"What do I talk to Angela about but my work and my reading? I haven't read a word since the birth." Hasty phone research on changelings was not something she would admit to Tom.

"You've read enough in the rest of your life to make up for it. Nobody's expecting you to have read anything. Maud is only four weeks old!"

She was silent.

"And Angela isn't a book perched on a body, at the end of the day. I know you are in awe of her, but personally I've always found her refreshingly easy to talk to. I had a nice chat with her about impending fatherhood at her Christmas party. She was telling me about her experiences as an auntie."

"It's different for you, and it's different for aunties."

"How so?"

"Fatherhood doesn't imply a loss of everything else. And auntiehood is like the golden ticket of the childless or childfree or whatever we're supposed to call them. It's the state of being that allows someone to proclaim that they love children, really, but can't see why you would want to have any yourself."

"And for you it's how, exactly?"

"It's bondage. It's slavery on a bodily level. It eradicates you mentally and reduces you to a bargaining chip in the service of evolution." She spoke resentfully to her glass of red wine. They only had one wine glass and she had taken it. Tom was drinking his from a mug. So recently in the past, she had been happy to drink wine from the mug. It had felt vaguely adventurous; shambolic adulthood, Famous Five go to uni, camping-in-the-living-room kind of fun, but now she had no wish for anything juvenile. She wanted to be an adult and surrounded by adult things. She held the wine glass delicately by the stem. The stem was everything. The stem meant she was a grown-up and could be trusted not to break things.

Tom abruptly placed his mug on the counter and went down the hall. She listened for the bathroom door to creak shut, and waited, a vague fluttery panic in her, for him to return. He did not. She waited longer, but there were no further sounds of footsteps moving either towards or away from her down the hall.

She placed the wine glass on the table and tiptoed down the hall into the bedroom. Tom stood in profile against the window, looking down at the changeling. She was sleeping half swaddled, but her arms had escaped and were thrown back. There was a kind of bacchic abandon in the way they lay, exposed, thrust outwards. Her head was on one side, moonlight and orange streetlight dusting her forehead, and her lips twitched with chilly silent laughter. Madeleine could see below the skin and organs to the twisted wooden core, the bundle of sticks made animate. Might she not tell Tom? Might he not see it, in this dim, bewitched light, for what it really was? He was not as strong as he needed to be, but might they not, together, be strong enough?

Madeleine moved tentatively into the room, and placed an arm around Tom. He did not move, did not acknowledge her touch in any way. His gentle, boyish face was cold.

"I don't know why you don't love her," he said. "That's just shocking to me. I know you *will* love her, but it's hard to hear you say these things."

Immediately she was chilled and wordless. She didn't know how to respond to such a charge. *I do love her.* Impossible. It would roll and echo through the room in all its falseness, magnify and distort like ancient fairy laughter, it would fill the room, and break the windows to burst out, and balloon higher and wider, a mushroom cloud of mirthless noise over the neighbourhood. She might say, *I do not know how to love this but I believe I loved the real Maud, the child with the cockleshell ears on a brand-new morning.* But what was belief in love, ultimately? There had been so little of the real Maud. She might say *I love you.* More impossible than the rest, because it implied, no, it demonstrated that love was not unconditional, a loved one was chosen, not born, and if her love of Maud was conditional upon Maud's not being a changeling, then perhaps Tom's love of her, Madeleine, was conditional upon Madeleine's loving the baby.

There was a coward's way out, and she took it. "It isn't like that," she said, and her voice quivered into tears. "It will come, what you want me to feel. I'm just so tired, and so alone—"

"So alone that you won't see Angela who might make you feel less alone—"

"So alone that I don't even know how to be with myself, let alone with anyone else. I don't know how to talk. I don't know how to be." She teetered a moment, and then she let herself cry, let the tears establish her helplessness, which he was sure to respond to, although this act also weakened her, and she did not want to be weakened before Tom. It was like an admission that she did not belong in the world, that Tom should be the one to live in the world, and she was the delicate creature who needed to be protected from it. It was a dangerous precedent to set. They had never been on this standing with one another before. Or maybe they had. Maybe she had agreed to this long ago, when Tom got a job and she remained the perpetual student, even though her pay was almost the same as his back then.

She accepted Tom's putting his arms around her and guiding her out again to the sofa. The changeling remained asleep, and for the rest of the evening she forced herself to speak lightly of other things, to ask him about his work and his colleagues. He smiled and spoke, gaining speed and animation, telling her things about the last few days, things he had not thought to mention at home. He drank wine and flushed pink as he always did, and sat trailing his fingers lightly along her neck and arms. He reminded her to pick up the photographs tomorrow. She agreed. She behaved like herself again. Herself, just a little overtired, that was all.

The fox, which is born in our fields, also crosses the frontier, going into the border of twilight at certain seasons; it is thence that he gets the romance with which he comes back to our fields. He also is fabulous, but only in Elfland, as the unicorns are fabulous here.

—The King of Elfland's Daughter, LORD DUNSANY

So, she must see Angela. She decided to take the pram. It was a faff to get out with it, but it would be more convenient when she was there, as long as the bumpy journey worked its magic. And the pram would give her something to hold on to, because the world seemed to be shifting beneath her this morning.

She was late and there was nobody to see her rush, so she jerked the pram through the front garden and over the difficult raised step. The usual struggle with the gate, which finally burst open onto the staring, thwarted face of the neighbourhood. She avoided eye contact and banged the pram sharply over the threshold. She quickly turned her back on the motorway intersection with its boarded-up windows and fluorescent smears of fried chicken shops, and headed right, pushing the pram past the wet hedges of the old tenements. After seeing Angela, if she didn't have proper answers, she was going in there, come what may. She realized she had left the plastic rain sheet behind. It looked like rain, but she was late.

The street was vague and wraithlike; it seemed on the point of evaporating. The changeling in the pram looked more solid and substantial than many of the people who flitted past. A great weight of sky bore down, hustling clouds of grey and brown and mildewed green, and there was a sickening rocking, the trees and houses tilting constantly on the edges of her vision. She focused on the face in the pram.

"Who are you?" she hissed. Not loudly. Not loudly enough to be heard above the light rain pattering on the canvas top. Yet the changeling stared back with guileful eyes. Dismay crawled through her healed stitches and clawed about in her stomach, her chest, her lungs. They passed a colourful mural celebrating the migrant community of the 1970s. Somebody's belongings were rolled into a hedgerow next to it. No sign of Greymalkin. Madeleine could see the neighbour shuffling by on the other side of the street. She lowered her head and hurried on, trying to ignore the sight of her shoes dissolving in every puddle she stepped in. She glanced again into the pram. The changeling opened its mouth and showed its toothless gums.

In recent days she had felt the road to be a ribbon of sameness. She had walked it hundreds of times before having a baby, but then she was part of the texture of life, she was needed by it. It was frightening how little the world needed her now, and all of life boiled down to this one line, forwards and back, forwards and back, over and over, the only constant thing beyond the four walls of her flat.

But even the road was at risk of washing away. If she stepped from the sidewalk, she would be engulfed into nothingness. The neighbourhood was just a mural; if she reached out, she could flake a little paint off it with her nail. Unreal city. Only the road was real, and it had begun to buck gently underfoot. It too would break from its usual route and run into all-swallowing mist. She must reach the high street before that happened. She must concentrate. She must not look into the puckered, puckish face of the changeling, and must not look back either. Looking behind would only show her a swirl of raindrops and concrete and shards of mural paint, dissolving neighbourhood, dissolving city grasping at her heels. Finally, she ran.

At the intersection with the high street there were students, and the girl from the art prints shop. There were the bars where she had danced to local bands, gift shops where she had bought expensive birthday cards for friends, in a distant lifetime. The famous chippy of blustery nights, and across from it, the café. All this was real, and all this would keep the world from moving underfoot.

There she was.

The puffy but beautiful face of a late Renoir, the many textures of black and the startling silver jewellery. Madeleine approached across the gently rocking floor.

Angela stood and gave her an awkward half hug. It was the embrace of academia itself. She had never experienced the strange, humbling sensation of Angela's physical bulk in such a way. Angela had never been a body before, and Madeleine, thin and static, felt a strangled desire to cling to that solidity. Harder rain fell outside and threatened to wash everything away. But Angela pulled back and leaned over the pram like someone in an art gallery.

"Well, now." The changeling was pretending to sleep, but there was a twitchiness at the eyes. "Isn't that a lovely baby. You must be very happy."

"Oh yes." Madeleine produced a smile.

"What shall I get you? You sit down. I suppose you're still not able to drink caffeine?"

It had not crossed her mind that perhaps she wasn't meant to be drinking caffeine. "Hmm. I do, actually. I'll have a cappuccino please. But I'll get them. I fancy a piece of cake or something. I'm a fiend for sugar since the birth."

"No, no. You sit down. I'll get everything." She sat and observed the café in bright, hard shards. Couples in artfully mismatching outfits, a young woman reading intently, gusts of rain on the window, the usual warm, caramelized-onion smell, the sleeping changeling, the rocking. Angela returned with the coffee and cake and a hot chocolate, of all things. She had never actually seen Angela consume anything more than a glass of wine before. They usually met in her office at the university, or at her house, where spaces appeared to be tailored to Angela's oil-painting appearance, or in class, a neutral space.

"You'll have to tell me about the birth. I hope it worked out as you were planning and you were able to have a natural childbirth."

Madeleine watched Angela stir the whipped cream below the surface of the chocolate. She had sudden mad visions of Angela at the bank, Angela putting petrol in a car, Angela flossing her teeth and spitting blood into the sink. Angela looked up at her, waiting, and Madeleine remembered the question. The birth. She shivered with contempt for her former self, shyly gushing one afternoon in March about natural birth plans, when the sun slanted unexpectedly down through the quadrangle outside Angela's office. She was ashamed of herself.

"No," she said, fascinated by a droplet of whipped cream on Angela's lip. "I was in labour for hours, then forced onto a table and sliced open." She held on lightly to the table; she was beginning to feel sick.

She saw that she had scored points for her wording. "Are you recovered?"

"I suppose I'm physically fine now," she said. "I'm not supposed to do certain exercises yet or anything. I don't like the memories though. I can't forget it."

"A friend of mine compared childbirth to being tortured," Angela said unexpectedly. "Is that frivolous? I told her about Jean Améry saying that torture is the shame of destruction, and it is difficult to return to the world from that. I don't know if that's the thing to say to a woman who has been through it. She didn't seem to think so."

Angela lapsed into silence, and Madeleine lowered her head and used the coffee spoon to draw a happy face on her cappuccino. "Everyone else seems to think I should just get over it," she said eventually, her face still averted. "I have difficulty finding things to compare it to. There aren't many babies in my field of study."

"My sister-in-law is an Anglo-Saxonist," Angela said. Madeleine looked up, quickly, for the café stilled in its rocking when Angela spoke. And Angela too was no longer a strange body, ill-fitting in the surroundings, but once again a radiant face with a seductive contralto voice. "She told me she had an epiphany during childbirth. For her it was several hours of what she called back labour." Angela paused uncertainly over the terminology. "She said she understood why epic poems were all written by men. Women, she said, took no vicarious enjoyment in the hero descending on a quest to defeat monsters and face death; they lived it. Beowulf is a hero for diving into the pool of snakes to finish off Grendel. But Grendel's mother is already down there. I'll leave the Freudian reading to you. What my sister-in-law said was that the surety of death comes to you in those moments, such as childbirth. A death that is mere brute suffering, and beyond the histrionics of heroes." Angela took a large sip of chocolate, looking slightly embarrassed. "The children would probably never recover if they heard us speak this way," she said.

"But you're an auntie," Madeleine replied, half bantering, half resentful. "You're allowed to say terrible things about children." She had not missed the neutrality of Angela's gaze every time it turned on the changeling.

"Well yes," Angela agreed. "There is that. I'm sure my sister-in-law would not admit to all this in front of my nephew, for all that they say he is wonderful with female psychology."

"That seems an unusual thing to say of anyone."

"Of his writing, they say that."

"Oh. For some reason I thought he was still a boy, or a teenager."

"No, my nephew, Gerard. You ran into him the other day. He's nearing forty now."

"The novelist?"

"Of course."

So much, Madeleine thought, for Tom's idea that we look after Angela in her dotage in exchange for a home in the garden shed. The thought of Angela as aunt to a man, a real man and not an abstract boy, began to dissipate the solidity of their talk, began to make the café windows ripple inwards, and not just with the rain; she began to see Angela growing and shrinking rapidly in her seat, saw a dusting of chocolate powder on her chin.

"Gerard says he'd like to have a chat with you one day. He probably wants to pick your brain for something he's writing."

"Hmm," said Madeleine. And then "I've been doing some research too, about changelings."

"Of course," Angela said with a smile.

Of course. She felt hope in a great lift that threatened to bubble out her throat as hysterical laughter. She remembered her friends' reactions, however, and improvised.

She could not trust Angela quite yet, not enough to mention the case directly. "I was thinking of *Goblin Market.* I believe I've been misreading it all these years. I think that Laura and Lizzie—the sisters—are changelings. They go to the goblin market and come back changed. That makes them changelings, doesn't it?"

"Go on," said Angela, nodding.

But of course there was nowhere to go on. She had made the suggestion at random so that Angela would correct her and they could obliquely approach the truth. "No, no," she said. "Then I thought that it was a silly idea, since changelings are children."

"Children or young women. Stolen child or stolen bride. But most often children, of course. One belief is that changeling stories represent societies' past traumas regarding children who were deformed or developmentally challenged. Children who had something wrong with them."

"Aha," said Madeleine, cunning as a fox. "Children who won't stop eating, or won't stop crying."

"Well yes, and extreme irritability. Failure to thrive for all their voracious eating. You know all this of course. These children represented a very real problem for families back then, struggling for mere survival."

"Who isn't?" Madeleine said, looking away. A silence settled. She could not bear for Angela to stop speaking, for when Angela spoke the world settled into recognizable patterns. Everything had a reading and therefore an answer, perhaps multiple answers, but in any case, an argument could be made, and supported. The weather, brewing into a storm, raged and licked over the doorstep every time someone entered the café, and then the door closed and they were sealed within, hiding, with everyone else, from the world outside. It would be a cold walk home. Fairies lurking in the hedgerows, cats in the garden, Tom and Madeleine's own small child lost somewhere, while Madeleine herself sat protected here and cared for a fairy replacement until she could find a way to make the change.

"Of course many terrible things were done in the name of curing a changeling or forcing an exchange," said Angela.

"Right," said Madeleine. "But what can a person do, really? What would a good solution look like? Apart from cooking in eggshells and beating it with a red-hot poker of course, or throwing it in the fire so that it leaps up the chimney."

"I beg your pardon?" Angela's eyes widened, and she cast a lightning glance at the sleeping changeling. The world tilted immediately, and Madeleine had to grip the table to prevent herself falling backwards.

"That's what they do in the stories." Madeleine forced a smile, creating a literary in-joke. "Most of the variants. Otherwise they beat them with nettles or leave them by the seashore."

"Yes. So they do." Angela frowned slightly, as though trying to recapture a train of thought.

"Tell me what I've been missing," Madeleine said then.

Angela misunderstood. She began to speak of banalities, of classes, of a conference in Bologna and how it was always a highlight of the year; they always chose sun-kissed locales to hold it in, and wasn't this the dreariest spring in living memory? Madeleine said she had never been to Italy, although Tom's brother taught English there.

"Perhaps next year I can bring you along," Angela said.

"You'll be back by next year. I suppose you won't have been back long enough to submit a paper, but perhaps we could arrange something in an organizational capacity. I have to spend my grant money somehow."

Madeleine looked out into a ferocious evening. Two boys were shouting on the street, lurching into each other's faces, jugular, spitting. Friends on both sides pulled them apart. When they turned away and left, necks still craned for a final insult, there was almost a swagger to both of them. Adrenaline. The appeal of violence. "Perhaps your sister the Anglo-Saxonist was right, about the epics," she said. "I feel like real-life violence is all around. I feel like slapping someone who would go looking for it."

"Could it be that a close reading is in your future?"

"I haven't read since the birth," Madeleine said. She forced herself to meet Angela's eye. "I thought I would be able to. I knew I wouldn't be doing—other things, dancing, parties, I thought I would read."

Angela nodded, unsurprised but also unforgiving. Forgiveness was not for her to give anyhow. Reading enough and deeply enough was like dieting. You might cheat and fool others, but ultimately you only cheated yourself.

"It happens," Angela said. "It will improve when you send her to nursery."

Madeleine murmured the cost of just part-time nursery.

"That seems like a lot of money."

A woman came in, peeling her soaking hair off her cheeks. Angela and Madeleine both looked at her, and for a moment Madeleine thought the woman—angular, with very long hair—was Marie. She opened her mouth to ask about Marie, or to confess, or even to cry out across the room for absolution, but it was not Marie of course. Angela began gathering her scarves and preparing to leave.

"I should make a start before it gets any worse out there. The forecast called for a storm, but not until later. Don't push yourself too hard," she said, swathed in all her black woollen pieces; still, somehow, the oracle. "Don't worry about reading the dense things now. Maybe a bit of fiction. Something light?"

"How will I ever finish my thesis though?" asked Madeleine, who had always finished all her studies in the exact time prescribed.

"You'll have to re-evaluate how long it will take." Angela gathered up her bag. "But don't worry about that at the moment. You're doing the most important job of all now."

It sounded ludicrous, coming from Angela.

"Oh, I'm sure I'll get back on schedule," Madeleine said lightly. The café was spinning, and to force it to stop she added, "when I make good on my impulses to leave the baby out for the fairies."

Did Angela recoil? Had her voice betrayed her, letting in that splinter of hatred? Did Angela, too, respond to that childhood fear, of the child hated and rejected by its mother? Madeleine was above and beyond that fear, had come out the other end. Life went on, past rejection.

"How will you get home?" Angela asked. "Are you getting enough help with the baby?"

"Of course," said Madeleine. "Tom has taken to fatherhood like a fish to water. He always knew he would. He must be almost home by now. I expect he'll come pick me up."

"Well make sure he does his part." Angela looked at her doubtfully, and glanced down upon the changeling, a glance of pity.

It was always the baby that was pitied, she thought after Angela had disappeared into the rain. The café shifted below her again, and she grasped at the moments of stability. Torture. Epics. Angela had all the information, really, but nobody, not even she, seemed capable of seeing where it led. And as always, the conversation had been rife with that strain of awkwardness that ran through all exchanges with Angela, despite her garrulous presentation to the world, her house parties, and her equal-opportunity hobnobbing with novelists, celebrated scholars, graduate students' husbands.

Her whole frame ached with hunger. Nursery was a year away. She ordered banana bread, shaking all her spare change viciously into her palm to pay for it, and called Tom.

"Just got home," he said. "Where are you?"

"I'm in Breadcrumbs. I want you to come get me."

She finished her banana bread and snuck the empty plate onto a nearby table so Tom would not know. The rain continued unabated, and most others left the café as closing time drew near. She barely stirred, slumped into her booth, cloaked in the warm, buttery light and the soothingly eclectic artwork.

The door pushed open at last. Tom was wet, red-eyed and irritable at heading out again after a long day. He sat across from her, removed his tweed newsboy cap, and thwacked it against the table. "This will be ruined if I wear it any longer out there. Better to get wet." He reached across to the pram and slid it underneath.

Madeleine watched him closely.

"So the promotion is a no-go. They are delaying creating the job. Probably it will never happen. Why bother giving us hope for the future, better pay, upward mobility, and all that capitalist-dream bollocks when they can just have us grinding away for the same old crap wages? We've got to economize. I've had a horrible day. I do wish you could at least have made it home from the café by yourself."

"I'm sorry. It was just."

"Madeleine. The baby is covered in her own sick."

She had not really looked at the changeling since Angela left. It had not screeched, nor demanded to be fed, and that was enough. She watched as Tom mopped it up, making clucking noises. "Where's the plastic sheet?"

"I forgot it at home."

"Why didn't you tell me on the phone? I could have brought it. It's pissing down out there."

They set out into a squall. The edges of things were blurred and shadowy, and a high wind had come up, tossing rain and leaves before them. The pavement pulled away from the ground; another gust and it would whirl away amongst the leaves. A woman in a black raincoat like a bin bag stood on the corner clutching tattered shopping bags. She alone stood still among the pitching and rocking. A witch.

"Let's hurry," Madeleine said.

"You don't have to tell me," Tom grunted a little as he pushed the pram up over the curb. "I think the wheel on the right is getting funny. We should have bought new."

"New was so expensive." Madeleine strode over puddles and hurried ahead. The rain racketed down, loud enough to hide hushed noises, but she knew there were movements in the bushes and eyes in the trees. Something dashed across the road and she stopped short, so abruptly that Tom and the pram collided into her from behind. The shape vanished into a nearby hedge, and twitterings and low laughter came out in its place.

She was so weary, of the fear and insomnia, of having to

feed the baby, of trying to keep her balance in the vertiginous shadows.

"Take her back!" she shouted into the bush.

Silence but for rainfall and a passing car. Tom looked around, tried to edge her forwards by pushing the pram gently into her hip. She did not move; she didn't so much as blink but stared into the bush.

"For fuck's sake Mads, move along. Let's get home!"

"I know they're here," she said.

"Who are here?" His voice soared with impatience, and the street gave a final lurch, doubled in on itself, and stabilized as its own mirror image.

They were in front of the tenement buildings, next to the gate with the broken lock. Madeleine pushed on the gate. Tom's voice faded into the rain. She was through, and stood within the garden. The derelict Victorian terrace house loomed at the end of a lawn, most windows dark, a few lit on the second floor where a blanket was strung across as a makeshift curtain, and one flat in the lower corner where an Ikea paper lampshade and a political poster declared student tenants. She tried to block out the lights and focus on the lawn, where the streetlight splashed over the hedge enough to see shadows curling away into deeper shadows. If she focused, she could just see the fairies. They were different sizes. They didn't look human, and they weren't all solid, and the shadows pooled over them so she could never fully make them out, but she saw twisting, spindly legs, matted hair, glowing eyes in different corners of the bushes.

She took a step, and was seized by precarious mud. The light was strong enough to see that her foot lay next to the four-clawed print of a fox. She fell to her knees on the soaking grass and studied it. The delicate texture of the tissue, one pad clearly scarred, the taut marks of the nails. And when she raised her eyes, the fox stood there, just out of reach. She had only seen foxes from a distance. They had been poetry and mange, hunger crossing through the neighbourhood gardens, vestiges of the wild woods in awkward harmony with the urban landscape, worlds colliding. This fox was so close she could see the rain on his whiskers. The streetlight reflected on eyes that encompassed both woods and rubbish heaps, eyes that had survived the erasure of the countryside.

Yes, said the fox, I have slunk down the sidelines of industrial revolutions, I have hunted rats on the borders of motorways, I have seen plagues, enclosure, migration. He stood before her with the dignity of a king, come forth from his home beneath a garden shed to meet her eyes and share the secrets of his long apprenticeship: Mad Elaine, he said, mankind may build and erase and civilize and drive the old world before him, may diagnose and anaesthetize, may strip the brutality from daily life and some of the pain from childbirth, but the wild remains, just beyond the edges, past the broken gate, in the short and paranoid walk home at night, in the dread of the day the bills must be paid, in the throes of labour and the alienation of the cold hearth of home. In fear.

Fear was what the fox felt every moment of every day, and fear was what the fox would never truly understand. Fear dwelt in the unknown, and the fox knew the certainty of all the many calamities of a life lived. The fox was not afraid of shadows. She was.

He turned and loped away across the lawn, a swift, black form, then a movement in the darkness, then nothing at all. Tom was shouting from the gate, standing with one shoulder propping it open while he held the pram wedged against the two steps beyond. He was leaning sideways towards her in a pose of pure aggression, one he rarely adopted, never with her. She shrank away from him.

"Madeleine, what the hell are you doing?"

She clambered to her feet, newly righteous. "Don't talk to me that way. I need to get our baby back. They kidnapped her."

She approached him. A few more cars swept past. He watched her. The changeling abruptly woke up, drenched and hungry, and began to wail. "Kidnapped our baby?"

Madeleine was losing the surety of the thing in his hanging jaw and the derisive bark of his tone. She stepped back from the streetlight and cupped her hands around her ears. Yes, yes, footsteps in the hedgerows, spidery laughter from the lawn.

"Haven't you noticed? She looks nothing like us. She is nothing like us. She's not what we wanted or expected. She screams and she eats constantly, and she watches me constantly, she is cunning. It was my fault though. I opened a window in the hospital and they came in, and Greymalkin is involved; the cat leads me on or tries to lead me to them. I can't decide. But they changed her for one of theirs, like in the old stories." The changeling was still wailing away, and Madeleine reached instinctively to take her up and calm her. Tom twitched the pram violently back, away from her.

"Changed at birth?"

"Yes."

Tom laughed sharply. He retreated a step, then came back at her.

"The only one who changed at the birth, Madeleine, was you."

They stood, soaked, by the spikes of the broken Victorian gate.

Madeleine took off her glasses, shook them, tried to wipe them on something, but everything was wet, so she put them back on.

"You have changed. Madeleine."

She watched him and he watched her.

"Children or young women," she said. A stolen bride, had Angela said? The language of some of the old stories flashed by her in the old total-recall way it used to. The mother, coming home after leaving her baby in the cradle, met a tailor who said: "You should be wary to be abroad at this time. The good folk are about; I passed them on the road." She had thought it a generalized warning, but it was personal. *You* should be wary, you, young mother.

Madeleine began to laugh, damp laughs, consumptive laughs, as though the night were wheezing out from her. "Of course it would be me," she said, and again, "of course." Tom's grey eyes were cold, they refused her a place in this new world of responsibilities and missed promotions, they did not believe her, they saw something different and diseased.

"If you find my old wife in the garden, send her back to me," he said. "I'm going to take our daughter home before she catches her death."

He turned and walked away firmly, pushing the pram. The baby's wails rose and fell and were swallowed by the storm.

She held on to the gate. The fairy voices chimed and caroused around her; the fairy faces protruded from the hedges, laughing and sticking out their tongues, beautiful faces made grotesque, hideous faces made exquisite, mere twists of leaves and branches becoming animate and all reaching out their shadowy arms to pat and caress her, but not to take her back, and not to release her other self.

So it was not the child who had been taken to the half-world, it was herself. Changed at birth. Or after. She thought of the creatures dancing in the garden, the fairy rade moving through the neighbourhood with its forest winds and dream-stealing sleeps. The girl riding astride the cat—not an older Maud then, simply a lost Madeleine. A stolen woman who had tried to come home, and she, Madeleine-behind-the-window, had tried to let her in, but it hadn't been enough.

The voices laughed and clamoured from the hedgerow again. She was the interloper, they confirmed gleefully. What a good joke! As in the stories she was an ancient fairy that no one wanted anymore, someone whose time had come. Either that or a piece of old wood glamoured to look like a person, due to rot away in time. Honestly, they couldn't remember which, they couldn't keep track. Fairyland was so invigorated by the lovely young woman that had been reeled in.

And then all the fairy faces withdrew from the bushes, though their laughter still rang out through the falling rain. She was cast out from her people. Thrown from the nest. Again. She stretched her arms up to the sky like bare, windswept branches, and touched the clouds.

I come, Graymalkin!

—*Macbeth,* WILLIAM SHAKESPEARE

Under the hedge, the cat was attuned to every drop that fell in an unexpected spot or with an unexpected rhythm, a patter before the pitter, the subtle signs of disaster in the wild. Eyes like lamps, ears flat along the skull, one half deaf, hip aching with the weather, waiting for the rain to ease.

Madeleine stayed out in the rain some minutes longer, searching every inch of the tenement lawn, shaking the bushes, slipping in the mud, calling into the hedges for fairy or fauna. Then she forced herself to stand and go home. The baby needed her.

She found Tom in the bedroom, rocking back and forth with the screaming baby. They were a couple that never fought. Once in four years Madeleine had slept on the sofa, and once Tom had. There was no question of that tonight. Madeleine crept under the blankets and Tom passed her the baby. Maud's eyes were red and inflamed, and there were tears on her crumpled cheeks, the first real tears she had ever produced. She took the breast offered, but continued to make angry noises, choking tearful sobs. Occasionally she pulled back her head to stare at Madeleine and emit an anguished shriek. Madeleine was frozen with guilt; she felt unable to generate heat. Her limbs lay heavy and cold.

The lamp on the dresser was lit. She raised her hand and examined it against the light; skin, bone, but also nail, claw, bundle of sticks. She let it fall. Tom was somewhere, lingering in the hall. Madeleine suspected he was listening outside the door.

The rain stopped, the clouds parted, the moon rose hard and cold. Streetlights blazed beyond the hedge and stained the sky but never touched the garden. The cat stepped out from under the hedge and stood proud and disdainful in the unmythical landscape. Greymalkin, monarch of this broken flagstone, was more than a little hungry, and open to what the night might bring.

Maud was asleep, the tempest past. Tom came in and began to undress, folding things, ordering baby paraphernalia on the dresser, reluctant. Finally he lay down, stretched in his own cold half of the bed like a stone knight in a cathedral, hands folded. She wanted to wheel into sleep with him, but it was so cold, and he didn't speak and neither did she.

Greymalkin moved towards the gate and then hesitated. A familiar noise was coming down the street; staggering footsteps, angry mutters, and wheezing. There was a crooked man, and he went a crooked mile. The cat remained still. The footsteps came closer, and the man, in his old, gaping parka, hove into view, leaned against the open gate, and took a swig from a bottle. His eyes looked into the gloom. "I know you're there," he sobbed, and clung to the gate and sobbed some more before heaving himself upright and shouting again, "I know who you are." Greymalkin was unmoved. Humans could not see so far in the dark. But he looked unlikely to leave in the near future,

and might begin to crash about the lawn. The cat turned away and headed deeper, loping towards the alleys and the back gardens, passing down the side of the tenements. Voices floated through an open window: "For fuck's sake. There's another nutter by the gate now. They'll never mend that gate. I'm not going out with ranters around." "You won't get out much then." "Heh."

And then Tom said, "Goodnight, Queenie," and turned off the light, and it was all right, or close enough; in the hierarchy of his names for her, Queenie was affectionate, if not as affectionate as Queen Mab. But that was better. She didn't want him calling her the fairy queen tonight. It was too cruel and ironic, when the real fairy court was feasting and laughing at the trade they'd made, a broken old thing for a fresh young girl. Meanwhile Queenie sounded domestic, like someone's real, fallible, but forgivable wife. She closed her eyes. The rain had stopped completely, had withdrawn like a stage prop that was no longer needed. The clouds, too, had departed. The moon had risen.

Sleep brought a cat padding through a mucky garden.

The fear was of a new kind, a catalogue of concrete risks rather than a generalized terror. There were signs, smells of friend or not-a-friend. There were places the cat had marked; places the cat had not dared to mark. The fears were new, but so too was the confidence, a light, lithe form, eyes that rendered the night visible, and an instinct for things that lurked in the shadows. The cat knew there was a woman there, and she came forwards and clambered astride its head.

They moved off together into the back alley. There was a strong smell of fox. Greymalkin continued unperturbed,

but the woman whispered "stop." She wanted to be brought face-to-face with the real, true wild. She wanted a confrontation. She wanted a bloodletting. Greymalkin tried to walk on, displeased, but her voice echoed and re-echoed and would not leave the damaged old head, and finally the cat drew up, turned back to the fox smell, and obeyed.

Greymalkin was old and reluctant, but mad: mad dogs and Englishmen go out in the noonday sun, but it's cats and mad maidens who stalk upon a midnight dreary. The cat could show her the wild, oh yes, could leave a gift from the wild on her front doorstep. Greymalkin ran back through the oozing mud, incautious for once, and leapt upon the fox cub, all claws, all blunted teeth and sharp bloodlust. The cub squealed and fell and tried to right itself, struggling to protect its throat and its belly. The cat was as inevitable as grey death. The cub screamed and writhed and lost great chunks of fur.

But Greymalkin pulled back with a howl of pain. A great sharp stick fell on the cat's head, accompanied by kicks and snarls. I know who you are. Get off, you demon. Leave the baby be. Blood dripped, hot and sticky, from the mauled ear, entirely torn away now, and the stick crushed ribs and cartilage. The moon looked impassively down upon it all. In agony, the cat sank its claws into the man's leg. He stumbled back with a curse. Greymalkin, torn almost to shreds, limped under a fence and hurried through a dangerous garden to a safe one. The woman's voice was gone, and Greymalkin crawled around and then into the depths of a prickly bush, and waited for the world to end.

PART III

The Host of the Air

I must confess that after months of thought I am unable to get the true bearings of this event. One or two consequences are obvious. The experiences of children will be taken more seriously. Cameras will be forthcoming. Other well-authenticated cases will come along.

—***The Coming of the Fairies,*** ARTHUR CONAN DOYLE

The world had stopped pitching and shaking. Madeleine felt a great stiffness though, in her arms and shoulders, in her legs. She felt the weight of many centuries of knowledge. She was old even in fairy terms; she had been put out to pasture. She shuffled down the hallway alone, bemused by the real-world silence of the morning, and dragged a blanket to the sofa. She opened her laptop. There was an email from Angela.

Madeleine,

Lovely to see you yesterday and to meet your bundle of joy. I hope you don't worry too much about keeping up with your reading. The thing with books is: they keep.

Madeleine snorted and gazed off into space momentarily.

I made it home through the tempest and remembered I hadn't actually referred you to the Yeats poem that backs up, to some extent, your Goblin Market theory. Perhaps you know it. "The Host of the Air," originally titled "The Stolen Bride." Of course, his stolen child has rather overshadowed the bride, but there's mention of women stolen by the fairies throughout his Celtic prose writings. Undoubtedly, I'm not telling you anything you don't already know. But it might make for some stimulating reading, if you wanted to flex your mental muscles a little. Mix business with pleasure, as they say.

Please feel free to write to me at any time. It doesn't have to concern your doctorate,

Angela.

She must have dozed off again, because she was woken by Tom hovering above her. "I'm going to take the baby for a walk," he murmured. "You rest. We'll bring breakfast."

"We shouldn't spend money. We'll end up like the man downstairs."

"I wasn't planning on a liquid breakfast. You relax." If he was making the effort to joke, they could probably avoid a fight over yesterday.

The door slammed and Tom was out in the day, feeling the breeze on his cheeks, whispering observations to the baby, bonding. Madeleine watched him set out across the street, and went back to her laptop.

She had been a girl who knew all Yeats once, but it had slipped away. She looked up the poem Angela had mentioned.

O'Driscoll drove with a song,
The wild duck and the drake,

From the tall and the tufted reeds
Of the drear Hart Lake.

And he saw how the reeds grew dark
At the coming of night tide,
And dreamed of the long dim hair
Of Bridget his bride.

The words lapped like water on a shore with their old magic, and she looked up from the book and away through the window to the tree outside, and blurred her eyes to cut out the bus stop and the trampled park. She needed more reeds and night tides. More trees. They should go to the country.

The poem continued. Fairy kidnapping of the bride. Sad music. Men and girls dancing. Bridget his bride. Yes, there were other stories like this. She hadn't thought of them as being changeling stories too. She never noticed these things in her studies because she was always reading critically. She was always searching for symbols or literary devices or biographical similarities. She never thought of the stories as simply being themselves.

The bread and the wine had a doom,
For these were the host of the air;
He sat and played in a dream
Of her long dim hair.

Madeleine touched her own hair. Not her hair, for she was not herself. Although she was, in some strange way, still herself. A changeling, a crabbed, stunted creature, immeasurably strong, immeasurably old, and lost. And yet also still in Madeleine's body, overlapping somehow with Madeleine's consciousness. The change was more complex than simply substituting a baby.

"Embrace complexity," she said to the room at large.

The bread and the wine had a doom. That was how the fairies ensnared you; they offered you food. And once you had tasted fairy food, you were beyond the sphere of human influence. Real-Madeleine had been spirited away in one of her outbursts of hunger. Meanwhile she, the interloper, was never satiated or complete. She felt the tug of hunger. There was a terrible hole in her; if she didn't eat, she might unravel altogether and be revealed as a decrepit old sprite, shuffling through the streets like the neighbour.

In the poem, O'Driscoll's illusion shattered. But Bridget was borne away forever, gone like drifting smoke, never was piping so sad, never was piping so gay.

She laid the computer down and made three paces through the room to the window and looked down through the eyes of the house. She saw nothing bloom. There was a rental van across the street, and a flustered young man was helping movers run things in while a woman stood guard nervously, as though their nice upcycled furniture and expensive kitchenware might evaporate. As indeed they might. She saw no trace of Greymalkin on the changeling face of Splinters Wood.

She returned to the computer and skimmed one of her saved tabs on changelings. The hunger, yes; and anger, yes; and seeming to belong to another age. Truthfully, that last had described Madeleine even before the change.

Moreover, sifting through the various stories, there was the fear of scissors. Shears placed in the cradle. She remembered watching the blades twist towards her, defying physics. It was because *she* defied the laws of the human world.

And the eggshells. She read those differently now too. The changeling always laughed to see a brewing in eggshells . . . and she had laughed even as she did the brewing, laughed until she cried. She had been quick to blame the baby, but Angela had set her right. She was the stolen bride. But where the mothers sometimes got their human babies back, the poem suggested that the brides didn't return.

She quickly pulled up Evans-Wentz's *The Fairy-Faith in Celtic Countries* on the computer and made various searches with shaking fingers. There was so little about mothers. They were mostly just trying to get their babies back. What there was didn't seem encouraging: "The fairies were wont to take away infants and their mothers," the text confirmed, and a list of preventative measures followed, including scissors in the bed and consuming obscure plants. Then came a stern warning that if these precautions were ignored, mother or child or both might be taken.

Well, but could they be recovered? That was even less encouraging:

> A girl in this region died on her wedding-night while dancing. Soon after her death she appeared to her husband, and said to him, "I'm not dead at all, but I am put from you now for a time. It may be a long time, or a short time, I cannot tell. I am not badly off. If you want to get me back you must stand at the gap near the house and catch me as I go by, for I live near there, and see you, and you do not see me." He was anxious enough to get her back, and didn't waste any time in getting to the gap. When he came to the place, a party of strangers were just coming out, and his wife soon

> appeared as plain as could be, but he couldn't stir a hand or foot to save her. Then there was a scream and she was gone. The man firmly believed this, and would not marry again.

There was no chance of rescue by a man, then. Though at least this woman's husband had believed her; he hadn't looked as Tom had looked last night, furious and disdainful. So much for Tom.

Still, in its way the story was evidence of this feeling she had, of her overlapping consciousness with the other Madeleine. It showed that you could be one thing and the other, if only for a time. And it showed that there was a chance of getting back, even if the young man in the story had bungled it. The possibility would have to sustain her hope, because she must reverse this change. Maud was a real human baby, and she deserved a mother. She had to try to break the enchantment.

How though? She could not continue creeping into gardens in search of fairies, chasing Greymalkin, avoiding mother and baby groups, entrapped by roads and walls, unable to catch a single miscreant. She needed an abundance of fairies, and soon.

She fished out her little paper, covered with her various fruitless plans and reflections. A new line: *We need to find the wild. I am the changeling. Need to find others, there should be more in the country?* Such a vague plan, but what did she have? As an afterthought she added: *Will try to find a fairy mound, failing that, the usual cures are by fire or by water.*

Then, if she were returned to the fairies or ousted in some way, her real-world double would return somehow. In the stories the baby reappeared lying in the cradle, or on the cold hillside. For a woman, would the double come, and would it be she, herself, or would this consciousness that was hers and not hers merely die? And was that something to grieve?

She went back to the window and saw Tom returning across the park. She would have to improvise. He was looking up with a troubled expression. He waved when he saw her, but his smile looked forced, and her answering smile certainly was. She could not take Tom into her confidence. She could not stand to have him look at her again like somebody crazy. She hurried to put on the kettle and store the laptop.

"I got two cinnamon rolls and one Danish and a croissant," said Tom, laying the greasy paper bag on the table with a flourish. "And I picked up the photos."

"Oh," said Madeleine, peering in at the pastries, starving. Tom had, in one morning, made the entirety of her life look simple. Dress the baby and take her out. Spend money in the bakery where pastries cost £1.50, rather than in the café where they cost £3. And pick up the fucking photos. It was a pity he hadn't topped up the electricity while he was at it. She took tetchy-hungry Maud and fed her on the sofa. She herself was so hungry she wanted to tear the paper bag with the pastries apart, but she needed to act normal, for Tom. As he went to get cups and plates, she opened the envelope with the photos.

Maud, Maud, more Maud. Bits of Madeleine's arm, occasionally bits of her face, a ghoul's face with purplish circles under the eyes, when the eyes weren't downcast and resting on the baby. And the one of Madeleine and the baby in the hospital, shortly before discharge, a dazzling portrait of mussed hair, chipped nail polish, fearless gaze, incidental infant accessory, soothing greenery.

She looked closer and closer still. Green tendrils of worry reached out and choked her. In fact the background greenery was not remotely soothing. The grain of the printed picture looked quite different to the camera screen. The bushes out the window, though gently blurred, were teeming with life, with small, twitchy fingers, with snarling teeth and belly guffaws, with gossamer wings. There was a fungal rot on her dewy, new-mother cheeks. They were not dewy so much as mildewed. *They* were in the bushes behind her already, at the bottom of the hospital garden, laughing and reaching out with their wet fingers. She dropped the photographs onto the coffee table.

They sat down to breakfast. Tom brought cups of tea to the table, piping hot and brewed strong, as she liked it. He took Maud from her arms and placed her in the bouncy chair. "We don't want to accidentally scald Maudie now." Despite his light tone, he never quite met her eye. She understood that he had resolved not to mention yesterday. If only his resolution would hold, this conversation would be much easier. Outside the window the beech tree was bright with new shades of green but oppressed by the heavy sky. She felt strongly that they must get out, find an origin point to their troubles. Her new getaway plan wasn't, perhaps, the most obvious origin point, but she suspected it was the right one.

"I would like to go see my parents."

Tom took a large sip of tea, swallowed painfully, and fanned his mouth. "How can we do that? It'll take us all day to get there by train. We would have to turn around and come back again tomorrow morning."

"You could leave me up there, with them." He bit his lip. She knew he didn't trust her, after last night. "We could rent a car."

"We're meant to be being frugal," said Tom. "Now you want to rent a car." He fished the Danish out of the bag and cut it in half, and then into quarters. It was the unnecessary quartering that told her he was stressed, that he was unsure of himself and that she could win; if she was cunning, she could make it to the wild. She would find her kinfolk. She would cast off the fairy consciousness, recover the Madeleine that was missing. And, barring that, fire or water.

"I know," she said simply. "This is important to me." And then to finish him off. "I should have gone with my mother last week, like you said. It would have been good for me to get away for a few days."

She did not think he would refuse her after that, and he didn't.

Walking among the sleeping birds in the hedges . . . she looked upon herself as a figure of Guilt intruding into the haunts of Innocence.

—*Tess of the D'Urbervilles*, THOMAS HARDY

They rented a car and a car seat for Maud. Madeleine drove. She always drove. She had learned as soon as she was old enough; it was the only way to get around in the suburbs, and though Tom had learned young too, it had been with his shouty father as instructor. Tom hated anything car related as a result and drove like a half-blind old lady. Even so, he reached for the keys in the rental office today. She scooped them up quickly, and he said nothing. Don't trust him, Madeleine, he doesn't trust you.

The city streets were quiet. They drove back through Splinters and past their own house. The whole area was only a few streets flashing by, and from the road the building looked insignificant. And then they were driving through the outskirts, following the directions to the bridge, the great white bridge that stretched from one country to the next, the strange, grey sweep, through rain and into rain, only water before them and around them and behind them and beneath them, the colour of Tom's eyes. Madeleine snuck a look at him as she drove, and he returned her gaze, smiling tight-lipped. If only Tom were her true companion in this, it would be an adventure, like everything they did together. But she was alone.

The road swept them up onto the bridge proper. The windscreen was spattered with rain, and the far side of the bridge was all in mist. On the other side of that mist, of that water, lay what? Was this the fairy highway? Fairyland was often described as walking into mist. It was where the borders merged, where the veneer of civilization wore away and the natural world was ascendant. She had been right to come away. She needed more than the city gardens. She needed the wild. In the meantime she had this chemical-smelling car, and the white arc of the bridge, with its tower lights blinking through the cloud, and Tom, worrying beside her.

"Mads," he said finally, reluctantly, as they began to descend again. "What you said last night."

"Yes, Tom."

"You'll admit it was an odd thing to say."

She was silent.

"Maddie, please." He had a sound of wanting to have the conversation here and now, so they could leave it behind them on the bridge.

"You said some strange things too."

"I was so worried. And Maud was so upset."

"She's always so upset. You're just not alone with her when she's like that."

"She was upset and you didn't care and then you started saying things . . ." So he was not going to spell it out. Tom had his limits. That made things easier.

"It wasn't meant to sound that way," she said gently. She could not expect him now to understand how he had given her the key to seeing the problem as it really was. It would worry him as much as what she said yesterday. Best to redirect him. "I was using a metaphor," she said.

A quick look between them.

"A metaphor."

"Absolutely. It was a manifestation about my deeper angst of worrying I'm not good enough." She smiled like the fox to the hen. It was easy to behave like a human, distract humans, sidle into their lives, and take things from them.

"Right," he said. He returned his gaze to the landscape.

They came down from the bridge in a splatter of bad weather, and then it turned. Joyful sunshine poured down. The motorway hissed with evaporating rain. They drove north, and the country became more itself, in explosions of colour and light. When she moved onto the B roads, clusters of hawthorn tossed alongside the road like freshly spun clouds.

"May trees," said Tom. He looked pleased for the first time all day. "Isn't it gorgeous? It's like we've been living under a cloud in the city for weeks. There was no getting out from under it. Maybe it was a good idea to get away, after all. Nice to see a few flowers."

She would not tell him all the other things hawthorns were. The plant of the fairy queen. Unlucky to have in the house. Even Nan, never superstitious, would have balked at it. Hawthorn had the smell of death. But Tom was still chattering away about the springtime.

They drove on, through sunbeams, through fresh leaves and a field with a gambolling black lamb, and through the flowering of everything, but she had begun to notice the dead things.

Some were just smears of fur or feathers or blood on the road, others were crumpled heaps next to it: mostly rabbits, a flattened hedgehog, more rabbits, and so many dead pheasants, and a fox, definitely. Reynard, Reynard, perhaps you were wise to move to the city. And then the sad bulk of a badger. How fast did you have to be going to hit something that big on a straight road? And more rabbits and perhaps a cat.

Death, said the road. Death, death. Death. Perchance to dream.

It had been beautiful too on her way up last year for Nan's funeral. She'd been almost a year with this tight, nauseous feeling in her chest. She had thought Maud Anna might ease that tightness. She might represent a carrying-on, of Nan or just of life, but that was a heavy burden to put on a baby. Maud wasn't anything yet really, and she certainly wasn't a continuance of Nan. Nan had expired gasping, staring up at a beige hospital ceiling, feebly moving her hands, just as these animals had gasped out their last breaths in shock upon the tarmac, until nature had finally relented and relieved them of their lives.

Tom was watching her sidelong again. She was clinging to the steering wheel. "You look like a Sunday driver. Like me when I'm driving," he said with a laugh that was nothing like his old, unfiltered giggle.

"All this death is just so random and pointless," she said, raising her voice to batter the unspoken things into submission. "Just some lowlife trying to get home five minutes sooner; all these poor creatures lying in agony on the side of the road until the shock or the injuries do away with them. Why are we so hateful and cruel? Why does everything grind inevitably to death and oblivion?"

Why had the Madeleine of a year ago thought having a baby might undo some of the death in life?

"I know," said Tom. "It's horrible."

"You don't think it's horrible the way I do," she said. "You just think so as a nature lover and a decent person." Her horror blackened the entire landscape. It was the horror she had felt at the hairdresser, before all the open windows.

"Thanks for not letting me have any depth," said Tom, drily. "Maybe I see it as a metaphor for the way all our children are doomed by the relentless forces of greed and destruction. Or a manifestation of the way our society kills everything it comes into contact with. You're not the only one depressed over articles of drowned refugee children. Yes, I've seen you reading them compulsively. I may have gone over to the dark side and have a corporate job now, but I still have a soul."

She laughed out loud, and so did he.

"Let's stop and eat," she said. "We've another few hours before we get there."

Tom rolled his eyes. "I see we're on the bankrupting ourselves tour of the UK this weekend."

Madeleine wondered, after fish and chips and ice cream, if she should be rejecting human food. *The bread and the wine had a doom.* It entrapped you. But depriving yourself of food had never been put forth as a solution in any of the old stories. In fact, it always seemed a bit one-and-done; you ate a fairy grape once, and that was you trapped forever.

It was after four o'clock when they turned into Nan's village. Madeleine was tired, of driving and of playing a role. Tom had been irritable since the lunch bill arrived, and she could feel his eyes fixated on the dashboard clock. So much expense for so little time. She also felt the weight of time. She wanted to get away alone, but first she would need to seem a good mother, so that he might trust her to stay on with her parents without him.

The front garden looked unchanged. Nan had always liked an abundance of flowers over tidy beds. It was a little overgrown, but nothing more than you would expect of two old people living behind the flowery curtains.

Inside, the house was echoey. The carpet looked more threadbare than before, the sitting room more deserted, though the afternoon light still poured into the kitchen, refracted into dozens of rainbows by a small hanging crystal that Carol had tied there some years ago.

"They've gone somewhere," Tom grumbled. "Why didn't we call ahead? We should have said something. That was stupid of us. They might be out all day, after we've driven all this way to see them."

"They must be here," she said. "They wouldn't just leave the door open."

"They might. What is there to steal from an elderly dead couple? That tin of expired pineapple rings? The charity-shop porcelain bits?"

Madeleine walked through the kitchen rainbows to the mantelpiece, where all the chintzy knickknacks sat, and laid her hand on the cool flanks of a porcelain pony. Nan had indeed bought the pony in a charity shop. It was rearing on both hind legs, and a hapless rider was frozen forever in the act of falling from its back. "I like the bad-tempered look in its eye," Nan had always said. Now it was chill and dusty in the house of death. She saw her mother's handbag slung over the back of a kitchen chair.

Carol was in the attic, sorting through boxes, looking drawn and stressed.

"Oh, what a lovely surprise!" she cried, holding her arms out. Madeleine hung back. Today she could only make the minimal effort at playing good daughters and happy families. Her whole body felt the wrong size and shape for the attic, and she couldn't trust her voice not to have a scratchy fairy lilt to it.

"This is who you'll really be wanting," Tom manoeuvred around Madeleine to hand Maud to Carol.

"Oh yes!" And immediately Carol was clucking and crooning, in her element. "I'm so pleased you've come!" she said. "It's not much of a holiday sifting through all this. All told, I think I preferred the neighbourhood tourism and even that freezing old ship! I hope you've been singing Maud all the eeriest lullabies in my absence."

"Ah, well," said Tom uncomfortably, but Madeleine thawed into a smile.

"Certainly I haven't been singing the namby-pamby ones," she said. She looked around the dusty attic. "Where's Papa?"

"He's off in town in search of some records for his genealogy," Carol replied.

That brought her up sharp. "I thought he was doing his own family."

"He's now started poking around mine as well."

"For God's sake."

"He enjoys it."

"I dare say he does."

"Shall we take a break, Carol? I'll make some tea?" Tom was in there like a dirty shirt to prevent the argument.

"He'll be back soon. Oh go on then, Tom, yes. There's so much to do, and not much time, but I must have a cuddle with little Maudie."

"Why is there not much time?" Madeleine asked as they went down the stairs, but Carol was humming to Maud and didn't hear her.

In the kitchen they waited on the kettle.

Tom and Madeleine were in different corners, observing Carol at the table cooing to Maud, and pretending not to observe one another. Tom looked tired and puffy around the eyes and the mouth, as though someone had tightened a screw at the back of his head to pull his face tighter over the bones and then released it again. Perhaps he might look less exhausted if the promotion had come through, if he had a wife who remembered to pick up the photographs and take the rain sheet for the baby.

"Smile for me, smile for me." Carol touched the corners of her granddaughter's mouth. Maud kicked her legs and widened her eyes, but did not smile. "I want your first smile to be for me. How old are they when they smile again?"

"I've no idea," said Madeleine.

"Four to six weeks," said Tom, giving her an exasperated glance. "So it might be a week or more yet before we can expect a real one. She does smile sometimes, but I read that it's an impulse, like a twitch. She even does it in her sleep."

"There's nothing so precious as those first smiles," said Carol.

"How do you know?" Madeleine said. "I was ten months before I came to you."

"You're not the only baby I've ever known, you know. We were here the summer your cousin Lily was born."

What a waste, Madeleine thought, to be so captivated by a baby's first smiles, only to have her grow up to be cousin Lily. Imagine Maud were to become like that, going through every bad phase like clockwork, from stroppy toddler to I've-just-got-to-powder-my-nose-raver, to I'm-not-racist-but. She leaned against the counter and glared at the kettle. Was this love, then? Being delighted by a toothless grimace? Would real-Madeleine go weak at the knees for this too? Frankly it seemed a poor sort of thing compared to the incandescent love she had been promised upon becoming a mother. But a baby had simply been handed to her. It might grow up to be an Angela or it might grow up to be a cousin Lily. Either way it could not compare to the love she had felt for Tom, whom she had actively, joyously chosen. Her chest expanded with the memory of those days, and with the rage that they were over. Her rage could fill the room. When she looked up again, she saw Carol was watching her.

"Madeleine," she said. "Are you alright?" A glance passed between Tom and her mother.

She forced her oversized, gangly form down to the size of Nan's kitchen. "Of course."

"You were just tapping your fingers on the counter about a hundred times a minute," said Tom.

"My hands are stiff from the driving."

"It isn't just that," Carol said. "You seem incredibly on edge. As you did in the city."

Madeleine's head wanted to burst. She slipped her fingers behind her glasses and rubbed her eyes. She felt her new self pulsing behind them. She must say something, however destructive, or everything else would come pouring out of her, all the things she absolutely mustn't speak of if she hoped to get out into the wild alone.

"I've been on edge ever since the Great Nondiscovery, years ago," she said. Well, that was said, at long last. She lowered her hands to look at her mother.

Carol didn't avoid her eyes, as she so often did in uncomfortable conversations. She had an earthiness here, in her childhood home, as if stripped of several layers of constructed self. "I can imagine what you're referring to," she said. "I'd be happy to talk about your feelings around that." Her voice had moved closer to the local accent of her childhood. The no-nonsense voice of Nan. Though Nan would never ask you how you were feeling. Most emotions were unmentionables. She would just bring you a cup of tea.

Madeleine's irritable fairy-self burst through again. "Would you!" she snarled, cat teeth bared. "You, who cried and cried about it, alone in your room at night. Who never spoke about it afterwards."

Carol blinked. "It was a hard time for me," she said. "Not only because of that; work was doing downsizing at the time, I was worried about my job just a few years shy of retirement. And your Grandy was going downhill already, and I was far away. I did get upset, with all the emotions of it. You weren't meant to hear. I'm only human. But as to the rest, I did try to ask you about it. It was natural enough for you to be curious. I should have been expecting it. You wouldn't reply to my questions so I was waiting for *you* to talk it through. You've always been the one who brings things up."

Madeleine's snuffling rage paced about the room, clawed up to the ceiling, and then deflated.

Only human. What she would give to be that. The kettle boiled. Madeleine scalded the pot and made the tea. She gave Carol a brief, wordless nod. She needed to hold her focus, which was finding the fairies, convincing them to take her in exchange for the Madeleine who was gone, the one who was a proper mummy, who would come forth and take her rightful place and help Tom. Maybe then he would look more like his old self.

"Honey, I'm home!"

Her father cast the front door open, arms wide, a parody of a 1950s patriarch. He'd always liked to make this ironic entrance, the return of the man of the house, although in reality both he and Carol worked, and Carol was inevitably the last one home through Madeleine's youth. Her father kept schooltime hours and often came back with something sweet for himself and Madeleine to snack on together, something Carol wouldn't have permitted on a weekday. He entered Nan's house holding a box of mini apple pies from the corner shop, an echo coming down the years.

Madeleine turned, and accepted his sudden smile of pleasure, his exclamation of "the prodigal daughter!" and his expansive embrace with unexpected tears in her eyes. Here he was in the flesh, her beloved, traitorous father.

With one arm still cast over her shoulders, he came to look at Maud. He clucked approvingly, but no more. And Madeleine in turn approved that he was not drippy.

"Well this *is* a wonderful surprise. I was sorry you hadn't come up with your mother."

They gathered at the table with the tea and shared the pies. Madeleine sat with the warmth of her father on one side and the cool window on the other, and looked into the garden.

"How is the photography going, Tom?" her father asked politely.

The garden was less wild than she remembered it being. It was overgrown, of course. There were piles of earth-clotted pots arrayed against the garden shed. The grass was full of leaves that had fallen and lain there all winter, and also outbursts of toadstools, but wild it was not. A whole host of fairies might hide in the brambles that had taken over the back portion, but no whispers came to her, no twitching leaves.

"I've been practicing my portraits, as you might imagine," Tom was saying with a self-deprecating laugh. "And baby parts.

Baby feet, baby fists, baby ears. I've graduated from birds to babies."

She had always thought of the garden as a little wilderness. Now she saw that the houses on either side hemmed it in, the flower patches were edged with carefully spaced stones, the trees had been pruned, once upon a time.

"Never work with children or animals they say."

"Heh."

Her childhood paradise, where she had lain on the grass and gazed at the sky and imagined fairies in the tangle of nettles along the far back wall, a small patch of village garden. Nan would have seen her lying there, from this same spot at the kitchen table. Nan would have known the names of the plants and the trees and the birds, whereas Madeleine was a city child and could only name the most obvious. But what did that matter? Why should she categorize everything like a Victorian? Her life followed a Victorian framework as it was, too much so. Poor Madeleine, lost girl. Who are you anyway, Madeleine? Who were your parents? What's your real, true name? Who does your child resemble? Blood will out, you know.

"And speaking of work," Carol added. "Did anything come of that promotion?"

"They seem to have cancelled that idea."

"Oh rats," said Carol. "Here I was hoping you'd be able to move."

"They may yet," said her father, meaningfully.

"We're not moving," said Madeleine. "I love the neighbourhood. What's that new tree out in the garden, with the blossoms?"

"It's a plum," said Carol. "Your Nan always spoke of wanting a living monument rather than a stone in the cemetery, so your father and I went last week and bought it. There aren't many blossoms at the moment. I expect replanting was a shock to its system. Probably more next year, though we won't be here to see them."

"One of these years you may make it over in the spring," Tom said. "It's been ghastly this year, but often there's a window of false summer in it—more reliable than the real Great British Summer. Perhaps I should take Maudie out there now and lie her on her back under the plum tree. She likes the patterns when she sees branches against the sky."

"Well you should take her out to enjoy it then," said Carol. "Sadly she won't get to grow up with it. We've had an offer on the house."

"What?" Madeleine, pouring more tea, lost control of the lid. It clattered onto the table like a delayed punchline.

"It's been a stroke of luck, really," said Carol. "A friend of your uncle's has made an offer."

"You can't be thinking of selling."

"We can't keep the house, Madeleine. What would we do with it, sitting here empty?"

"Family holidays."

"To come once a year for a few weeks, it makes more sense to rent something. Something more comfortable, and probably closer to you and Tom. And the two of you don't get up here much."

"Villages shouldn't be left full of empty holiday homes," her father said. "It's best that someone come and live in it. It's as it should be. Julian's friend wants to make an open living area and put in one of those glassed-in extensions here at the back, so that it leads directly into the garden. Update it properly."

She looked around at the house that had been an unchanging

part of her childhood. At the remains of her grandparents' possessions. The tins on the shelf, the porcelain horseman, the outdated curtains, the books, romance, crime, politics, classics, and some of her old fantasy novels, still orderly on the shelves. An old couple's home, down to the framed pictures of unremarkable-looking grandchildren, including herself. Though of course you could identify Madeleine in a family photo from across the room. In a sea of petite light-haired people, there was Maddie long-legs, black-haired and gangly. Always the cuckoo and the changeling.

"Just look at those big, dark eyes," said Carol.

Madeleine turned and glared, but her mother was in fact poring over Maud again. The face turned sour, upset, the mouth opened, the Maud wail came out.

"I guess she's hungry," Carol said reluctantly, and passed her across the table. Madeleine took her, fed her, and continued to stare over her mother's head at the photographs. She willed herself not to look tired. She did not want to show even a shred of weakness. She did not want everyone asking if she was feeling all right.

"They're really distinctive," her father said. "They must come from you, Maddie."

"What do?"

"The eyes."

"Actually," said Tom quickly. "I think they're from my father. The shape at least. I have a baby picture of him, and he looks just like Maud."

"Oh for God's *sake*," Madeleine said, a beat too late, that extra moment when she considered not saying anything, leaving it all be. "There's always this obsession with the physical."

"It's hard to see much in a baby's personality, so the physical is all we have," her father said.

"Who cares?" said Madeleine. "Why do we need to talk about the baby anyway? Let's all poke and prod the baby, let's put bits and pieces under a microscope. 'The baby looks like you, Madeleine, she's your double.' Newsflash. That's because she isn't related to the rest of you. You can all move on now."

"She's related to me!" Tom tried to joke.

"She's related to more people than just the two of you, of course," said her father. "If you took me up on my offer of a DNA test, you might even track down that birth mother of yours."

Through her childhood her father had read her so perfectly, only to fail so spectacularly now. Tom chewed his lower lip. Carol looked appalled.

Madeleine considered the laminate tabletop before her with a small, bitter smile. "I do not want a DNA test, Papa. Not now, not ever. I do not want to know my blood mother. Maud will make her own choices, but I do not want and have never wanted a DNA test. I wanted this information to be *given*. In the absence of that I reject any knowledge. I consider myself a member of this family—" She stopped speaking. She could not go through the whole spiel again, choosing her family as they had chosen her. It was all so empty.

"I'm tired from the drive," said Tom. "You must be even more so. Let's take Maud out and lie her under the tree. We can take some pictures to remember it by. Maud and your Nan, together in some way."

She was not tired. If only it were so simple. Tom, who had claimed to love complexity, was so simple; things moved in logical patterns for him, and difficult times could be attributed to logical events. *Tired.* She was the reverse of tired, with nervous energy flowing through her limbs so that it was a conscious effort to keep them still. They no longer felt stiff. The blue of the sky was deepening over the garden; she could see it happening in real time, each second, each fraction of a second a distinct step in the process of time running out. After this there would be no more chances. The house would be gone. The edges of the sky had begun to flicker with lights and colours that did not stabilize, and that evaporated when she tried to look on them directly. Crackling energy was rising in her. The garden was empty of fairies, but the potential for them was now, at last, everywhere. Something floated by, part way up the garden at the level of the plum tree. Floated by and was gone, over the neighbour's hedge, carried by the light spring breeze.

Paul and Carol started to move up the stairs. Tom waited for her by the side door, holding Maud in one arm and reaching the other out to welcome her back into the fold. His physical presence had always been a homecoming. She remained where she was.

"I'll just pour another cup of tea and come out."

He nodded. She watched him come around the side of the house into the garden and move towards the plum tree. His back was to the house.

She slipped her shoes on and followed him out the door, turned the opposite way, and walked in the direction of the village. Abandoning Tom, abandoning the baby. And with that act, abandoning the moral high ground, rather like her other mother.

Fairies are invisible, but they cannot always manage to be inaudible . . . A fuss about nothing, a midge-bite madness, a fit of the tantrums.

—*Kingdoms of Elfin*, SYLVIA TOWNSEND WARNER

The village was unchanged, offensively so. The sky was the eternal bruised pink of millennia of sunsets. The road proceeded slow and dignified, with flowering bushes in well-kept gardens. It curved away down the hill to the main road, which was only a busy highway with a corner shop and a post office that had closed down two summers back.

It was all too staid, too kept. In her memories the gardens and surroundings were clustered with wildflowers, but in fact they were planted and weeded to within an inch of their lives. Beyond the green hills were moors, wilder, but she knew what Tom would say: the moor was only a manicured patch of rustic land and sky at the disposal of the grouse, which were at the disposal of the guns.

A black-and-white cat sat on a gate post, licking its paw. It was noticeably better fed than Greymalkin, more solid, less real.

"There is nothing wild left in the country either," said Madeleine to the cat. "Unreal village. I thought the city was unreal, but it is as real as can be."

"You don't say," said the cat. It stuck its leg out provocatively and licked itself with gusto.

"You will talk to me but Greymalkin won't?"

"I am here to force the moment to its crisis," it said, bored, between licks.

"Of course."

"The gap of danger where the demon waits, that sort of thing."

"I know that's from something . . ." Madeleine said, but the cat yawned. She hurried away. She passed the shop and carried on down the hill to the woodland and the river. Though "beck" was perhaps a better word for it, and "woodland" was misleading too. It was only a narrow stretch of trees along the edge of the beck, trees that no one had ever cut back because there was no economic benefit in doing so. You could stand at the discontinued train station and see through the grove to the field on the far side.

Nonetheless, the woodland and the river were the only "walk" a person could get at easily and on foot from the village, for though the fields rose up all around it in waves of idyllic green patchwork, all were private, and most were inaccessible except by car. Past the river, a public footpath older than any house in the area snaked through farmers' fields, but even it never arrived at the moor, or not without crossing a lengthy section of road. In any case, it was too far. The river would have to do.

She crossed the railway tracks. No trains came here anymore. Few people from the village ever wandered down this way either, with the shop in the opposite direction. Sometimes there were groups of teenagers, but not today; there were only trees of all ages, from slender saplings to a beaten and bowed willow draped over a pool in the river. It was that moment of the evening when the air takes on a thickness that clouds the vision. The warmth of the day lingered. She sat in a crook of a root and looked into the pooled water. In the fading light, old words, memorized many years ago, rose bright in her mind:

"They are fatherless creatures, and their whole ancestry is hidden in a past of demons and ghosts."

She would have liked to speak to Angela's sister-in-law; the Anglo-Saxonist, mother and braver of the epic depths. Was it a good translation? It was a beautiful one. She remembered more, if she didn't think too hard; the words bubbled up from some long-ago cramming session.

A frost-stiffened wood waits and keeps watch
above a mere; the overhanging bank
is a maze of tree-roots mirrored in its surface.
At night there, something uncanny happens:
the water burns . . .
On its bank, the heather-stepper halts:
the hart in flight from pursuing hounds
will turn to face them with firm-set horns
and die in the wood rather than dive
beneath its surface . . .

The pond was quiet and unruffled, with the old willow crouched and waiting at the far end.

There had been a mountain lake once, turquoise, freezing, with a glacier lodged in splendour and menace at the far side in just that attitude. This had been out west, on a summer trip with her childhood friend Madison. Maddie and Maddie. "Come on, let's swim," Madison had insisted, and they had swum in their underwear, or rather they had forced themselves in and swum each in a small, squealing circle, and then come out gasping, and dressed shivering, and jumped until they were warm again. The clean feeling of her damp hair against her neck, so clean it could carve through to the bone, had stayed with her all day. That was the year before university, before the Great Nondiscovery, before her decision to move abroad. The last hurrah of old school friends. She had invited Madison to her wedding, but Madison couldn't afford it. And once she was married, she no longer went off on semi-spontaneous hiking trips with friends that lasted days. She hadn't noticed the shrinking of her world. Instead, she had gone on to have a baby, blithely unconscious again of all the forces this arrayed against her, rejecting the accounts of isolation and loneliness. Those fatherless monsters had stalked her this far, and cornered her here.

She tried to imagine Nan sitting in the curve of this same root. Nan was always back in the house, doing grandmotherly things like baking cookies, or ungrandmotherly things like having the local women over and giving them homemade perms, singing along to the radio whether it was Vera Lynn or Michael Jackson. Nan was always a personality and a half, an outsized presence, but, now that she thought about it, an outsized presence always in her own kitchen. Or, well, down the shops or in the next town, but never more so than in her own kitchen. Nan had been pushed into that kitchen once upon a time, and she had never really come out; she'd just rattled and brawled from the inside. If once she had sat upon this root, she had not returned to throw herself into the cold water, and to come out clean and different. Marriage or motherhood had done for her as it had done for Madeleine. And now all that rattling and brawling had subsided. Few people remembered her, fewer every year. The house would be sold.

"The gap of danger where the demon waits is still unknown to you. Seek it if you dare," she said.

She was here. Might she not slip into the water? Might it not close around her like a lullaby? It was not the wild, but according to graves in the churchyard, children had drowned in it down the long, sleepy centuries. Madeleine removed her clothes and took a little breath and then stepped down into the water.

It was shallow. The deepest part of the stream came to just above her knee, and so there was no possibility of swimming, only of lowering herself down and feeling her skin slide on moss-covered stones. She heard her own small gasp at the cold, but as something detached from herself. Mostly she heard the murmuring of the water over the rocks, a murmuring that was like a language.

The sky above was enormous from her seat in the water, and still full of colours. It was like sitting within a rainbow, and the water tingled about her in the same rainbow hues. She too was filled with colour and with warmth. She was warm, warm: she might make the water boil around her. Her stomach, shrunken but still puckered from pregnancy, was hidden in the radiant water; she was all radiance but for her protruding knees, and bright water sluiced off them. She leaned back until her head was cradled in the branches of the willow, pulled out her hair elastic, and let it float free.

Two flies floated lazily over the pond, tracing patterns.

The sound of the falling water at the entrance of the pool was in her ears; that was all that was in her ears; she wouldn't have heard another thing, not if someone had stood beside her and spoken.

There were more flies, one drawing a figure eight between her raised knees.

The voices running over one another, speaking an old

language, impossible to parse the meaning into words, no matter how she listened. Her hair floated, her knees dripped. Her submerged body was detached and weightless.

A whole swarm of flies came pouring over the bank side, dripping daintily just above the surface of the pond.

Fairies can come in a swarm of flies.

She didn't dare move, fearful that they might leave. She watched with her head still reclined in the willow, and tried to see the forms beneath the blurred wings clearly, but the light from the sky and the light from the pond refracted in a prism of brilliance that left nothing clear.

A blackbird was singing. *Vel oo cheet? Vel oo cheet?*

"The word of a bird is a thing to follow."

There were voices, bark rough, cozy-croak like a frog, liquid bluebell purple, moth-flutter. The swish-swish of wings humming and hammering. Bluebell wanted this and frog said no, and moth wanted to know why not. It was the vocabulary she didn't understand, rather than the meaning.

A dead spider floated by in the water, and as it passed under the swarm of flies its legs began to twitch.

The fairies are the dead, some believe.

And with that thought, there came, on the trickling waters, human voices. They were caught among the thirsty roots of the willow, had been held there many years, and they pulled free at last and eddied among the coloured waters. The spider passed under and away from the flies and was motionless once more, but the voices became clearer. A boy, taunting, and a girl whose tone was a study in neutrality and suppressed violence.

"They say your mum's a madwoman."

"My mother's dead."

"That's not what I heard."

"What do you know about anything anyway? If I say she's dead, then she's dead."

"My mum says she tried to set her hair on fire and now she's locked up. And that she tried to kill your baby brother."

"That is a lie, Billy Robinson. Say that again, and I'll hold your head under water until you won't know which way is up."

And like the spider, they were pulled away in the current and were gone, leaving a little curl of mist, a bubble, then nothing.

Madeleine frowned in the cooling water. "I don't understand," she said, though she didn't think the fairy voices would know her words any more than she knew theirs. "I need more than that. Please." That had merely been a fragment of something, village memory; it might refer to anything or anyone; it had nothing to do with her.

The other voices, moth and bluebell, mustard and cobweb, rose to a pitch. They were aware of her, and they were conferring. One voice shouted down the others. Frog-croak, restoring order. Frog was speaking slowly, as to a child or a foreigner, but she still didn't know the words, and the others pattered in again, trickled and tripped in the waters, trying to get a word in edgewise, their voices rising in confused frustration. *How can you have forgotten us, your people?* Forgetting that they had cast her out. And frog was shouting them down again with that raking call of hers. A conference, and they all settled down to a barely audible hum.

She heard people coming over the bridge that crossed the beck behind her. Footfalls on wood, though the bridge ("the new bridge" Carol called it; there had been another one before) was metal. Despite her nakedness, she didn't try to hide. A woman and a little girl had crossed, and stood side by side and looked down into the pool, but with unseeing eyes. They made no reaction to Madeleine, glowing and dripping there.

"You have no grannie, she's dead," said the woman. "You have your father's mum if you want a grannie."

"Why is she dead, yours?"

"We all have to die, love." The woman's delivery was clipped, and the girl seemed well used to that way of talking. Still, she cast a shy glance up and asked:

"When did she die?"

"Long ago. Long before you came along."

"Was there something shameful about the way she died?"

"Why?" asked the woman sharply.

"Dunno."

"Don't listen to village gossip. People love to spin tales. And it's nothing to do with you anyway. The only behaviour you're responsible for is your own."

There was a cadence in the voices that she knew, even as she watched them turn away from the pool and follow the path along the beck, where the waters chopped their voices into bubbles and ripples and carried them away. The hum of the others was fevered, like crickets in high summer. She knew who the mother, with her perfectly curled short hair, and the girl, with her flaxen braids, had been. Nan, the shadow of her, and Carol.

Madeleine rose from the pond. Her body, where it had touched the water, was translucent. It was burnished and rosy and smudged blue like the sky. She stepped onto the path, over the roots of the tree, and followed Nan and Carol. Even young, the usual posture and the usual space was between them. Nan correct and motherly, but not warm; Carol fearful but devoted. They went like fog, bright nothings at the edge of the trees, drifting out and dispersing.

She kept walking, past the old station and to the hill leading out of town. She would walk up the hill, she would walk into the hill, she would find wherever the hidden door was that led to the underground world of the fairies; she would go through the pavement like fog herself, into the belly of the world.

She was a crystal prism, colours and light carving forth from her. Everything wet was transparent; only her knees and her head that had touched the air were still solid. She tossed her long, dim hair in the languid night.

The wide road swept upwards, and she walked along the grass ridge in the middle, right down the centre, pulsing with light. The sky grew larger and the world was smaller. She walked in beauty like the night. She walked towards fairyland, and it was not a grey and misty place; it was the human world that was grey and misty; the fairies lived in an unfading dawn of fruit and fire. The human world was shadow at her feet, squat houses fading into darkness and coloured blurs whirring past like flies, cars with their lights switched on. They were distractions buzzing around her ankles. She had grown large; she was a giant stepping over a toy village. When she reached the moor, her wet footprint would make a crater, and these small grey humans would walk through it and believe they were in the wild. She tossed her hair and watched scalding bright drops rain down. The wind was full of song and music. The swallows rushing to the nest, the blackbird settling down in the dusk, *Lhondoo, lhondoo.*

It was the last of the light now, and she could not find her way into the hill. The road was paved over this last century at least. If there had ever been a door into the hill, she couldn't get to it, and she stopped in frustration and stamped her feet in fury on the ground. And as the light faded, the sky crushed down, the marble-sized houses at her feet rose up to meet it, and there were hands clutching at her, forcing her to shrink.

A car was halfway up on the grassy verge with the doors open and the hazard lights on. She was still on the road leading out of the village, and cars of day-trippers were rushing by on their way home. People stared at her through the windows. Tom and her mother were grasping at her, with mouths that hung slack and garbled words she didn't understand, and her mother was pushing her into the back seat.

The drive home was less than a minute; the cottages, the black-and-white cat sitting like a sentry in the same place. It winked at her as they flashed by.

Nan's tiny kitchen was rent with screams. Her father pacing two steps one way, two steps the other with Maud in his arms, turning with arms half extended before his mouth too went slack and his eyes wide with fear, while Carol said "not now," pushed Madeleine into the chair, and threw a blanket over her.

"Who did this to you?" Tom demanded, crouching before her.

She didn't reply.

"Did somebody—hurt you?" He cast a wild look at Carol for support. "Should we call the police?"

"Nobody hurt me." Two worlds rubbed uncomfortably against each other. She was angry they had taken her away when she might have been getting somewhere, but that wouldn't be the right thing to say. "I'm not hurt, look." She waved the blanket vaguely. She was no longer radiant, merely naked in Nan's kitchen. Her father, dumbfounded, twitched the curtains closed, though they only overlooked the empty garden.

"Where are your clothes?" said Carol. Madeleine looked at her silver-haired mother in a purple fleece dusty from the attic, and saw a flaxen-haired girl dissolving into mist.

"I took a dip in a pool down the river," she said.

They all remained staring at her. This would not do.

"And a boy stole my clothes," she added wearily. She held out her arms for the baby, saw them all exchange glances. "It was just a dumb joke."

She lay in Nan's old bed pretending to sleep. Maud was crying downstairs again, immune to Carol's mothering. Beyond that came the heavy, ugly sound of Tom crying too, sitting at the bottom of the staircase, and her father's voice, unintelligible, and Tom's rasping replies: "different," "but I didn't know," "just very tired."

In the garden, the blossom-patchy plum tree stood guard, like a spindly child, or a skeleton. The house is in uproar, she thought. She liked the thought. I have turned the house upside down.

Down the dark narrow passage, through the dark narrow door (which she did not forget to close behind her), and along the wide gallery she fled like a hare, and was just going down the wide stairs into the wide hall when, what did she see, through the window, but Mr Fox dragging a beautiful young lady across the wide courtyard!

—"Mr Fox," English fairy tale, retold by FLORA ANNIE STEEL

"Stupid, bastard, unsignalled exit." Tom was driving in his hunched-over grannie style, going too slow, and even so missing the exit to their part of town. Madeleine said nothing.

In fact, she couldn't remember what day it was, or what they were doing here, or why she had let Tom drive.

"We have plenty of time anyhow," said Tom.

"Time for what?" she tried.

"Our appointment is at two. I thought it safer, to give us time to get back to town."

Asking what the appointment was for sounded risky. "Aren't you working today?"

"Of course not."

She turned her head. Maud slumbered in the car seat. "Shit," Tom said. Another exit sailed by.

"Why don't you move over, then you'll be ready for the next one."

"There was that bastard lorry. I've been signalling for about ten minutes."

"Just go," she said, looking over her shoulder, and Tom lurched over, tension palpable in every sinew of his arms and neck. They had to take a longer way around through the city now. The harbour swam into view through another grey day, and they could see the old sailing ship directly below them as they left the ring road. The masts plunged into the half-mist like stakes impaling it.

"I wonder why we've never bothered to go visit that ship," Tom said.

"I took my mother."

"Right. But we've been here almost two years."

"We always said it was a Ship of Theseus and probably not really worth it."

"Yeah, I guess."

"It's interesting," she said. She wanted to tell him, but she didn't want to sound crazy, so she spoke in a clipped, academic delivery. "I think you could apply it to people too. Is it the same person if everything about them has been changed piece by piece?"

"I suppose that's why people get divorced," said Tom, and she hated him in that moment, peering priggishly into oncoming traffic. Why had she never noticed his slight tendency to jowliness?

He looked over when they were safely stopped at a red light. "I wasn't talking about us."

"Of course not."

"Haven't I always said, I'm not going to fuck things up like my dad did? How could you think that? You'll never catch me walking out on my child. We'll find a way through this." He channelled all his old charm into his eyes.

"The light has changed," she said.

They drove home. Tom said he would return the car later. It wasn't due back until evening, and they might need it again.

"Is that a new mural on the corner?" he asked, craning his neck. "We really need to get out of Splinters. I hate being part of this. I'm sure the painting's beautiful and all but the neighbourhood is being changed and it's losing something essential."

She only saw that all the trees in Splinters gardens tossed in a stiff breeze. Never had it looked so much like a forest as that half-block walk home.

"I'll change Maud," she said.

"No, never mind, I'll do it. You rest." Every word he spoke was stilted, and each seemed designed to avoid another word. She could only vaguely recall what had caused all this awkwardness between them in the first place. Maud was sleeping in any case, so Tom propped her, still in the car seat attachment, on the bed and began tidying up around the flat. He disappeared down the hall with a pile of books and oddments. Madeleine sat on the sofa and browsed the news. It was all bad as usual, comfortingly so in this case. She allowed tears to leak down her face indiscriminately, at all the bad news.

It wouldn't do for Tom to find her weeping by herself in the front room. She didn't know what "the appointment" was, but it was clear he trusted her less and less, and so the appointment was not going to get to the heart of matters. Yesterday he had conspired with her mother to pull her away, so she couldn't trust him either. To stop the comforting flow of tears, she went back to reading about changelings. That dried her eyes immediately.

And so it was that she finally read the account that had passed glancing by her at every step along the way.

Are you a witch, or are you a fairy? Or are you the wife of Michael Cleary?

She had read it before of course, at some point in her studies. And she had forgotten it, and here it was. Of course, Bridget Cleary.

> Bridget Cleary was an Irish woman killed by her husband in 1895. Prior to the murder, their marriage was said to be a happy one, but her husband became convinced that she had been abducted by fairies and a changeling left in her place. At the time of her death she had been ill for several days. As her illness progressed, Michael Cleary called both the doctor and the priest, but as medicine and religion both failed to cure her, he became convinced of a supernatural explanation. Belief in changelings was widespread in Ireland at the time.
>
> Bridget Cleary's body was discovered in a shallow grave not far from their house, a labourer's cottage that was rumoured to be built on the site of an old fairy ring. She had been set on fire, either just before or just after death. Several people, including her father and cousins, were implicated in her disappearance. Witnesses attested that she had been carried before the fireplace and sprinkled with urine to cast the fairy out. Her husband threw her to the ground and threatened her with a burning piece of wood, before bundling her into the fireplace and throwing lamp oil over her. Witnesses fled as Cleary cried that

> it was a fairy rather than his wife who burned, and that she would soon return to him. The jury, after viewing the extent of her injuries, found Michael Cleary guilty of manslaughter. He served fifteen years in prison and upon his release emigrated to Montreal.

Flutterings, swishings, chitterings in the artificial quiet of the house, and when the screaming began, she bent in upon herself and tried to block it out. After a minute, something about it rang home, and she forced herself upright and along the hall. A baby was crying, contorting out of her car seat. She had forgotten there was a baby. But more startling was Tom, sitting on the bed and reading and ignoring the baby. He leapt up; they both approached the car seat. His face was white. She took the baby and lay down on the bed to feed her. Next to her head was a book. Her theory book. She didn't dare look up at Tom. He had a small square of paper in his hand. He wasn't looking at her either. He slid the paper into his pocket as though it was nothing. But his movements were strange and jerky. He was turning in circles around the room. Madeleine held Maud, as though the baby could protect her.

Tom's phone dinged. He looked at it and nodded, relaxed slightly. "Your parents have confirmed they are leaving this evening. They'll be here tonight."

"Oh," she said.

"They'll be here to help with Maud in the event of unforeseens."

"Unforeseens?"

He wouldn't look at her. He hid behind the project manager hands again. "We should probably get some formula."

"Why?"

"We may need it at some point."

"Where will my parents sleep?"

"On the couch, I suppose. Maybe we should sleep on it, though, and let them have the bed."

"The sofa bed is impossible for more than one person. It collapses in the middle."

"Hmmm," said Tom. "We'll figure something out."

She had begun to shiver. She tried to catch Tom's eye, but every time he glanced at her he looked quickly away again. Not before she caught a flicker of knowledge though. She thought of him in the car, on the bridge, disbelieving her. She recalled suddenly seeing her clothes on a chair in Nan's kitchen earlier, before all memory stopped. Someone had gone to the stream to get them. They knew she had lied about that. They knew what she was. And he had her paper, so he knew everything. Suspicion had become knowledge.

"How can we figure something out?" she whispered in a frightened voice.

"Don't worry about it, Maddie." He had turned his back and was pretending to fold baby clothes.

There would only be one sleeping on the sofa bed. She wanted to ask what he was planning, and yet she knew, and if he knew that she knew, he might act sooner, he might not wait for her parents' help in overpowering her. Tom always faced up to his responsibilities. He could do it alone if need be.

Had it been difficult to convince her parents? Perhaps not. Her mother would understand when he said she had been stolen by fairies, and her father—well, he no longer saw family connections beyond the ties of true, red blood. She went with Maud and huddled in the armchair by the bedroom window and looked down into the garden. No Greymalkin, no help there. They could bury her in the garden, under all the rubbish.

Maybe a new woman would ride forth from the fox shed on a white horse. Madeleine the true daughter, true wife, true mother, Madeleine in the first person, Madeleine with no memories of a terrified changeling, only a brief period of grey mist, soon forgotten.

Tom seemed to be circling her endlessly, seldom leaving the room, and Maud was cranky and could not be put to sleep.

"Why don't we go out for a coffee?"

"We just got home," Tom said.

"We have time before 'the appointment.'"

"I think we should stay here."

"I won't," said Madeleine, sitting up, holding the baby close. Tom hesitated.

"Okay, we can. But Maddie, can we talk?" She nodded briefly. Anything to leave the house.

They put their shoes on again. Madeleine strapped the baby to her chest. Tom would never hurt his child. He would not attack her with a burning branch while she carried the baby.

Eerie silence in the yard. She hadn't heard a sound from the downstairs neighbour today. She had never noticed how constant his music and other small sounds were until they were silent.

"Where's the neighbour, I wonder," she said lightly. She must keep up some kind of normal exchange, enough to get out of the front garden and into society, wilderness, the neighbourhood.

Tom shrugged. "Maybe he's gone away." Ah yes, gone away, paid off, perhaps. Out of the way. Maybe they would burn her, burn the house, start over. No one would think anything of a house in Splinters catching fire. If not, they could bury her in the garden with no witnesses. Once night closed in. He was taking her out, an appointment with the doctor and the priest, but they had not cured Bridget Cleary, and they wouldn't cure her.

They were out on the road that led to the high street. A life narrowed and crushed until it only ran along pace with the dingy pavement, backwards and forth, forwards and back. Off for an overpriced coffee. But the destination hardly mattered. The journey was the destination, her mother would say. Life is the destination. Live in the moment. Enjoy every moment. They're all so precious. They grow up so fast. It's over so quickly.

At the corner was the new three-day mural. Injustice had ground the neighbourhood down, but love would save it. She had seen it a few days before, but Tom hadn't, and he stopped to look. Madeleine stood some steps ahead and waited. It was the first professional wall art to make it this deep into the neighbourhood. The colours were too bright; they reflected on Tom's face with a demon glow. This was what happened when you tried to paint over reality with rainbows.

A bus drew up and the doors opened, and she realized she was standing at the stop. "Ah no, sorry," she said to the driver. And then, in the moment when the doors were about to close but had not yet closed, she changed her mind. She stepped through, and they swung shut behind her.

"You said—" the driver accused.

"Yeah sorry, I thought you were the other one." A nonsensical comment, there was only one. The bus pulled away and through a green light. She peered through the back window from a distance and saw the moment when Tom looked around and realized she was gone. There was naked fear and horror on his face.

Well, now he would not be able to burn her and get his wife back. Safe on the bus, her escape no longer seemed entirely a triumph. He wanted to cast out the changeling, and so did she. She herself had written that fire was the usual way, or water. But she would not be thrown in the back garden and buried there among the live rats and the marauding foxes, a fairy corpse decomposing to the beats of the neighbour's music. She turned her back on Tom's terror and sat down. She would find another way.

Escape by city bus was ridiculous. She would laugh if she were not afraid he would catch up to her, his cheeks flushed pink from running and his eyes shining, and his teeth. A murderous Mr Fox. *You may go anywhere in the castle, save this one room. Do anything you choose, but never look under the bed.* When she looks under the bed, Mr Fox is there, Tom with a fox face, smiling at her with pearly teeth. Her heart ached to think of it, now that her fear of capture was subsiding. What had happened to Lancelot?

When they pulled up to the stop just past Hartley Road, she stepped off, then walked rapidly two blocks down to the next bus stop. She mustn't stay in Splinters. It would be too easy for him to find her here. She took the next bus that came. It was headed for the wharf and the Ship of Theseus. To the water. So many fairy brides had fled by water, fled back to their own forms, selkies, mermaids, fishes. Oh, to be a fish in the waters.

At every stop she tensed and prepared to run if Tom or her mother or an army of foxes boarded. But it was quiet. There weren't even any old ladies on this bus, and usually there were. Indeed, her experience of taking buses was very much grounded in the idea of the old lady, the crone of public transport. Nan had taken her on outings into the market town, and these had been her first forays away from the dominance of cars. She had loved those outings, standing next to Nan at the stop and then trundling between the green fields, chattering. Nan listened in a way few adults did. Though Carol did. Or had, when Madeleine was a child.

Leafy suburbs, then the rehabilitated factory condos, then the harbour. The quayside bustled disconcertingly. The restaurant terraces were all full of people talking and laughing, happy uproar to her right, monotonous, lapping water to her left. She might turn to the side of life, join them, insert herself at a table of strangers, ask for help, ask them to keep her away from the water. But Maud's breath was a gentle whistling at her chest. And no, there is more than glass between the snow and the roses, Maudie. Asking for help would only result in her being foisted on Maud longer, keeping Maud away from a real mother, leaving her with only the empty husk of a fairy bride.

She unbuttoned her shirt so that Maud's downy head rested directly against her skin. She was so cold, and the baby's head was the only warmth that could penetrate it. Maud's lips twitched into the reflex of a smile. She snored lightly. Madeleine wrapped her arms around the carrier.

People were looking at her from the terrace of the last restaurant on the quayside, so she hurried on and climbed up on the lock.

Another story from long ago. A woman realized one day that her daughter was a changeling and so took the child to the edge of the water, and called out for the good folk to take her back. After a long while the baby was taken, and another baby left in its place. She lived with the new daughter with her heart full of joy, until the child was seven and said, "I must be returning home now," and left without a backwards glance. And when the mother ran to the shore in search of her, she found the old, rejected baby on the beach again. She realized that it was her own child she had rejected years before, and that it was the changeling she had raised and loved as her own. And she waited year in, year out, for the changeling child to return, but she never did.

The old stories all told the truth, but told it slant. Madeleine sat on the edge with her legs dangling over the water. When she tilted her head back, the prow of the old ship came into view with its golden mermaid. She would hear the mermaids singing. Looking down into the water again, she saw the fish swim out from under a canal boat and turn its frozen green-gold eye upon her. Below it the water hugged the old Victorian walls and fell quickly away into blackness.

The fish swam back and forth beneath her in its pre-world loneliness, and waited.

She cupped a hand against the baby's head and felt the stubborn warmth of life. A moment passed and another, moments of being. But it wouldn't do. By waiting she risked Tom finding her here, approaching with his burning branch and his sharp, smiling teeth. So she pulled to loosen the carrier and eased the baby out. A line appeared between Maud's eyebrows, and Madeleine held her breath. But it didn't matter really if she cried. Better that she cry, as the lock was deserted but someone from the quay would hear and come running.

She placed the baby well back from the edge. It wasn't much in terms of protection, but it would have to be enough.

The fish swam away under the canal boat again. Well, she would follow it, trap herself there so she might never surface. The water spread and deepened, below was water, the sky was water, and the old stones where she sat were water too, buckling under her and losing their shape and waiting to plunge her below, and she turned in sudden vertigo and clutched at the railings, but they were water too.

Crone hands grasped her and held firm, and human voices called to her.

"Now, now," Angela was saying. "There, there." And continued, "Now, now. Now, now. There, there." Angela in all her solidity, standing alone before the gaping emptiness and the siren depths, restful and alive.

"But how did you know?" Angela asked, wringing her hands, and Madeleine realized it was a different crone who held her shoulders; it was the community worker, Dorrie, who helped her to her feet, threw Angela a grim glance, and said, "I've seen faces with that look before. Pick up the baby." Maud jerked and twisted and wailed in fury on the ground.

A group had gathered not far away. A woman darted forwards and picked up the baby, tried to rock her.

"Call an ambulance," Angela said. "Somebody call an ambulance." Her easy air of speaking to the public was gone; her voice was insistent but nervous. Dorrie called out to the group. A few spectators detached, negotiated rapidly who would call, and an elegant woman walked in circles as she did so.

An angry waiter approached brandishing a bill. "Take that away," Angela said. "We'll get to that."

"We were having lunch to celebrate when we saw you walk by," said Angela. "You were staring at something we couldn't see, and your mouth was moving strangely."

"Let's just wait for the ambulance," said Dorrie.

"I can't calm her," said the woman holding the baby as Maud howled and howled, real, startled tears upon her cheeks. "She wants her mother."

"She'll have to wait," said Dorrie firmly. "Her mother needs a moment."

Madeleine shook her head, held out her arms mutely to

receive the child, though whisperings rose from the water. She was marshalled by women back to the quayside and onto a bench. A businessman talking on his phone at the other end of it gave the women an alarmed glance, for they were mostly women, a few standing back and muttering to one another, Angela loose as a ragdoll, looking like she needed to sit down herself. And there was another group of women, all older than Madeleine, unconnected but firm in their focus upon her. They all wore a look of stricken recognition, and they stood around her like lock keepers, holding back the water. So many people looking, for once, not at the baby, but at her.

A seagull passed overhead with the usual inhuman scream. The woman holding Maud approached discreetly. There were murmurs among the baby's wails, but Maud was handed over and Madeleine fed her, and so the noise stopped and an uneasy silence fell. In the hole left by the silence some of the women began to shift on their feet, to realize that they were standing in a group of strangers, to notice Madeleine's own numbed inability to speak or communicate.

"I don't think you should let her have that baby," exploded someone from the back. "She could be a danger to it. You hear about women doing awful things to their babies. A mother threw hers down the canyon a few years ago."

"She didn't do anything to the baby," said Dorrie, her hands still on Madeleine's shoulders. "She carefully placed it out of danger in fact."

"A woman who would do that might do anything!"

"Don't you think you should step back a bit and let her get some air?" said Angela, rallying. "We're waiting for the ambulance. I don't think this contribution is helpful." As always, Angela's sheer presence in public exerted its influence. The speaker fell back, as though it had been her own idea, and eventually left, even as the siren call of an ambulance some streets away displaced the siren call of the water. And then it nosed its way onto the old quayside and fell silent. It was the lights, finally, like stained glass flickering upon her retinas, that drove out the vestiges of fairyland, and Madeleine stood and walked towards them.

What time
Subaqueous
Cell on cell
Experience
Very slowly
Is forming up
Into something beautiful—awful—huge.

—*Paris,* HOPE MIRRLEES

Where? At the mother and baby unit, a psychiatric ward for new mothers. They are lucky there was a vacancy. The room is small and evenly illuminated with warm yellow lights that fail to conceal its institutional feel. There is a daybed, a cot, an armchair, and a television, switched off.

Who? Madeleine, ashy-faced, staring off to one side, unseeing. Her movements are shy and nervous.

And Maud? *Yes.* A brief beat of the eyelids.

Also, Angela, outlandishly dressed. Feathered and furred, topped with a vintage Chanel bathing cap and glitter-bedazzled children's dress-up wings.

Madeleine is there but not there. Trying to remember to hold the baby. Shards, fragments, rattle around her mind.

Sputter
and
fizzle

Occasionally a run-on sentence rushes through like a great belch.

"Why Angela what large wings you have you look like you belong in the pantomime you should have paused upon entering like a dame holding a pose for the hoots or applause but how nice of you to visit how nice, welcome to my parlour, welcome to my room small and yellow, whose neutral surfaces curve away into infinity, an infinity of inert shadows and echoes enclosed and amniotic and revealing—will you reveal things to me Angela?"

Taxis hoot in the street.

"A literature review," Angela says, hoisting a large shopping bag onto the daybed. "I've concluded some books on the subject do more harm than good. Nonetheless, literature will come to your aid."

Oh, yes?

"I left some of the useless ones at home. Can't fly with all that extra weight. But we'll just run through them."

Useless:
What to Expect

European Children Don't . . .
That one about hypnobirthing
The one about breastfeeding
And that other one
And some novels, though not as many as you would think

Angela says: "Though societal ideology in the Victorian period tended to posit the mother as saint or holy vessel, there is in fact a dearth of this representation in the literature that has survived to the present day. One famous example of the mother-as-saint is Marmee in Alcott's *Little Women*, her very name suggesting that something infantilizing is occurring in her portrayal. Yet elsewhere, Victorian novelists seem to have largely realized that a saintly character is not an interesting character, and so these mothers are relegated to bit parts or removed from the action altogether, as can be seen in mothers in works by Dickens, Eliot, Hodgson Burnett. Where mothers are present and unsaintly, they are not played for rage but for laughs (Austen, Thackeray, Dickens again, occasionally Hardy in a lighter mood). It is clear, with a little thought, that if we don't laugh *at* Mrs. Bennett of *Pride and Prejudice*, we would have to cry along *with* her. Elsewhere, swathes of fictional mothers are dead, perhaps to advance the plot, perhaps to allow sainthood to exist without the need of an actual living saint on the premises. Where nineteenth-century fiction is concerned, it would seem that the best mother is a dead mother, an idea that has been handed down and still regularly occurs in children's literature today."

Angela tosses a few books into a corner of the room with something like a snarl. Madeleine watches them thud against the linoleum.

More books follow. Out of the bag and over Angela's angry wingtip and into the corner of the room. "These are more contemporary. The hand-wringing, wryly traumatized, war-journal-type memoirs. *Oh haha, children say the darndest things. Hahaha, aren't husbands just the silliest, the most clueless? Is it wine-o'clock yet?* A number of people recommended them. I read some. I disliked the wink-wink tone."

"So what's left?"

Angela pulls a short pile out of her shopping bag. "We made a collection for you. My sister-in-law, Bronwen, myself. Marie sent a book too. Don't expect a patch-up. She's not the forgiving kind. But she can never resist recommending a book."

Useful:
"The Yellow Wall-Paper"
Killing Kanoko
A Life's Work
Madame Bovary
Die, My Love
The Tenant of Wildfell Hall
Medea

Madeleine drops the last as though burned, raises sudden, panicked eyes to the fairy godmother.

"*Medea*? Is this supposed to make me feel better?"

Angela is an actual fairy now, laughing head thrown back, hahahahahahaha! Her wings burst into flames and Madeleine cowers away.

It settles it all settles nothing is burning Madeleine steady yourself sorry wasn't meaning anything by the *Medea* never mind there there let's look at something else.

The room looks as though it has been squeezed in a large fist and hastily straightened out. The books lie tumbled on the floor. A playing card, with arms, legs, and an unmistakable builder's swagger comes. It begins to pick up the various books and pile them up around the bed as though building a wall with them.

Angela is now holding a magic wand made from a chopstick with a cardboard star taped on the end. "And now I am here in my capacity as the ghost of Midsummer Eve past." She waves the wand.

Marie is there. Marie is talking. Marie is standing, an incisive figure, long hair thrown back and slightly tangled, as always, face bare but eyes smudgily made up. As always; Marie.

"Damn it," says Angela, "Midsummer *past* I said, not midsummer present." She shakes the wand fiercely but nothing happens. With a hiss, she removes the cardboard star and tries to attach it to the other end of the chopstick.

Marie says in her flat Midlands tones, like someone arguing with herself in the mirror, "If you weren't such a genre snob and an Anglophile, you would have found all kinds of material to give you different ways of understanding the situation. Honestly, Madeleine. You think you're going to find the key to what's going on in your head in Yeats? It's the first thing those of us who aren't married to the classics know. It's the reason there's a movement to diversify the canon, for fuck's sake. If you want insight on something that's probably actually pretty universal but you know concerns some second-class citizens like women or ethnic minorities, you don't go dredging through Dickens or D. H. Lawrence. You go straight to the outer edges. You'll find it in science fiction maybe, in horror definitely. And ten to one you'll find it in translation. There's more good material every year. There's no excuse for not knowing these things, if you could just get your head out of T. S. Eliot's ass for five minutes. What does T. S. Eliot know about being a woman? According to him we're all talking of Michelangelo! Dumbass."

"You need to read the classics to judge the new stuff properly," Madeleine retorts. "If *you* understood that and didn't just dump theory into every paper, blah blah Lacan this, Deleuze that, you'd be more interesting as a scholar; actually, you'd be unbeatable." She has to lean sideways to look around the pile of books, which the playing card is building in front of her. "Take a long jump off a short pier, Marie."

"Like you tried to?"

"And *dumbass* sounds all kinds of stupid in your accent."

Silence.

"I'm sorry about the other day," Madeleine whispers behind her wall of books. She has to stand on the bed to see over it when Marie starts talking again.

"Yeah well, it doesn't matter if you think looking at things through a Lacanian lens is stupid, and it doesn't matter if you are the foremost analytical genius of our age, Madeleine, or at least were, or at least were a *promising doctorate student with a good memory* before motherhood blew your mind apart. It doesn't matter if you hustle the baby into childcare to come back to finish that dissertation. It doesn't matter if you never come back and become a glowing, radiant, drinks-gin-while-the-kids-are-in-the-bath-stay-at-home mum. None of that matters, Madeleine. Neither of us will ever live in a little fairy-tale house like Angela's in a leafy suburb of a great city, not by studying literature, because there are no jobs.

There are no jobs that pay shit.

There are no jobs.

No jobs no jobs no jobs.

Temporary contract

if you're lucky, luv.

We

are

all

fucked,

fucked,

f

u

c

k

e

d

d

d

d

d

."

Mid-harangue, she's frozen, like a bad video-call connection.

"Is *this* supposed to make me feel better," Madeleine wants to know.

But she can't see Angela because the playing card has put the last book in place; she has been walled in by books, buried alive, the only sound a low, dull, quick sound, much such a sound as a watch makes enveloped in cotton. Two watches, her own heartbeat, and Maud's, hark, louder, louder, entwined again! She is pounding on the wall of books. They are bricks now and do not give. She will die here; she will not be discovered for half a century.

BOOM.

Angela has blasted through the wall with her magic wand. "Sorry, sorry. I've got the right channel now. So as I was saying, consider me the ghost of Midsummer Eve past. Not your past, long past. *Abracadabra.* Here we go."

> *Now it is the time of night*
> *That the graves, all gaping wide,*
> *Every one lets forth his sprite.*

A woman. She is real. Madeleine and Maud are the ghosts. A woman in a narrow-fitting skirt, blouse, and red cardigan. The getup of the prewar era, though it's hard to tell because this basic silhouette served many women their whole lives. Hair soft and brown like a mouse. Pale eyes, abstract. She tilts her head and listens to noises that Madeleine cannot hear.

A quizzical look at Angela.

Shrug.

They watch.

What's unusual is how she crooks her arm as though carrying something always, sometimes holding the invisible weight in both arms. It is the angle of Madeleine's crooked arm, holding Maud. The woman doesn't interact with the space; it seems as though she's merely frozen that way.

And then she leaps, a diver in space, her body stiff as a board, and falls heavily to the floor with a thud, and begins contorting, flailing to the sound of her own laboured breathing and the banging and tapping her movements make. She's trying to propel herself forwards on the floor, and the movements are familiar, but wrong. She is swimming.

There's a girl watching at the door, in a short dress and overlarge brogues. She is seven or eight, with bobbed hair. There is something definite in the set of her jaw. The woman is facing away from her, swimming hopelessly across the floor towards the window. The girl watches narrowly, with her shoulders raised defensively so high that the collar of her dress almost touches her chin. She seems aware of being watched, and she schools her face into neutrality and then, gradually, into contempt. The woman has battled across invisible waters and reached a shore, heaves herself up from her imaginary lake, and gasps and sobs and tries to wring water from her perfectly dry hair. She looks back towards the door. The girl abruptly turns on her heel and leaves.

"Tom?" the woman calls in one of those old-style voices, thick country accent. Madeleine stirs uneasily.

"What's this about?" she asks Angela, who just raises her eyebrows knowingly.

"Tom, we've known each other since we were nineteen," the woman calls. "You know I'm not a danger to them. You must know that. Why don't you make them let me out?" She paces to the door. It is closed now. She paces back to the window. It looks out upon trees. The streets and the taxis are gone.

"A fit of madness," she says. "I'm well now. And Annie will not see me. She does not forgive me. And they have told me the boy is not dead but . . .
I saw the fish
Feeding on his small blue body."

Crash.
She throws herself back to the floor.
Swimming
Swimming and sobbing
Searching among the fish
Those are the pearls that were his eyes
Sitting afterwards on the floor with her arm crooked and empty, crying.
"Tom, I would not have believed it of you."

"'You'd think it was O tragic and that dying-looking one,'" Madeleine is muttering.

Angela is pulling Madeleine towards the window. "Come, we have a date on the other side of the country. Bear but a touch of my hand and you shall be upheld in more than this." And passing through the glass they are off, through thick clouds, Madeleine clinging to Angela's arm and holding Maud with the other hand and shivering in her hospital gown until a ray of sunshine pushes through the cloud, and then another, and they are on the hills, following in the wake of the girl Annie who runs through the sunshine, runs full of rainbows, runs with her face turned decidedly away from the shadows and the room and the swimming woman, and she keeps running, through the years, Madeleine and Angela and Maud gliding discreetly in her wake. She runs, a child with the mousy, bobbed hair. She runs, an older child in plaits. She looks like Carol only fiercer. She runs through the hills, and shards of life spring at her and run with her, a little boy who tears adoringly after her, friends on bicycles keeping pace then falling behind, boyfriends laughing at her side, replaced by others. Annie is open to all experience. *She always was*, Madeleine thinks, *always open to life with her arms held out to welcome more of it to her. Open to all life*. There's one man now who has kept pace awhile, and finally he and Annie run into a little house and come to a stop. Or not a stop; Annie is sewing curtains at a twinkly new Singer, she is frying a pork chop, she is thickening and filling out like the full moon, she is standing in the kitchen late one night drinking a cup of warm milk.

"But look behind her," whispers Angela, and so Madeleine looks into the shadows and sees what Annie was running from all that time. There's the woman from the locked room, older now and bloated from neglect and despair, in a vaguely institutional gown, though still with her old red, now-threadbare cardigan. Her arm is still stiff and crooked and empty, and she is pacing behind Annie, who is drinking milk alone and unruffled in her kitchen. The woman is pacing, trying to narrow the half-circles of her steps, trying to encroach on Annie's vision. But Annie, open to everything, is not open to this. There's a steely grim resolve in the way she looks ahead, only ahead.

"There's rue for you, and here's some for me," says the woman in the darkness.

"No," says Annie, reading the newspaper without looking up. Her face is tighter and older now and swish! Her shoulder-length hair falls; she has the short, permed helmet she will keep, in one form or another, until her death. Her face is shifting like a time-lapse video, and in each moment she is more obviously Nan.

There is a knock at the door and Annie opens it to an old man, short and ruddy and white-bearded.

"But Lancelot mused a little space," Angela whispers to Madeleine, wafting her glittered wings.

Nan looks questioningly into the old man's lined face. "Yes, Dad?"

And he replies: "'She had a lovely face. God in his mercy lend her grace.'"

"That's from something you've read," Angela says confidingly.

And Annie turns slowly around and looks for the first time into the corner where the woman would pace behind her. It is empty.

Madeleine can't see Annie's face from this angle. Does it all catch up with her? Does she shed a tear? Her shoulders are up around her neck in tension again. That's all.

It is cold among the clouds again, so cold, and all Madeleine can feel is Angela's arm upon hers. They are gone from the ghost world as quickly as they entered it, back among the hooting traffic and the scattered books.

"Where has she gone?" Madeleine screams suddenly.

"Who, my dear?"

"Maud, Maud!" She gesticulates to her own arm, crooked, empty. "Where is she?"

Angela turns and peers into the corners of the room. "Slipped away, did she? Really, I don't remember seeing her go. Perhaps she'll show up. In any case, she wasn't what you wanted or expected, was she?"

Madeleine rushes around the room on tiny legs. "I've lost the baby! I can't believe I've lost the baby. I don't deserve to—" She bangs against the door with the hard plated back of her new insect body. She tries to reach up to the handle; it cannot be reached. "Angela," she screams.

"I am transformed into a monstrous vermin!"

The door bursts open to the stark glare of fluorescent lights from the hallway, and playing-card people rush in to pin her to the ground. She leaps back at them, six tiny legs, wings and feelers flailing. "Begone!" she cries. "You're nothing but a pack of cards!" Still, they overpower her and hold her down, and needles, and tranquilizers, though she is growing, growing, but also falling, losing consciousness. Angela, now tiny, fairy-sized, takes flight with an alarmed squawk, and flies out the window.

This thing of darkness I acknowledge mine

—*The Tempest,* WILLIAM SHAKESPEARE

Madeleine started up. Maud, lying on her back on the carpet and kicking her legs, did not notice. Madeleine's father was attempting to entertain her by raising and lowering a finger into her line of vision, but Maud's coos were beginning to give way to crankiness and tears. Her father stood and lifted the baby and walked the length of the room, backwards and forwards with his granddaughter over his shoulder, patting her back.

"Let's see if the movement will get her to drop off again," he said.

"Never mind, give her to me."

He handed Maud over with an apologetic expression. "There are times when she just wants her mother, it seems."

"Of course," Madeleine replied sadly. "We are mad Madeleine and maudlin Maud. Who else would she want?"

"It was an education having her those first days," her father said, taking a seat in the armchair. "A re-education. You think you know how to change a baby . . . that is, to change a diaper. But you forget. Still, I think Maudie and I are good friends now, though of course she's glad to get back to you."

Madeleine said nothing. She tried to work out what it all meant. That Maud had been gone, that she, Madeleine, had been somewhere and her parents had been looking after the baby.

"They are so much work. Later they get older and have different challenges and you forget just how knackering they were when they were small. Though I suppose we didn't have you when you were as small as this, and so I've never known how much work they are. I wish I had known."

"You couldn't have known," she said. Was it her job to be comforting her father on his visit to the madhouse?

But it was obvious that he was just nervously making conversation, waiting for an entry to say whatever it was he'd come to say. She knew that look on him well, jiggling back and forth on the armchair, his hands loosely intertwined on his lap, his politician's shock of white hair falling across his forehead. He had been her best friend, before Tom became her best friend.

"She's much better in here with you," he said, possibly in what was intended to be a soothing tone.

Madeleine bit her lip. It was hard, so hard not to reply that nobody was better anywhere with her, that everyone, indeed, would be far better off without her, especially poor Tom—where was he?—and Maud. She recognized this was not the kind of thing you were meant to say in the mother and baby unit, where you were supposed to be getting better, so she did not say it. She could not believe, as they claimed they did, that she would get well again, or rather see things their way, but perhaps they might be persuaded to let her out.

Her father abruptly stood and began pacing around the room again. Maud fell asleep, her head hanging backwards into space and her opened lips giving a clear view of the roof of her mouth. Madeleine looked at her numbly, and beyond her saw a pile of books on the table by her daybed.

"Books," she said.

"Your tutor brought them," her father said.

"Angela was here? Really here?"

"She insisted on coming, and Tom said he thought it would be all right. Angela said she should have known something was up, that you didn't seem yourself the other day. She wanted to visit and bring you some books, she said."

Madeleine cast a practiced eye along the spines. *Medea*, the cause of her distress, had been removed.

Her father was standing next to the television, looking shattered, as though he had not slept in days. "Come sit down, Papa," she said.

He came and sat next to her on the daybed.

"With all my many years of training," she said with their usual playful, pseudoscientific tone, "I recognize this as a moment of importance. I expect I should pay attention and listen well to whatever you have to say and are not saying."

He smiled the delighted old conspirator's smile. "It's true that I asked Tom and your mother to go for a cup of tea," he said. "I wanted to tell you a bedtime story."

The light poured through the yellow curtains and lifted them and the bed on a wave of sunbeams, as though they and Maud were alone above the world on a magic carpet.

"You know of course that I've been doing my genealogy research."

She turned her head away. The magic carpet came back to earth.

"No, hear me out. I know you have been feeling alone and you don't like my new interest, but I want to tell you a story from the family history."

"This would be your family?" she said, quickly arraying

them all in her mind, standing stoutly before the mythical house in the backwoods, a quick sliver of moon flying up above them to the frantic cry of a violin. They all tapped their feet to the music.

"Your mother's family, as a matter of fact. Though I suspect what you are really saying is that I'm not speaking of your own, genetic family."

"How well you read me."

"I know I've been insensitive, Madeleine. And by 'I know' I mean your mother and Tom told me. I accept it and I apologize. I can only offer that I was a child in possession of a new toy. You and I are both prone to these obsessions. But it was always the stories I was after, and what they could shed on our experience. The blood is a connection, but only of any importance in terms of the stories it brings to light."

"Ah," she said at length, deliberately. "Fine" (as long as your sympathies were always on the side of life).

"Well then, this is something dredged up from your mother's family. About your Nan, and her mother, whom she never had any time for. I don't know if you knew that."

Madeleine considered. She would not mention the woman swimming on dry land. She was not sure what that had been, a dream perhaps, a hallucination. (I met a lady in the meads.) "I knew it by omission, absences, conversations brushed over. What were her parents' names?"

"Ellen and Thomas."

"Another Tom."

"It was a common name. Still is."

"Yes."

"At the funeral, you remember Sarah Clifton saying Nan had stayed with her family for a while as a girl? Afterwards I went and asked her why. I remembered it, without ever having fully been aware of being told. She told me that Nan's mother had been sent away, and gave me to understand it was a breakdown of one kind or another. Nan never talked about it, and neither did any of the adults of the time."

"Papa," Madeleine said. She felt nauseated and dizzy and wasn't sure if she wanted him to continue or not. (World is crazier and more of it than we think), she told herself, and not only because it was incorrigibly plural, but because it was crazier. Crazier meaning crazy. People went crazy.

"She didn't have the full story because she'd been a child, younger than Nan, and the whole thing had been clouded in what you could or couldn't say, and Nan refused ever to hear a word about it." (I am unable to get the true bearings of this event.) "I wonder if that would have been the case even a few years ago, but like so many of these crucial things in the lives of our parents, it was too late to ask. My theory, Maddie, is that people like myself end up doing genealogy because we've missed our chance to really connect to the past. Our parents die and take their memories to the grave, the ones they would have told us and the ones they never would have breathed a word about—and there were plenty of the latter among older generations. I tried to float the story by your Grandy, but he was very confused in those last few days we spent with him. He just repeated that Nan and her mother hadn't been close, that her mother had died but they hadn't gone to the funeral. But then he said that Nan's mother had been institutionalized until she died."

(Down the dark narrow passage, through the dark narrow door.) Madeleine was thinking of the woman pacing in her old red cardigan. And thinking, too, of the woman swimming down the silver river (with the convulsive, corkscrew movements of a great fish, threshing from its neck to its tail). "Orphan Annie," she said, then frowned. Ellen had effectively been orphaned in that same moment, cast back into a waste of waters, no home, no family, no voice.

Her father licked his lips and settled into his story. "Orphan, no. She had a father, and a brother, and she was in her thirties before her mother died. This winter I requested the records—your mother had to sign for them of course, and it was what you would call a total pain doing it all internationally; they took ages to arrive. I thought of asking you to go in person but you seemed awfully prickly on the whole subject. And who knows, they might have some outdated law about adoption and such things, like the passport office. The institution itself is long gone. It was disbanded under Thatcher, for better or worse. Your great-grandmother was dead by then of course.

"Her file seemed so slim. It contained almost nothing for half a life. But in reading it there was so much. I have copies here for you." He reached for a folder full of papers next to the pile of books, and paused. "There are letters in the file. Your mother has read them. One or two from Nan, in the first days of her mother's confinement. She was only seven. They read a bit stiff, like a school composition, but heartbreaking too. That was the period she was sent to live with Sarah's family. Shortly after the birth of her little brother."

(O love, how did you get here?) Madeleine sighed.

"There were letters from Ellen's sister, explaining that her behaviour had been unprecedented. She had been a wonderful and happy mother. She adored her daughter, Annie. She was sad that another child had not come along in so many years. There might have been miscarriages. The letters don't say. But she *did* fall pregnant again. It was a difficult pregnancy. She had trouble moving and couldn't walk for the last few months. Nan was frequently at Sarah's house even before tragedy struck."

Ah, tragedy. (Ineffable, effable, effanineffable tragedy. An infant crying in the night.) "Do I want to know about this tragedy?" Madeleine asked, her voice carefully neutral, as in all conversations down the years in which her father had explained the workings of the world to her.

"I'll sum up," he said, also using his professional voice. "The baby came a month early, small and weak and sick."

(And it was her last afternoon as herself.)

"I don't like stories with dead babies, Papa," she said lightly. But she remembered. *They have told me the boy is not dead.*

"That's not how it happened," he said. "Surely you knew your Nan had a brother, Stanley? This isn't a story about a baby; it's a story about a woman. Stanley didn't die, but he didn't thrive for a long time. I don't suppose he slept much either. After a few days with Maud I have a new appreciation for what that means."

(I stand at the pale of my being.)

"Your great-grandmother was convinced something was wrong with him and that somehow it was her fault for birthing him too soon. Her sister came around to help, swore that nothing serious was wrong, he was just scrawny."

(Want something to eat! Want something to eat!)

"He was even growing, but Ellen couldn't see it. It's all recounted in one of Tom's letters to the institution."

"Tom!" flashed Madeleine. "Leaving her to moulder there forever. Did he remarry?"

"You should read his letters, Maddie. They aren't like that at all. He was an articulate man, though not a writer by nature. He argued long and hard to have her released, but her aquatic fantasies never went away. He eventually gave up, stopped writing. He may indeed have had a companion at some point in the intervening thirty years before his own death. Can we blame him?"

"Aquatic fantasies?" She remembered the thud of the woman falling, the frantic swimming, the wringing of her hair. Ah yes. (They are beyond me, are fishes.)

"She was convinced the baby had died. When her sister came around in a panic, it was to find baby Stanley screaming on the bed and your great-grandmother trying to drown herself in the bathtub." (A figure of Guilt intruding into the haunts of Innocence.) "There was worry that next time she might try and drown the baby. Ellen's sister wrote that everywhere she looked the house at once seemed full of dangers, from the fire to the sewing scissors." (Scissors and razors are weapons.)

Madeleine looked blankly through the television. The room was overheated and stuffy. She felt a gentle harbour breeze on her cheeks. She saw the still water, the trout lazily turning in its depths.

"Is this supposed to make me feel better?" she wanted to know.

"It was a different time," her father said. "They didn't have antipsychotic medication back then. A woman changed by childbirth might struggle to recover from the stigma, or to recover at all with the treatments available. It means you aren't alone. It means you're one of the family. It depends what you mean by feeling better."

This was what she liked about her father.

It was never fully quiet in the mother and baby unit. There was always a baby crying somewhere, or a mother, though the babies cried with lusty outrage, and the mothers in muffled bursts. It was approaching summer; it had been a clear day and the light had not fully faded; the institutional yellow hovered around her as evening settled through the room, the light framed the blind like a portal. The noises of the ward and the sighs and the cries were currents of a diminished river, one that had drowned people in times past, when misfortune in life was taken for granted, but now was merely enough to wet a woman's toes in tragedy. The river in the village, with its bridge over the pooled waters.

Mad Ellen crossed the bridge, the old bridge, in her red cardigan, and was swallowed by the mists of fairyland. Long dead and little understood, contained in a handful of letters, mostly written by other people about the time before and the crisis itself, never the woman after. (The fox, which is born in our fields, also crosses the frontier at twilight. It is there he gets the romance.) The picturesque, tousled version of madness conferred by books.

Annie, short-haired, hatchet-faced, and heavily pregnant, not yet mellowed into beloved Nan, sat on the rock by the willow. Looking briefly around, she removed her shoes and soaked her feet in the water. She picked up a stone and weighed it in her hand prosaically. If she heard Mad Ellen's footsteps crossing the bridge, she did not look up, but rubbed her stomach and flexed her swollen toes in the water. This was her second child, the moment when it had all gone wrong for her mother, but Annie was made of sterner stuff. You just needed to learn to hold things together; you needed to grit your teeth, and grin and bear it, for the sake of the children. Ellen had obviously possessed some key weakness, some fatal character flaw that had prevented her holding things together. Annie was well-read in a small-town-library way; she had read most of Catherine Cookson but also Shakespeare and the *Iliad*, and if she could not discuss tragic character flaws in the style of a graduate-level seminar, she recognized them when she saw them. She knew her own flaw was that she was as hard as nails, and that her refusal to see people as victims made her fundamentally, in the case of Ellen, unjust. She saw the madwoman swimming, swimming through the same old illusions, and was unmoved. (A fuss about nothing, a midge-bite madness, a fit of the tantrums.) Annie pressed her lips together and skipped the stone neatly across the pond. Then she stood. It was time she was home, past time. The girl needed her bath.

Carol, ethereal, glowing, leaned on the bridge on a golden summer evening in her mid-thirties. She suspected she was pregnant (something beautiful—awful—huge). But she wasn't, of course. Years more of disappointment and a battery of tests would confirm her infertility. But on this evening, she was late a day or two and imagining a rosy-cheeked, flaxen-haired boy, yes, a boy, because mother-daughter relationships were fraught; she had had a bust-up with her own mother earlier in the day. Her mother with her hardness and her expectations. This would be a bonny, untroubled boy, and Paul would teach him to play the fiddle and she would bring him here on summer holidays to see the old village, but he would grow up away from all this, in the new country. Years later she brought a gangly, black-haired girl (so wild, and never, never but half your child) down by the river path, a girl who liked books more than music. And everything was different than she had imagined it (they accepted their reciprocal existence as divine fact), everything except her capacity to love the child and to subsume herself entirely into its person and interest. The glow that lit Carol's pale eyes that long-ago evening did not come from hormones, as she hoped and imagined, but from longing and excitement. She was transformed before the fact of motherhood. She would always insist she was transformed for the better.

And Madeleine languished in the tower, weaving the web in her mind's eye (because I seek an image, not a book), medicated to numbness and fragments of verse memorized with her once-exceptional memory (because whom the gods wish to destroy, they first call promising). She reached for the different threads of the tapestry, seeming grey on the borderlands of fairyland, yet pulling together in her hands to a gaily coloured web of magic, sights long gone, sounds long lost in the falling water, a voice calling *Elaine, beware*, a song on the evening air, heard Carol's low voice chanting, mournful, holy. She did not think a woman could stay here forever on the borderlands; twilight fell on the human world while fairyland beyond remained in everlasting dawn. She must cross the bridge (I come, Graymalkin) or turn back from it, but turn back to what, precisely? Turn back to responsibility, to acceptance? Maud needs a mother; Carol needs a daughter. And, probably, Tom needs some help. Turn back to Lancelot?

"It's time to take our medicine, mummy," said a nurse with a throaty voice.

Madeleine looked at her experimentally, closing first one eye and then the other. Through her right eye she saw a nurse, through her left eye a fairy. And so she hesitated over the pills, looked around the room, the threads of tapestry intruding through the window, the pile of books, a folded slip of paper on top of them. She had not seen that before, and reached for it.

> Maddie love, sorry I couldn't see you today. Your father was ages and visiting hours were over. Tomorrow.

I know you'll be better sooner or later though and then we'll be free of this arcane Victorian setup.

Take your medicine. You have a lovely mind.

Tom

She closed her left eye and opened her mouth for the pills.

"What are you doing?" asked the nurse, once she'd swallowed them.

"I'm ignoring that you're a fairy."

"Can you see me then?"

"Aye, through my left eye."

"Open it then."

"No, I want to get better. And I have heard a whisper say . . ." And yet with dread temptation she did open it. Threads of half-formed web, balloons of mist, a window to the outside world, a little withered old fairy, beautiful as the moon.

The fairy blew on her left eye, and it all disappeared. Madeleine was drifting into sleep and "yes," she said, "yes, this thing of darkness I acknowledge mine."

One's sympathies, of course, were all on the side of life.

—"The Death of the Moth," VIRGINIA WOOLF

"Well," said Tom. He shifted around and seemed to debate whether to tell me or not. "He died."

I was looking out the bedroom window. The hedge had grown and blocked our view of the fox shed, but the yard below was clean, the rubbish all gone, even the sagging, water-rotted armchair. "There was a literal rats' nest in the armchair," Tom added, following my gaze.

"I don't understand," I said. Maud was tightly swaddled, asleep on the bed. She took longer naps at more regular intervals now, and she also smiled. The smiles helped enormously.

"He died before you went into hospital. He was already dead that day, probably a day or two before. Drink."

"Drink," I said, but knew that drink was just the cold, daylit face of Greymalkin. "Oh god. Poor you, Tom. He didn't start to smell or anything, did he?"

"Yes."

"Oh god."

"The place isn't let again yet. They've probably got to fumigate or at least paint it, but I took the opportunity to chuck all that crap in the garden. Your father helped. The landlord didn't, the wanker."

I looked down on the quiet yard. It was scrubbed flagstones, with hardly a weed daring to show its face, but it could be nice.

"I did talk the landlord out of raising the rent though. Appealed to his better nature, new baby and so on, and the yard work. For the time being he's holding off. So we're here for another year anyway. I hope that's all right. I didn't know what to do, and the lease was up."

"Poor Tom," I said again.

He shrugged, but his face confirmed it. He sat down on the bed. "I'm glad you're home. I haven't much liked being here by myself, knowing a man died downstairs. It gave everything a grim cast. I look at the people on the street and wonder how long they've got left; wonder how long I've got left. It's put me right off the neighbourhood."

"Died." It seemed impossible, after the two years of skulking about, avoiding the neighbour, lying in bed listening to his binges. I'd had only two conversations with him; an argument about his bag, and that talk in the garden.

And he was dead. No help had come for him, as it had for me. What had become of that photograph: a lost mother and baby?

"Sorry for bringing all that up," Tom said, and I went and joined him on the bed, lying down with a sigh next to him, with Maud a kernel in the middle. Our arms and legs touched but we were both too tired to move.

"Dorrie's given me a lead on a future possible area of work, facilitating community consultations and things," said Tom unexpectedly. "I might go back and do another master's, once you're working and we're a bit more sorted. I'd like to do something useful. And also move."

"Okay," I said. "Whatever you need." I took Tom's hand and felt swellings of love. I thought of Maud and felt the usual dense exhaustion. Sometimes there was love at the sight of her, little purple bruises of it, but not today. They promised it would come, that reality would not be this bland performance of my role forever, that one day I would enjoy it. For this I held back the mists; I renounced and foreswore the fairies. I called my conditions by their proper names: depression, psychosis, hallucinations. And yet I saw no difference between things with their proper names and the things called faerie. I could accept—I did accept—that not everything had been quite as I experienced it; call it madness, call it metaphor, but that did not make it untrue. I kept these thoughts to myself, went to the psychiatrist, behaved myself, kept the aquatic fantasies at bay. The wild hovered, just out of eyesight. It had come for the man downstairs; it had come for one of the fox cubs. We had met the teenage daughter at the bus stop, and she said one cub had died; they'd had to call pest disposal services. We both stood around looking depressed about it and Tom looked nervous, and I wanted to tell him that it was fine, the death of a fox cub wasn't going to send me over the edge. And so I'd looked at Maud to avoid further conversation, and she was in the pram, looking up at the pattern of leaves against the sky with her eyes focusing and unfocusing with the effort of it, but under all that an expression of wonder.

"Euhhhhh," she trilled, and that was one of the flashes of unexpected feeling.

"Adored, beautiful little Maud," I said, and in that moment it was true.

A year and a month later, on Midsummer Eve, I celebrated a quarter century of life. Everyone approved that I wanted to throw a small party.

Two weeks before, I informed them all it would be fairy

themed, and that I expected everyone to be costumed or otherwise festive. Tom was, I think, furious. I told him the psychologist had said it was fine. I hadn't asked her, of course.

We put Maud to bed first. Guests were told to arrive no earlier than 8:15, and were to call to be let in rather than ringing the buzzer. I lay next to Maud on her low bed and heard the first people arrive, their stealthy feet passing in the hall.

Maud was already asleep, her cot surrounded by towering piles of library books. I was back to working on my thesis again, driven by unflinching productivity in any little half hour I could carve away. I suspected I would not go into academia after all, at the end of it. Which was a shame, in a way, as I found myself a much better scholar now, more imaginative and intuitive, more relaxed. I knew what I couldn't control, and that I was my own person outside of literature, in all my contradictions.

I could hear the downstairs neighbours, the young professionals, laughing in their garden. Students couldn't afford our corner anymore. The new couple had hung lights out there, and bought a table and chairs. The weeds were forcing their way back between the paving stones, but there was no whisker of neighbourhood fauna. So there would be no escape to the enchanted forest this Midsummer Eve, only to the front room, packed with the small collection of people I had not lost along the way. I had picked up a few as well, but they were not here, because the front room wasn't big enough for all their babies. One was stressful enough, upending the potted plants, pulling books off the shelf, tottering up to electrical outlets.

"I can stay with her until she's asleep," Tom had crept into the room. "Go and be with people."

"She is asleep," I said. "I was just making sure." I climbed up, and Tom and I looked down on her a moment. The wild, black, newborn hair was long gone, replaced with sleek, chestnut-brown locks and two perfect ringlets at the neck. She was apple-cheeked and jolly awake, remote and otherworldly when asleep, like all children.

I tied on my mask, a cheap gold cardboard affair that I had pasted green paper ivy leaves onto. I was no artist, and the result was more uncanny than ethereal. In the mirror I saw Tom wincing. He was reluctantly wearing a pair of tulle butterfly wings, his love of fancy dress dwarfed by his feeling that my party was in bad taste. I offered him my arm ironically, and we went into the hallway, now a photo gallery in homage to Maud. My picture that first week in the hospital took pride of place. I had never told Tom what I had seen there, but I kept a strict eye on the greenery. It was bushes, nothing more. My left eye remained blind.

In the front room I had hung paper streamers. I had printed out photographs and paintings of forests and pasted them on all the walls.

For a moment I felt what seemed an enormous rock pushing on my chest. It all looked a bit deranged: people, my parents, a couple Tom knew from work, Bronwen, all wearing fairy accessories and smiling politely, sheepishly.

Then my mother opened the oven to remove some appetizers. A cloud of steam billowed out, and through the haze I saw the same faces transformed into the good folk. And there were Angela and Dorrie, flamboyantly masked and winged, and next to them the novelist in a rubber donkey's head, which made me laugh. He and I had struck up an uneasy friendship in the past year. He was always picking my brain, turning my experiences into set pieces, and I knew I would appear in his next novel in some form. From him I got occasional updates about Marie.

They were also friends, or perhaps more. I missed her, but I never tried to apologize or to see her again, and neither did she.

In another moment of my life I might have thrown this party and stood in front of them all and . . . quoted. In another moment I wouldn't have thrown this party at all, but I would have faced any situation with a quote. But I had made my point already. I had brought them all to my lost land. So I rewarded them by being normal, by saying "thanks for coming and humouring me." And I poured drinks, discussed the price of rents, university politics, someone's recent breakup, how hot this summer was, not like that dreadful, wet apocalyptic spring we had last year when Maud was born.

I pushed the windows gaping wide for the muggy summer air, swept out a couple of dead flies, spared a dying moth, and breathed in the last days in Splinters Wood. We were leaving at the end of the month. The sale of Nan's house had been channelled to us as a deposit on somewhere further out and a little leafier. I had tried to make a case for one of the nicer tenement flats nearby. But the truth was we were already priced out. Splinters was taking off. Murals were being commissioned and painted depicting the most significant citizens of the area, even as their descendants moved further out in search of affordable rooms. Anyhow, Tom said, he had too many complicated memories here. Please, Queen Mab.

"They'll get their feet on the property ladder," my mother was explaining to Angela as they placed sausage rolls and spanakopita on plates.

"Oh yes, I've heard that area's very up and coming," said Angela.

"So away we'll go," I said to the novelist. "As if we'd never been here. A bubble on the surface of the neighbourhood, like all the other students. You know, I wanted to be *from* here, in some way."

"Your mother told me the new place has a square of garden," he said, or rather brayed, because he was trying to stay in character. "And she plans to turn it into a little wilderness for Maud." He whuffled and pawed the ground with one foot. I laughed. Tom, winged and moody, was lurking in the background, he who had never been the least bit jealous.

My father was topping up wine. Angela, at least, was drinking with abandon. "I always wondered about you, Maddie," she said, brushing past me rather unsteadily. "You seemed so reserved. I very much approve of this party."

"It's going to get better," I said, because this was a Brodeur party, and I knew what was coming. My father would produce his fiddle with a flourish, as on so many other occasions.

Before he could though, there was a wail from the hallway, and he darted out. He came back with Maud, who glowered around in fright at the paper masks and rustling wings.

"Oof," said Tom. "I knew it wouldn't work. It'll take ages to get her to drop off again."

"Oh never mind," I said. "Why shouldn't she stay up?"

So when my father did at last bring out his fiddle, it was Maud's sturdy legs that led the dance. My mother danced with her. Tom gave in to it all, shrugged his wings, and led me to a heavy stomping jig among all the people and around all the furniture. I reeled past the ass's head, Angela's good fairy, past my mother who was sensibly keeping Maud from impaling herself on the table corners. The young professionals downstairs clamoured angrily and banged on the ceiling. My mother threw off all her responsibility and hollered down at them to cut it out, people were allowed to live, it was Thursday, they could get through one day at their pretentious jobs a bit tired. She taught Maud to stomp extra hard for them.

My father was playing the old, haunting French-Canadian jigs and reels that were the backdrop to his childhood, then mine. Tonight they sounded different. He knew it too; the fiddle caught on stray notes; there was something harsh and angular about the sounds, but also alive. I saw suffering and celebration, a dark forest, hidden water, a pregnant moon. The faster he played, the surer the notes sounded, and so, abandoning himself to some long-submerged dream, he played fast, and faster.

And I danced. I leapt and I twirled and I stamped my feet. I paused only a moment to blow out the candles Tom was lighting on my birthday cake. I danced until all the cobwebs fell down.

I might have laughed forever. I might have danced on the ceiling, or pirouetted my toes clean off and danced on, feather-light, on the stumps of my legs. How hard, what anguish it was, to stop.

A shrill sharp on the fiddle and we both broke off at once, my father and I. He looked shaken, started to play something quiet, then stopped almost immediately, and put the fiddle away. I pushed my mask up on my forehead and leaned against the window frame to catch my breath.

In the rosy twilight, the teenage neighbour and some friends were gathered in the park, drinking slush ices from the corner shop and giggling madly. The moth had recovered with the music and flown away. But the streetlights were already stronger than the daylight, as was the glare of passing cars, and the neon sign of a new restaurant. The human world was bright and clear; the other fell into mist, and onwards into night.

On the corner a cat prepared to cross the road, waiting, like all cats, until a car accelerated towards it before streaking in front of the wheels. It escaped by a whisker into the park. And disappeared there under the hedge, little more than skin and bones, clearly ill, limping and disfigured but still alive. Greymalkin, familiar spirit, old friend.

A NOTE ON SOURCES

As Madeleine says early on in *Queen Mab*, her world has shape if she can find a quote for all the important moments, and the text has many allusions in thought and dialogue. Apart from the epigraphs opening each chapter, and the literary references that are discussed more fully in the text, I took a Victorian approach, and most quotes are unattributed in the moment. Below, however, is a list of those references.

Page 8: Madeleine mentions the plot of a short story, which is Samanta Schweblin's "Preserves," published in *Mouthful of Birds*, translated by Megan McDowell.

Page 9: Madeleine misquotes the final line of Virginia Woolf's essay "The Death of the Moth."

Pages 22–23: Tom and Madeleine quote the gander/goose lines of Theodore Roethke's 1954 poem "I Knew a Woman."

Page 26: The novelist quotes the famous opening line of T. S. Eliot's *The Waste Land.*

Page 26: Madeleine mentions "the drunkenness of things being various," a reference to Louis MacNeice's 1967 poem "Snow."

Page 29: Mrs. Danvers is from Daphne du Maurier's *Rebecca.*

Page 33: Madeleine's "turning and turning in the widening gyre" is from "The Second Coming" by W. B. Yeats.

Page 39: "Roar my terrible roars and gnash my terrible teeth" is a play on lines from Maurice Sendak's *Where the Wild Things Are.*

Page 43: "scuttling ragged claws" is an allusion to T. S. Eliot's "The Love Song of J. Alfred Prufrock."

Page 44: "Nature was red in tooth and claw" derives from Alfred, Lord Tennyson's *In Memoriam A.H.H.*

Page 44: "A drowsy numbness spread," is from John Keats's "Ode to a Nightingale."

Page 45: The red room is from Charlotte Brontë's *Jane Eyre.*

Page 48: Madeleine recites part of W. B. Yeats's 1899 poem "The Song of Wandering Aengus" to the newborn Maud.

Page 51: "Time passes" is from Virginia Woolf's *To the Lighthouse.*

Page 54: Tom names Greymalkin from John Masefield's 1927 children's novel, *The Midnight Folk* (although in fact the main cat there is Blackmalkin, and Greymalkin is a background figure. Tom, like me, had a mental lapse at the time of naming).

Page 55: A passing reference to the French-Canadian folk song "V'là l'bon vent."

Page 58: Tom makes reference to Cyril Connolly's famous line that "there is no more sombre enemy of good art than the pram in the hall," appearing in his 1938 book, *Enemies of Promise.*

Page 61: This chapter contains many references to John Keats's "La Belle Dame sans Merci."

Page 75: Madeleine makes reference to John Clare's 1845 poems "I Am" and "The Old Year."

Page 77: Dodie Smith's 1948 novel, *I Capture the Castle.*

Page 78: "Man hands on misery to man" is from Philip Larkin's endlessly quoted 1971 poem "This Be the Verse."

Page 82: Madeleine recites part of W. B. Yeats's 1934 poem "Meru," and again from his "The Song of Wandering Aengus."

Page 85: Verses from Alfred, Lord Tennyson's 1855 poem *Maud.*

Page 88: Reference to the Haitian lullaby "Dodo ti pitit manman."

Page 88: Verses from the traditional Scottish "Highland Fairy Lullaby."

Page 97: Descriptions of the fish reference D. H. Lawrence's poems "Humming-Bird" and "Fish," both from his 1923 collection *Birds, Beasts and Flowers.*

Page 99: W. B. Yeats's 1886 poem "The Stolen Child."

Page 99: John Keats's "La Belle Dame sans Merci."

Page 101: The changeling legend Madeleine reads was written by me, but based on various different versions available online through the University of Pittsburgh: https://sites.pitt.edu/~dash/britchange.html.

Page 104: The dead mothers of fiction mentioned are from Emily Brontë's *Wuthering Heights*, Virginia Woolf's *To the Lighthouse*, Ernest Hemingway's *A Farewell to Arms*, Thomas Hardy's *Far from the Madding Crowd*, and Louisa May Alcott's *Little Women*.

Page 124: The brewing in eggshells recipe is a mash-up of traditional changeling tales, predominantly "The Brewery of Eggshells" by T. Crofton Croker, accessed on the University of Pittsburgh site, with some detail and dialogue from the 1889 novel *A Reputed Changeling; Or, Three Seventh Years Two Centuries Ago* by Charlotte Mary Yonge.

Page 128: T. S. Eliot's "The Naming of Cats."

Page 133: Madeleine describes the hair salon in the titular words of Ernest Hemingway's 1933 story "A Clean, Well-Lighted Place."

Page 144: "Vexed to slumber" misquotes W. B. Yeats's "The Second Coming."

Page 151: A reference to Angela Carter's 1966 poem "Unicorn."

Page 152: Marie tells the story of the plant baby. This is Catalan writer Joan Perucho's "La tendra història de la planta bebè," and it's probably unlikely that even Marie would come across it, but it was too good a changeling tale to skip.

Page 153: Lauren Sandler's 2013 article for *The Atlantic* titled "The Secret to Being Both a Successful Writer and a Mother: Have Just One Kid."

Page 162: Tom makes reference to the madwoman in the attic, from the 1979 book *The Madwoman in the Attic: The Woman Writer and the Nineteenth-Century Literary Imagination*, by Sandra Gilbert and Susan Gubar.

Page 169: Madeleine imagines the neighbour crying through the lock, as in the nursery rhyme "Wee Willie Winkie."

Page 183: The Jean Améry statement mentioned by Angela comes from *At the Mind's Limits: Contemplations by a Survivor on Auschwitz and Its Realities*.

Page 185: Madeleine and Angela discuss Christina Rossetti's *Goblin Market*.

Page 197: A reference to the nursery rhyme "There Was a Crooked Man."

Page 199: The line "mad dogs and Englishmen go out in the noonday sun" passed into common parlance from Noël Coward's 1931 song, while "a midnight dreary" comes from Edgar Allan Poe's 1845 poem "The Raven."

Page 206: Echoes of Alfred Lord Tennyson's "The Lady of Shalott."

Page 207: Extract from W. Y. Evans-Wentz's 1911 book, *The Fairy-Faith in Celtic Countries.*

Page 215: "Perchance to dream" is from *Hamlet* by William Shakespeare.

Page 229: The black-and-white cat speaks of forcing the moment to its crisis, in echo of "The Love Song of J. Alfred Prufrock," by T. S. Eliot.

Page 230: Seamus Heaney's translation of *Beowulf*, 2000.

Page 233: "The word of a bird is a thing to follow" is from "The Changeling," by Charlotte Mary Mew, and "lhondoo" and "vel oo cheet" are from the Manx rhyme "The Lhondoo and the Ushag-Reaisht," or "The Blackbird Sings."

Page 236: Lord Byron's 1818 poem "She Walks in Beauty."

Page 242: I wrote a version of the story of Bridget Cleary based on a hodgepodge of sources around the web.

Page 248: Madeleine recalls Fiona Macleod's story "Fara-Ghaol," published in *The Sunset of Old Tales* in 1905.

Pages 249 and 250: "The mermaids singing" and "human voices" are references to T. S. Eliot's "The Love Song of J. Alfred Prufrock."

Page 249: "Pre-world loneliness" is from D. H. Lawrence's "Fish."

Page 253: References to and structures borrowed from *Giacomo Joyce* by James Joyce.

Page 254: References to and structures borrowed from *Paris* by Hope Mirrlees.

Pages 257 and 265: The playing cards reference *Alice's Adventures in Wonderland* by Lewis Carroll.

Pages 257, 260, and 263: References to the ghosts of *A Christmas Carol* by Charles Dickens.

Page 260: "The Cask of Amontillado" and "The Tell-Tale Heart" by Edgar Allan Poe.

Page 260: *A Midsummer Night's Dream* by William Shakespeare.

Page 262: "Those are the pearls that were his eyes" is from *The Waste Land* by T. S. Eliot.

Page 262: "You'd think it was O tragic and that dying-looking one" is from Molly Bloom's monologue in *Ulysses* by James Joyce.

Page 264: "There's rue for you . . ." is Ophelia's line in *Hamlet* by William Shakespeare.

Page 264: "Lancelot mused a little space" and "She had a lovely face. God in his mercy lend her grace" are from "The Lady of Shalott" by Alfred, Lord Tennyson.

Page 265: Madeleine is transformed into a monstrous vermin, in the vein of *The Metamorphosis* by Franz Kafka.

Page 266: This chapter contains all the quotes that were the epigraphs of previous chapters.

Page 277: Nods to Molly Bloom's monologue from *Ulysses* by James Joyce and quotes *The Tempest* by William Shakespeare.

Page 285: A brief allusion to "fast, and faster," drawn from the children's book *Madeline* by Ludwig Bemelmans.

The epigraph from Vladimir Nabokov's "Razor" on page 131 was translated by Dmitri Nabokov. The epigraph from Franz Kafka's "A Crossbreed" on page 140 was translated by Willa and Edwin Muir.

For general fairy knowledge, I found the following books invaluable: *Strange and Secret Peoples: Fairies and Victorian Consciousness* by Carole G. Silver; *The Fairy-Faith in Celtic Countries* by W. Y. Evans-Wentz; *The Celtic Twilight* by W. B. Yeats; *The Fairies in Tradition and Literature* by Katharine Briggs; and Terri Windling's sadly defunct *Myth and Moor* blog, parts of which may still exist on her Substack: https://mythandmoor.substack.com/.

ACKNOWLEDGMENTS

Sandra Pareja, for your care and stream-of-consciousness voice notes from all time zones, thank you. Jenna Johnson, it's been a privilege. Thank you for your insight and guidance. Thanks also to Lianna Culp, and to Tracy Locke, Gretchen Achilles, Emma Moore, Nina Frieman, Bri Panzica, Nancy Clements, Justine Gardner, tracy danes, Debra Helfand, Scott Auerbach, Daniel del Valle, Hillary Tisman, Nicholas Stewart, Caitlin Cataffo, Sam Glatt, Jonathan Woollen, Isabella Miranda, Grace McPhee, Sarita Varma, Sheila O'Shea, Spenser Lee, Devon Mazzone, Pauline Post, Flora Esterly, Nalie Borihane, and anyone I may have missed.

Thanks to Laura Macaulay for your most helpful notes, and to Juliet Garcia and everyone at Pushkin.

Rosa Rey, Irene Pujadas, and Julie Thevenet, thank you.

To the past, present, and future members of my writers' group, all good friends, my sincerest thanks. In particular: Andy Allen (who read a short story and said "this should be a novel"), John Bentley, Maria Di Mario, Elaine Foreman, Joel Graham, Vic Hutchinson, Kate Lith, and Keith Rosser. For your encouragement and frequent pointed criticism, merci!

Thanks to my bookish friends, online and off, for making me spend an absolute fortune on books.

For the invaluable experience of being edited day in and day out, thank you to Phil Seager. Thanks also to Marta Comín and to all my work pals.

In 2019 I asked various friends to "describe labour in three words." Absolutely no one stuck to the brief, but all those words were invaluable. Thank you Roser Cabré-Verdiell, Maria Di Mario (again!), Mallory Girod, Molly Girod, and Emilie Marzinotto.

Thank you to Lana Bastašić, for friendship, and for teaching me everything I know about Joyce and Woolf.

Thank you to Mònica Tomàs White, who read an early draft and hyped my novel when it mattered: at midnight, at the bus stop.

Others who read early: thank you Míriam Cano, Alicia Izquierdo, and Aga Sikora. And for many and varied things, thanks to Laura Camps de Agorreta, to Guillem Izquierdo, to Daniel Segura, to Gema Suárez, to Susanna Gürocak, and to Lucía Benavides.

Thanks to Dan Keeton, Eric Ball, Florence Roy, the Thomson/Phillips family, and in particular Ginny Thomson for excavating a file folder, you know the one.

Eternal thanks to Magda Tur and Eugenio García, for the practical help, the sleepovers, the gift of whole weekends to make deadlines. Thanks to the whole García/Tur/Racero family.

And of course, all my love and thanks to my own family. My favourite line in *Goblin Market*, no mean feat, is "for there is no friend like a sister." Thank you to mine, Morna and Shona McBride. And endless thanks to my parents, Jan Keeton and Stephen McBride, for support and encouragement, for raising me in a house full of books, for thinking an English degree was a good backup plan, for allowing their home to be an impromptu summer camp and writers' residency each August.

To Ivy, Sibyl, and Isidore, for first mornings, second chances, third helpings, thank you.

Víctor García Tur, *stupid husband*! Gràcies per tot.

ONLY KILLERS AND THIEVES
DUST OFF THE BONES
Paul Howarth

SYMPATHY
Olivia Sudjic

DINNER WITH EDWARD
Isabel Vincent

LITTLE GODS
Meng Jin

THE OTHER'S GOLD
Elizabeth Ames

MACHINE
Susan Steinberg

SHE COME BY IT NATURAL
Sarah Smarsh

IN THE HOUSE IN THE DARK OF THE WOODS
Laird Hunt

THE INLAND SEA
Madeleine Watts

THE EXTRA MAN
Jonathan Ames

THE BEAUTIFUL BUREAUCRAT
Helen Phillips

AMONG THE LIVING AND THE DEAD
Inara Verzemnieks

THE OUTERMOST HOUSE
Henry Beston